OK
Book

# THE TRUTH ABOUT BEN AND JUNE

# THE TRUTH ABOUT

# BEN AND JUNE

## ALEX KIESTER

PARK
ROW
BOOKS

PARK
ROW
BOOKS™

Recycling programs
for this product may
not exist in your area.

ISBN-13: 978-0-7783-1195-9

The Truth About Ben and June

Park Row Books
22 Adelaide St. West, 41st Floor
Toronto, Ontario M5H 4E3, Canada
ParkRowBooks.com
BookClubbish.com

Printed in U.S.A.

*For my mom and dad*

# THE TRUTH ABOUT

# BEN AND JUNE

# MAPLEWOOD

# ONE

———

On the day everything fell apart, Ben awoke to the sound of the baby crying. He swung his legs out of bed, and as his heels struck the floor, pain zinged from the backs of his calves up to his temples. His stomach flipped threateningly.

From down the hall, he heard Mikey shudder in a breath and wail harder. "Coming!" he shouted, and a fresh throb of pain shot through his head.

He glimpsed the other side of the bed where the covers had been thrown back, the sheet twisted into a tight rope. He wondered where June was. The empty space in bed was normal—his wife hadn't slept through the night since Mikey was born—but at this point in their baby's crying, Ben usually heard her trying to talk him down. *It can't be that bad*, she'd murmur. Or *Mikey-boy, you're acting like a real baby right now.*

In his crib, Mikey's hands were balled into tiny angry fists. His face was so contorted from crying he didn't see Ben approach, and his eyes widened in shock when Ben scooped him up. Thankfully, the surprise took the cry right out of him. Bouncing in his dad's arms, he caught his breath in jerky gasps. Ben kissed his soft temple consolingly. "Mikey-boy," he murmured against his little head. "You're acting like a real baby right now."

Ben laid him on the changing table, put on a clean diaper, then tugged back on his pajama bottoms and settled him on his hip. Mikey took a trembling breath and sneezed in Ben's face.

"Bless you," he said, wiping his eyes with his forearm. "Now let's go find your mom."

But June wasn't in the kitchen as Ben had assumed. He frowned, dumbly turning his head to one side then the other as if maybe she'd stuffed herself into a cabinet.

"June!" he called, but the house was still and quiet.

Ben squeezed his eyes shut, trying to remember if June had told him about an early appointment that day, but other than the few words they'd exchanged late last night when he'd slid into bed, he couldn't actually remember the last time they'd spoken. He felt a surge of anger at Clark & White for robbing him from his own family, but he swallowed it down. After all, it was his job there that allowed him to pay for the very house he was standing in.

He looked into his son's face to find it pouty and dejected. "Oh, relax," he said, hitching Mikey up on his hip. "She's here somewhere."

But June wasn't in the living room or the dining room or the downstairs bathroom or the two upstairs bathrooms or the guest room or his office. She didn't respond when he called her name, and he didn't see her outside when he looked from the windows. Even though she'd clearly not been in their bedroom or the nursery earlier, Ben checked again. Still empty. When he discovered their car untouched in the garage, he didn't know if he should feel relieved or not, but found that he wasn't. It was the first week of March in New Jersey and outside looked blisteringly cold. June would've had to have a very good reason to go out on foot.

He made his way to her closet. If her heavy-duty boots were gone, it would mean she'd just stepped out for something—to the store for milk. It would've been odd but not implausible.

At the doorway of her walk-in closet, he flicked the light switch, illuminating her clothes with harsh white light. Standing at the mouth of his wife's wardrobe, which smelled so uniquely like June—coconut shampoo and the funk of worn clothes—Ben's chest lurched with something like regret or nostalgia. The scent of his wife felt uncomfortably like a memory.

On the floor was a tangled mass of dark, dirty laundry. Blouses and dresses and coats hung limply in two rows around him. Above, a wraparound shelf burst with haphazardly folded leotards, pairs of tights, and all her different dance shoes— thin black ones, ballet slippers, tap shoes, and those ugly beige ones with the stumpy heels. And there, in the middle of her shoe rack, were June's heavy-duty boots. She hadn't walked to the store after all.

Then something at the top of her closet caught Ben's eye: a gap in all that stuff, about three feet long, the wall behind it stark white and empty. It was where June stored her suitcase.

He stood there, staring at that empty space for a very long time before he flipped the light switch, plunging the closet back into darkness. He strode to the master bathroom, his legs moving like they'd been powered by an electricity surge, but his mind felt oddly blank, as if it were unwilling to comprehend the evidence before him. At their shared vanity, in their shared toothbrush holder, was one toothbrush—his. The counter space around June's sink was completely bare.

No, no, no.

Back in their bedroom, he laid Mikey on the bed and grabbed his phone from the bedside table. The screen was blank—no calls, no texts. He called June, but it went straight to voice mail.

No, no, no.

Ben looked at their brand-new son. June wouldn't leave them; he knew that with a certainty inside him like a stone. And yet, she was still very clearly not here. His brain grinded to a halt as if his gears had gotten stuck on these two conflicting truths: June would not leave; June was gone.

He took a deep breath and willed his shoulders to relax. He just had to think it through. First of all, the doors were locked and the house was untouched, so it wasn't as if she'd been snatched from their bed. Odds were she just had some early appointment that he'd forgotten about in his overfull brain, the details of which would perfectly explain the missing suitcase and the not-missing boots or car. She'd probably walk in the door within the next few hours and they'd laugh about how worked up he'd gotten about her very benign appointment to the…dentist. And yet, while the pragmatic part of his brain told him there would be an ordinary, logical explanation, the rest of him prickled with dread. Her absence just felt…*wrong*. He called her again, and again it went to voice mail.

Before they had Mikey, June hadn't been particularly good about keeping up with her phone. She'd kept it on silent during rehearsals and sometimes forgot to respond to texts or calls until hours after getting them. But since she'd become a mom, she'd practically tethered herself to her device, frantically returning to rooms where she'd left it, as if at any moment Mikey might be near death and she'd have to dial 911 to save him. Ben called again—voice mail—and again and again and again. Voice mail, voice mail, voice mail.

He stared at his screen, trying to think of someone who could help, someone who might know where she was. June's mom was dead and her relationship with her father—without that dutiful card on her birthday each year—could probably qualify as estrangement. Maybe he should call the studio. Even though June wasn't technically a member of the Martha Graham Dance Company anymore, before Mikey was born, that was where she'd spent most of her time. He didn't have any of the members' numbers in his phone, so he Googled the studio, but when he called, no one answered.

He decided to call Moli next. They hadn't seen June's best friend since she'd come up a few months ago to meet Mikey, but Ben assumed she and June still talked all the time. In fact, now that he thought of it, it seemed possible that June had made plans to go to her friend's for a long weekend—hadn't she mentioned wanting to do that recently? At just after six in the morning, it was far too early to call, but Moli did have a baby, so she was probably awake too. Feeling guilty, he dialed.

"Ben?" Moli answered.

Ben knew immediately from her confused tone that June was not with her, and his heart dropped. "Hi, Moli." Though every part of him was filling with fear, convention took over and he added, "How's it goin'?"

"Uh…fine," she answered, but it sounded like a question. "I'm a little sleepy, because it's six in the morning. Is everything okay?"

"Sorry, I'm—" He tried to keep the creeping panic out of his voice. "I just woke up and, uh, June isn't here and she isn't answering her phone. I'm sure it's nothing. I'm sure she's…" But he couldn't finish the sentence because he wasn't sure of anything. He had no idea where his wife was or why she wasn't where she should be. "I'm sure everything's fine."

"Wait, what? I don't understand. Is she—where's Mikey?"

"In my other arm."

"And June's not there? Is she on an errand or is she, like… missing?"

"She's not *missing*. She…" Ben didn't want to finish the sentence, but how could he not? "She took a suitcase with her."

There was a long silence, then, finally, "She left?"

"No. God. No." It sounded so harsh.

"Well, why else would she take her suitcase?" When he didn't immediately answer, Moli continued. "What's been going on with you two lately?"

Ben shot a bewildered look at his phone. "What? What is that supposed to mean?" Ben had known Moli almost as long as he'd known June. They were friends. And the implication of her words—that he was somehow responsible for this— felt like she'd reached through the phone and slapped him.

There was another silence, but it was shorter this time. "I just—I mean, I haven't talked to June in weeks. I don't know what's been going on with her."

Ben frowned. He thought June and Moli talked, or at least texted, almost every day. He opened his mouth to say something, but then closed it. He had more worrying things to focus on at the moment. "Look, Moli, I gotta go. I'm gonna keep calling around for her. Call her for me, too, will you?"

After Ben assured her he'd keep her updated, they hung up and he continued to scroll through his contacts, stopping when he came across the number of June's mom's studio. He didn't think June had been there in a long time, but at least it would be open. They always had some sort of early-morning workout dance class.

But Dee Dee, the woman who ran the studio, didn't know where June was and hadn't spoken to her in months. Ben managed to play the whole thing off as something innocuous and vague—June didn't have her phone and he'd forgotten where she said she was going—and he thanked God Dee Dee bought it. He couldn't stomach another line of off-based questioning like Moli's. *What's been going on with you two lately?* As if you could simplify everything in a marriage to the goings-on of the past week. His mind flashed to that moment earlier, as he'd stood at the mouth of June's closet—her scent like a memory—but he buried it. It didn't mean anything. He and June were good.

Ben dressed in a rush, blindly putting on whatever he grabbed first from his closet. Mikey, he left in his pajamas, shoving on his tiny socks and boots, grabbing his tiny coat and hat. Catching a glimpse of the two of them in the long mirror propped against the wall—he with his hair mussed from sleep, Mikey with his rounded tummy peeking out from between his NASA pajama set—Ben felt like they were two lost castaways, helpless without June there to anchor them. He felt a longing for his wife like a hook in his sternum.

Mikey started crying again and Ben switched him from his right hip to his left. "Okay, okay. Let's eat."

In the kitchen, Ben opened the refrigerator and reached to grab a full bottle of prepared formula, but his hand paused midway, a stack of Tupperware catching his eye. That was odd; usually their refrigerator was almost empty. He frowned, grabbing the bottle, then he closed the door and opened the freezer. Even odder. Normally bare except for the occasional frozen bag of berries, today it was packed to almost overflowing with row after row of single-serving lasagnas. There were flavors of every kind: lasagna Italiano, lasagna Floren-

tine, chicken lasagna, vegetarian lasagna, spinach-ricotta lasagna. He stared, eyes wide. He couldn't remember the last
time he'd eaten lasagna.

He scanned the rest of the kitchen and caught sight of the
recycle bin brimming with empty bottles: wine bottles mostly,
but one of Jameson whiskey too. Ben felt a sudden, itching
need to get out of there. He couldn't just continue to spin in
circles in their empty house, hoping June would burst out of
a cabinet. He needed to look for her. He grabbed the car keys
and the milk bottle from the counter and strode to the door,
passing the recycle bin on the way. The acrid scent of alcohol
wafted up to him and turned his stomach.

The air outside was biting and Mikey burst into a fresh
round of wails. "I know," Ben said, and his voice had an un-
intended edge to it. "This isn't my favorite morning either."

As he walked out onto the landing, his phone dinged with
a message and he stopped short. Heart racing, he dug a hand
into his coat pocket and pulled it out. But when he glanced
at the screen, he let out a sigh. It was only Moli.

Calls have all gone to voice mail. Keep me updated. I'll keep
trying.

"Dammit," Ben muttered, shoving his phone back into
his pocket, but as he did, it dinged again—again, only Moli.

I just don't get this. Did she say anything before she left?

Ben let out an indignant huff of breath that turned white
against the dark morning sky. Maybe he was being paranoid,
but her question felt pointed, like, if he truly understood his
wife, he'd intuit where she was now—it was just another it-

eration of her question before: *What's been going on with you two lately?*

What had been going on with them two lately was that things were fucking hard. They had a four-month-old baby. He was swamped at work and—he wasn't blind—he knew June was swamped at home. But like everything June did, she'd set the bar so impossibly high. Before having Mikey, she'd binged on historical documentaries so that "her ignorance didn't rub off on the baby;" she'd stocked up on all-organic food and plastic-free toys; she'd read literary novels aloud, angling her mouth toward her belly for better acoustics.

So now she was having to adjust to the reality that parenthood, at least for the time being, was far less about tranquil teachable moments and far more about dirty diapers and cries that woke them a dozen times a night. She was having to adjust to the reality that she would not and could not be the "perfect" mom. On top of that, the sleep deprivation and Ben's long work hours had taken a toll on their relationship. He couldn't remember the last time they'd sat down together for a meal or had a conversation that didn't revolve around Mikey. And yet, despite all that, he and June were good—honestly. They might not be thriving at this particular point in their marriage, but they were okay.

Just last night, he'd come home from work around two in the morning to a dark and silent house, his head already starting to throb from the drinks he'd had at the office as he reviewed his latest merger contract. He'd slid quietly into bed next to June, thinking she was asleep. But then, in the dark, he felt her body shift, turn toward him, and in a soft voice she'd whispered, *I miss you.* Sure, the basic sentiment of the words was wistful, but it was also a declaration of their bond, a way to say that she was looking forward to catching up with him, once they caught their breath.

Standing on the stoop now, their son perched on his hip, Ben's throat tightened at the memory. He clicked his phone off without responding to Moli. As he began to walk down the steps toward their car, the heel of his boot scuffed against their welcome mat. It shifted slightly and a glint of something underneath caught Ben's eye. He turned and, with his foot, flipped up the corner of the mat. There, in the place they used to hide their house key when they hadn't yet made a second copy, was June's shiny gold one.

Ben gazed down at it for a long time, a frown etched on his face. Ever since they'd made that second key, June had kept it on her keychain, between her library card and a kitschy charm of a ballet slipper her mom had given to her only somewhat ironically. To his knowledge, June had never taken the key off because she'd never had a reason to. The only explanation for removing it now was that she was leaving it behind, that she wasn't planning on ever opening their front door again.

Ben shook the idea from his head—it didn't make any sense. After all, just last night, June had turned to him and told him she missed him. And while he might've been pre-occupied with work and dulled by a hangover and distracted by Mikey's cries, he was clear about one thing: people who missed their husbands didn't leave with the intention of never coming back.

# TWO

————

It was just after seven in the evening of the day June disappeared when Ben pulled up to the Maplewood police station. He'd called in sick to work that morning, for what he thought was only the second time since he'd started at Clark & White almost seven years ago, and he'd spent the day taking care of Mikey, juggling the work calls and emails that stopped for nothing, and hunting down his wife. When it was clear that June wasn't going to show up for Mikey's bedtime—something she hadn't missed once since becoming a mom—Ben grabbed his keys, stuffed Mikey into his carrier, and drove the few blocks to the police station.

He felt like an idiot going to the police—June was not a missing person—but he didn't know what else to do. That morning, he and Mikey had driven around town for hours, darting into coffee shops and stores, searching for her. He'd called the numbers of June's friends that he'd had in his phone, but all of them claimed they hadn't seen her in months. He'd even gone so far as to call June's dad in California, keeping his tone light and questions vague. He'd said that June was out of town and he hadn't been able to reach her. He was just wondering if they'd spoken recently. No, Ben wasn't *worried* worried. He just wanted to check in. New baby and all. New dad jitters. He'd been surprised at how easily convinced June's dad had been with his clearly bullshit story, but all Richard had said at the end was a genial *When am I gonna meet that little guy anyway?* as if he couldn't quite remember Mikey's name.

It was at that point Ben decided to stop making calls. Contacting her close friends and father was one thing, but he knew his cover story would sound absurd if he started calling acquaintances. He'd wanted to reach out to June's friends here in Maplewood, but they were all married to the guys he worked with, and he didn't want to poke a hole in his sick-and-working-from-home story while he still had to take care of Mikey; nor did he have any desire to be the center of Clark & White's rampant rumor mill. So he'd gone to the police, because it was the only thing he could think to do.

Inside the station, a middle-aged woman behind a glass-paneled desk looked from Ben to Mikey in his carrier then back to Ben. "Can I help you?"

Ben's heart pounded. He came from a long line of people who believed marital issues belonged behind closed doors, people who would've been mortified to hear he'd gone to the police about a matter as private as a missing wife. "Um, yeah," he said, clearing his throat. He couldn't quite hold the woman's eye. "I'd like to talk with someone. My wife is... missing. Well, she's not technically missing, I guess, not legally. But she's...gone and um, I don't know what to do."

The woman squinted at him. "So you're here to file a missing person report?"

"No," he said a little too loudly. "Because no one's missing."

"I thought you said your wife was missing."

Ben paused, the first inklings of panic creeping up the base of his neck. What if this woman turned him away for misusing police resources or worse, shunted him into an interrogation room with a detective? He just needed help. He took a deep breath and chose his next words carefully. "I'm trying to navigate a situation I don't know how to navigate. I don't think I need any official police involvement, but I— Could I just speak with someone? Please?"

The woman stared at him. "Well. Our detective is on vacation—he's the one who'd normally handle something like this—but I suppose I could find an officer to help you."

Ben's shoulders slumped in relief. "Thank you."

He followed the woman through the doorway in the lobby and into an old-looking hallway. The top half of the walls looked like they were bulletin, flimsy and beige. The bottom half was fake brown paneled wood. The whole effect was both depressing and suffocating.

"You caught us at a weird time," the woman said over her shoulder. "The day shift is wrapping up and the night shift hasn't quite settled in yet."

They approached an open doorway, the scent of freshly brewed coffee and decades of stale coffee wafting through it. "Looks like Officer Moretti's in," the woman said, leaning her head through. Over her shoulder, Ben could see a woman in plain clothes standing by a coffee machine. She had pale skin and short, dark hair tied back into a little ponytail.

The woman looked over at them. "Cheryl."

"This man here would like to file a missing person report," Cheryl said.

"No, I—"

But Cheryl interrupted him. "Oh, right. His wife's missing and he wants to talk to someone, but he *doesn't* want to file a missing person report." She threw him a glance. "My mistake."

Moretti's eyes flicked to Ben. "Sure. I'll talk to him. Thanks, Cheryl." Cheryl walked away and Moretti turned back to the counter, pouring coffee into a mug that said, *Well I Hate Fridays!* "Coffee?"

Ben hesitated. Was she talking to him? "Huh?"

"Would you like a cup of coffee?"

"Oh. Um…" Actually, coffee sounded good. His hangover had somehow intensified over the course of the day and now it throbbed through him like an insatiable monster. The caffeine might help, not to mention he still had a long night ahead of him to catch up on work, but it also felt vaguely like a trap. Although he knew June wasn't technically missing, this woman didn't. He wanted to say *Did you hear Cheryl? She said miss-ing per-son!* "No, thanks."

Moretti turned to face him and took a sip of coffee. "All right then. Let's do this in the conference room."

The conference room was only a little bigger than Ben's office at Clark & White. While he hadn't exactly been expecting a bustling hub of police activity in the quaint town of Maplewood, these headquarters were almost comically parochial.

Moretti put her coffee mug at the head of the long table, turned to Ben, and extended her hand. "Officer Elise Moretti."

"Ben Gilmore." He lifted the carrier. "This is Mikey." He expected her to make some sort of comment—*He's darling* or *Hi, there, Mister Mikey*—but Moretti just glanced at the baby and nodded. Ben placed the carrier on the floor and sat on the edge of the seat. As Moretti went to fetch a piece of blank paper from a nearby copier, Ben took off Mikey's hat and coat then took off his own. The conference room was stifling.

"So, Mr. Gilmore," Moretti said after she'd settled in with a pen and paper. "What's going on?"

Ben noticed his knee was bobbing and he pushed a steadying palm onto it. Then he told her about everything that had happened that morning: about waking up to find June gone, about the missing suitcase and toothbrush, about how he'd spent the day driving through Maplewood and their neighboring town of South Orange, searching futilely for his wife. But as Ben heard the story come out of his mouth, it sounded off. It didn't capture the wrongness of it all. June wasn't just some faceless woman who'd disappeared to a hotel for the weekend. She was *June* and she was *gone*. There was no note, no text, no voice mail. No explanation.

When he finished, Moretti leaned back in her chair, crossed her arms. "Well, I have to agree with you that your wife's not technically missing. It's not illegal for a grown woman to leave." She hesitated. "So I'm not quite sure what you want."

"I know that, but…what if something's happened? What if she's hurt or something?"

Moretti stared at him with narrowed eyes for a long moment. "The best I can offer you right now is a request to locate."

There was a soaring in Ben's chest. A request to locate sounded so official and yet also unserious. The perfect balance of gravitas and casualness. "Okay. Great. That sounds good. What is that?"

"Exactly what it sounds like. If you file an RTL, we'll keep an eye out for your wife."

Ben nodded. "Good. That's good."

"Then let's get some information." She leaned forward and took the cap off the pen. "What's your wife's name?"

He took a deep breath. With the introduction of ink on paper, everything seemed so real, so official. "June Maxwell."

Moretti jotted it down then proceeded to ask a series of mundane questions—What was June's birthday? Her height? Weight? Skin color? Hair color? Eye color? Did she have any distinguishing marks?—and Ben felt dumbly proud when he was able to answer them all: December first, 1986, 5'6", 120 pounds, she was white, had dark brown hair, blue eyes, a small scar on her right knee.

Moretti made a note of it all then looked up. "Do you have any reason to believe your wife is a danger to herself or others?"

Ben envisioned June's dainty wrists and fine fingers. He thought of how easy it was to lift her off her feet, as if her bones were hollow. "No."

"No mental illnesses or anything like that?"

This time, Ben envisioned the ease with which June laughed, her wide, open smile and sparkling eyes. He thought of how confidently she moved through the world. "No."

"And do you have any reason to believe she's in possession of anything that could pose a threat to herself or others? A gun, for instance?"

"No," he said, a flare of annoyance in his voice. "My wife isn't traipsing around with a gun."

Moretti's face remained neutral as she made a note. "And what about your relationship?"

Ben frowned. "What d'you mean?"

"Is there anything going on between the two of you that could be the reason for her leaving? Anything you can think of that could have her distressed? A recent fight, maybe?"

Ben shifted in his seat, her words eerily similar to Moli's from earlier. "I'm sorry, what are you implying?"

"Mr. Gilmore," Moretti said, placing her elbows on her desk and leaning forward. "I don't want to make any assumptions, but you smell like alcohol. It's...pungent. And if you were drinking last night and your wife left shortly after, an argument between the two of you could be one option that fills in the blank."

Ben balked. "My wife and I—we're—" But he stopped short because what he'd rather idiotically been about to say was *We're Ben and June*, as if they were the fictional "It Couple" from some made-for-TV rom-com. And yet, to Ben, a half of that whole, they were an establishment. Of course, with work and the baby they'd had a hard time these past few months, but that didn't change the fact that they'd lived side by side for almost a decade. They'd created a life together that was imperfect, yes, but also so, so good.

How could he convey to this stranger all of his and June's shared history, all their inside jokes, the way June leaned into him when he came up behind her as she washed dishes? He couldn't, so instead he said, "Look, I'm not delusional. We're brand-new parents. Things haven't exactly been easy. But we have a good marriage. And frankly, I'm not entirely sure how this line of questioning helps me find my wife."

Moretti tossed her pen down onto the table. "Look. Ben. I'm a cop, not a marriage counselor. But your wife took a suitcase with her. She left the house stocked with food. It doesn't take much reading between the lines to make a logical guess as to what happened here. So I think, if you really want to find out where your wife went, you might want to start by being honest with yourself about why she left in the first place."

With those words, the reality of Ben's situation, the truth he'd been pushing down deeper and deeper all day, finally, and with the force of a geyser, crashed upon him. He'd been underplaying—even to himself, even in his own mind—everything that had transpired in their marriage over the past year. The truth was he couldn't remember the last time they'd laughed at an inside joke, couldn't remember the last time he'd walked up to June as she did the dishes.

His mind flashed again to the previous night. He had staggered into their room and slid, exhausted, into bed, head pounding, eyes burning. Through the fog of pain, he remembered June turning toward him, saying something. But now, in the harsh light of the police station, in the wake of what Moretti had said, he wasn't entirely sure what that had been. Had she said, as he'd thought, *I miss you*, in a show of uncomplicated sweetness? Or had it, in fact, been *I'll miss you*, as in *I will*—a declaration about the future, a clue to the morning that had yet to unfold?

He thought back to her shiny gold house key, glinting on the stoop, and realized, with the sensation of a stone sinking through water, it had been the latter. June had left him.

Rage tore through him like a flame. His wife—the one person he was supposed to be able to count on, the one person who'd vowed to love him and live life by his side, the one person who'd promised to never give up when it came to the two of them—had done just that. Life had gotten hard and she'd thrown up her hands. With a tight throat and clenched fists, Ben gazed at poor, motherless Mikey in his carrier and thought something he'd never thought before in conjunction with his wife: *That bitch.*

# THREE

———

*Seven years earlier*

June Mary Maxwell and Ben Robert Gilmore met in the waiting room of Mount Sinai Queens Hospital in Astoria four minutes before the start of 2011, which, both would later attest, was highly unlikely and therefore highly auspicious. It was unlikely for a couple of reasons; the first of which was that Ben hardly ever went to Queens. He'd been in law school at Columbia at the time and rarely ventured out of his apartment, let alone Manhattan.

The reason Ben had left the city that night was because the cousin of his friend Mihir was in town from India and wanted to visit Queens, the birthplace of his hero, Martin Scorsese. Somehow, Mihir's cousin—whose name Ben had forgotten by the first time he ever told this story—had convinced Mihir to spend New Year's Eve at a bar in Astoria. It was an inconvenient location for all their friends, but Mihir, who was arguably the most charming of the group, had somehow spun the story to persuade them that this would fulfill his cousin's only American dream.

The other reason for their meeting's improbability was because Ben, who was typically too busy, too distracted, or too timid to approach women, had been feeling uncharacteristically bold that night. His latest human interaction—the same interaction that landed him in the hospital—had left him feeling confident bordering on reckless.

Earlier that evening, he'd started reading *Letters to a Young Lawyer*, and had lost track of time, another thing he rarely did. By then, all his friends had already left for Queens, so Ben had to get there alone. On his walk to the bar from the subway, he spotted a young woman in a coat not warm enough for the weather, thin black tights, and high-heeled boots, teetering along next to a strung-out-looking man.

Ben watched anxiously as the guy grabbed the woman's upper arm and she shook him off. He grabbed again; she shook again. They did this over and over, stuck in a loop, zigzagging along the sidewalk, as Ben hesitantly followed a few yards behind. He was not the type to insert himself into strangers' relationships or public scenes, but he had a bad feeling about these two. The man's grip seemed unnervingly possessive, the woman's arms breakable. And from the glimpses Ben caught of her when she veered sideways, her eyes were rolling unfocused in her head.

Finally, it seemed the man had been shaken off one too many times. When the woman did it next, the man ducked his head and bulldozed her into the nearest wall like a rhinoceros. Then—Ben couldn't believe his eyes—he reared back and spit on her.

"Hey!" Ben shouted, his heart pounding. He ran over, but when he got within arm's length of them, he froze. What was he supposed to do now? Punch the guy? Neither the man nor woman had registered his presence, and he was feeling more and more ineffectual by the second. He regretted everything that had led him to this moment—giving in to Mihir's request, getting lost in that book, his own bizarre fit of courage—but now that he *was* here, he couldn't turn back. Because what he feared even more than being beaten in the streets was turning out to be a fearful man.

Ben wanted to be the kind of man who helped the innocent and stood up for what he believed in. He wanted to be the kind of man who would have taken a Nazi bullet for harboring Jewish people in his basement or the type who would have aided the Underground Railroad. He constantly thought back on the events of history like some retroactive morality test—*Would I have been brave enough to sacrifice myself for a stranger? Would I have risked my life for a cause?* Even that line of questioning made him feel weak and guilty, like he was appropriating someone else's suffering for a petty litmus test of his own goodness. But now the twenty-first century had given him a chance to prove himself. Even though it was a feeble, watered-down test of his valiancy, he felt like he was standing before a threshold.

"You can't spit on people," he said, and he could hear the incredulity in his own voice. He never would have guessed he'd have a need to utter those words in that order. He grabbed the guy by the scruff of his shirt like he was a pound dog, both relieved and disturbed by how insubstantial the man was beneath his winter clothes.

It was only then that the man registered him, and Ben seized the opportunity of his delay. He shoved the guy toward the wall and aimed a fist into his face. But he'd never thrown a punch before and it didn't have enough heat behind it. The guy was merely boggled and now his fury had transferred to Ben. But before he could retaliate, Ben tried again.

This time as his fist descended, the guy ducked, swiveled, and Ben's knuckles collided with the brick wall behind him.

"Motherfucker!" he shouted.

The yell was born purely from pain, but the strung-out guy clearly thought Ben was cursing at him and he turned on his heel and ran. Despite the throbbing in his hand, Ben was delighted by the unexpected turn of events. He looked to the woman, but she just peered back at him unevenly, slurred the words "*I dunno you, mothufucka*," and teetered off.

Despite this rather anticlimactic ending, Ben was still feeling courageous by the time he'd walked the six and a half blocks to Mount Sinai Queens Hospital, which was the nearest twenty-four-hour urgent care facility he could find on his phone.

June, who had stayed in her apartment that night with what she thought was a bad cold, had been feeling progressively worse as the evening went on. With her two roommates, Moli and Emilio, gone to a party she'd been planning to attend, June took the subway—there were no cabs—while drugged on Nyquil, at 11:30 pm on New Year's Eve, to the nearest place open that could give her something harder.

She'd arrived moments before Ben and blearily watched the newcomer present his inflamed hand to the nurse at reception. Clipboard of paperwork in his intact hand, he scanned the waiting room. His eyes skipped over the drunk white girls in tight dresses, each with a swollen wrist or ankle, then on to a large Hispanic family, of which the sick or injured member was indiscernible and who were all playing an enthusiastic game of UNO!. Finally, his gaze landed on the emptiest corner where June sat, puffy coat over pajamas, only very slightly drugged. He made his way over and settled into the chair two over from hers.

They both filled out their paperwork, intermittently watching the coverage of Times Square on the small, outdated TV hanging in one of the corners of the lobby. Though they hadn't spoken, Ben felt a silent camaraderie with the young woman two chairs over. They both smiled as a little boy from the UNO! family did a victory dance and they made anxious, wincing eye contact as one of the drunk girls tripped on her way back to an examination room.

The urge to talk to her grew inside Ben, and by the time the TV announcer declared that they were only four minutes from the New Year, it had grown unbearable.

He turned to her and grinned. "Hi."

June looked sideways at him, first with just her eyes, then with her head. Though she felt really terrible, there was something in this stranger's look that made the night suddenly seem like an adventure, as if they were fellow hostages in a very low-stakes, slightly hilarious situation. She found it impossible not to smile back.

"Hi."

"I've just been thinking and…since it's tradition to kiss at midnight, and as the only two people in the room who are not drunk or"—he nodded to the family in the corner, three of which had just shouted overlapping *UNO!*s—"engaged in a serious card game, do you think we should, you know, uphold the tradition and bite the bullet?"

June cocked her head to look the guy over. He was around her age, maybe a few years older. He had sandy hair with just a hint of red and matching stubble. He'd tossed his overcoat on the chair beside him so she could see his outfit—a puffy, athletic-looking jacket, black jeans, and brown leather boots. He was more conventionally good-looking than the type of men June was typically attracted to. All of her previous romantic interests had been the brooding, artistic type, who drank whiskey at noon and composed sonatas. Or they were fun-loving eccentrics who bought everyone drinks at the bar, shouted to cab drivers to "surprise" them with a destination, and ended up in Atlantic City for the weekend. They were always exciting and charming until suddenly they were not.

June studied the stranger across from her now and decided that she found his guileless way of speaking and his practical clothes rather refreshing.

"Hmm," she said. "Well, since it's tradition in Spain to eat one grape for every stroke of midnight, and since that's how I've celebrated ever since my friend Moli and I stayed with her grandmother in Madrid over winter break two years ago, we should probably do that instead of the whole kissing thing."

"Absolutely," the guy said, nodding. "I would not want you to break such a steadfast tradition." He stood up from his chair, injured hand cradled to his chest. "I'll just pop over to a bodega and grab a bunch of grapes." He turned to leave, paused, slowly turned back. "But actually, now that I'm thinking about it, a bodega probably wouldn't have fresh grapes and none of the markets are gonna be open at midnight." He stroked his sandy-red stubble. "What tradition could we do instead? Oh! We could go back to the kissing one?"

June grinned and shrugged. "Why not?"

At this, Ben, who would've been delighted by nothing more than a conversation with this girl, felt as if he'd both won the lottery and was sitting down to take the bar exam all at once; his palms began to sweat. He crossed the distance between them in two strides then sat down in the chair next to hers. "Wait, really?"

She smiled and nodded. From the TV across the waiting room, they heard the announcer start the countdown. "Ten!... Nine!..."

June's heart fluttered in her chest. "I'm sick," she said, suddenly remembering about germs.

Ben's face was now close to hers. "I think I broke my hand," he said back.

"I don't want you to get sick."

"I don't want you to break your hand."

June laughed, and before she knew it, the announcer was saying "Three, Two, One!" and the guy from the hospital waiting room, whose name she didn't even know, was kissing her, and for a moment, her headache and bleariness all fell away and she was kissing him back.

Throughout the years to come, every now and then, Ben and June would go over all the unlikely things that had to happen for them to meet and wonder at the precariousness of it all. If just one of these had been altered even slightly—if June had gone to the doctor when she'd first gotten sick; if Ben hadn't opened *Letters to a Young Lawyer* that day; if Mihir's cousin hadn't been in town or if he hadn't seen *Goodfellas* at the age of eight and fallen in love with Scorsese—if even one step in the series of events that night had been altered, Ben and June never would have met. And they both agreed: their meeting was so unlikely, so highly fortuitous, surely, they were meant to be together.

# FOUR

——

June's disappearance—her betrayal—fell like a dark veil over Ben's eyes, coloring everything with a black, desolate tint. Their home, a white colonial with blue shutters, had, at one point in the not-so-distant past, been a beacon of solace and warmth. Now, as he walked up the path to their front door after his visit to the police station, the sight of it made him sick. It was like looking at the husk of something dead—hollow and cold.

The inside, however, glowed with an unfamiliar cheer. It was warm and bright and smelled like something fresh—a roast? Vegetables? Ben's heart leaped. June was back. She was back and she was cooking. He'd walk into the kitchen and find her in her ripped, baggy jeans, holding a glass of wine as she stirred something on the stovetop. But as soon as he'd conjured the vision, it vanished. June hardly ever cooked, and she wasn't back and, for that matter, as much as he wanted her safe and found, his wife was not the person he actually wanted to see right now.

"Ben!" His mom's voice rang through the house.

*She* was the one who was here, of course, because he'd

asked her to come. Earlier that evening, when it began to sink in that June would not be home in time for dinner, Ben had finally broken down and called his mom. Because while your wife running away was a crisis, it wasn't the type of crisis that allowed you to take off work two days in a row. June hadn't been abducted—she'd absconded—and now he needed a babysitter.

His mom, who considered herself a mother before anything else despite all three of her children being grown and out of the house, had responded just as he'd known she would. Before he'd even finished with an explanation, she had walked out of the monthly meeting of her book club to pack a bag and drive the two hours from New Haven to Maplewood. He was so grateful for her help that the feeling somehow folded back in on itself and turned into guilt.

Ben set Mikey's carrier on the floor, clicked the front door shut behind him, and slumped against it, drawing out the moment as long as he could before his mom appeared in the wide entrance to the living room.

"Hi, honey," she said, smiling warmly.

He tried to return the look, but his own smile felt tired and threadbare. "Hey, Mom. Thanks again for coming."

"Oh, don't mention it. It was Nancy Cooper's book pick this month so *you're* the one doing *me* a favor." She walked over, pecked Ben on the cheek, then turned to Mikey in his carrier, her face lighting up as she did. "Hello, darling," she cooed, her voice morphing into the sweet, gushing one she reserved for her grandson. She straightened and looked again at Ben. "Oh, Ben, you look exhausted. Have you eaten? Why don't you get some food while I take little man? It must be close to his bedtime." She leaned over to unbuckle Mikey and pulled him into her arms.

"Past, actually."

They walked through the entryway together, Ben peeling off toward the kitchen while his mom and Mikey headed
into the connected living room. He grabbed a fresh bottle of
Jameson from a cabinet and made a show of slowly unscrew-
ing the top, lazily choosing a glass from a shelf, when what
he really wanted to do was tear the thing off and drink from
the bottle. But he didn't want his mom to see how automatic
his need for alcohol was at the end of the day. When *had* it
gotten so automatic anyway?

He watched as his mom perched on the couch, resting
Mikey on her thighs. "I'm happy to put him down in a few
minutes," she said, her fingers wrapped around his calf, pressing his toes to her mouth. "I just want to get a little bit of
Mikey time in first."

Ben frowned. Something about the way she was with
Mikey seemed off, unfamiliar. At first, he thought it must
be the contrast between the two—her pristine cashmere and
pearls next to Mikey's unwashed NASA pajama set—but after
a moment, he decided that wasn't it. Whatever it was, he
couldn't quite place. "That'd be great. Thank you."

"Stop thanking me. I *never* get to see my grandson. This
was the best thing that could've happened to me. Well. Not
the best, of course. Sorry. How's June's dad doing? Have you
talked to her?"

Ben blinked, lost, but then he remembered: the lie. When
he talked to his mom earlier, he'd told her that June's dad
had called that day with a medical emergency and June had
bought a last-minute flight to California to be with him. It
was the only thing he could think of to explain her sudden
absence and although covering for June made him burn with
resentment, he couldn't tell his mom the truth because he

knew she would freak if she heard it. There would be much fuss over *what to tell the neighbors* and *considering Mikey's future.* And what was the truth anyway? Because although he now remembered June's parting words, her cruel abandonment didn't make any more sense than it had that morning. He'd gone over it and over it in his head all day. The pieces of the puzzle did not add up.

"Yeah. I talked to her a little bit ago," Ben said. "She said her dad's okay for now. Stable and in the hospital." Lying was tricky. He had to come up with something bad enough to explain June's absence, but not too bad that his parents would be expecting a funeral anytime soon.

"Do they know what happened yet?"

Ben pressed his fingers to his forehead. "Uh…they think it was a very mild heart attack. Hopefully, he won't need surgery, but he'll have to stay in the hospital for a while longer. And June wants to stay with him. Do you think, um, do you think you could stay here for a few more days?"

He couldn't even speculate about what would happen if June decided to come home without warning just as she'd left. Her absence was hard to explain, but what would her unanticipated arrival look like? Ben drank his whiskey.

His mom gave him a surprised look. "Really? She's gonna be gone that long?"

Dread bubbled inside Ben. He didn't know what he'd do if his mom couldn't stay to help. "Yeah. Sorry I didn't tell you earlier, but I didn't know— Is that okay with you?"

"Oh, please, I'm happy to stay," she said, turning her face back to Mikey. "I just worry about poor Mikey without his mom for that long."

Irritation crept up Ben's spine. "Well, he still has me."

"Of course he does," she said, looking up. "But you have

a full-time job. It's different. Anyway," she continued before Ben could respond, "are you gonna eat? I saw you had lots of frozen lasagna, but I ordered out for dinner. Steak and asparagus. Yours is in the fridge."

"I'm not hungry," he said, surreptitiously pouring himself another whiskey, this time almost to the brim. He'd promised himself this morning as he lay in bed, Mikey's wails cutting through his hungover head, that he wouldn't drink that night. But morning-Ben hadn't had his world flipped upside down like he had. If he ever needed the numbing efforts of alcohol, it was now. "I have some work to catch up on if you're okay with Mikey. Sorry I'm not much help, but…" His voice faded. "I'll be around if you need me."

His mom shooed him away with wiggling fingers. "Go, go. We're fine. I raised three children of my own and they're all perfectly well-adjusted."

Ben laughed, but it came out weak because, good Lord, with his wife missing and his overfull glass of whiskey, nothing felt further from the truth. He carried the drink by his thigh where he hoped she wouldn't see, deposited a kiss on Mikey's head, then walked heavily up the stairs.

There was so much he needed to do. Moli had texted another half-dozen times; Dee Dee had left him a voice mail; his boss had called that morning, and Ben had to have gotten at least another fifty work emails since he'd last checked. It all weighed down on him with impossible heaviness, but even more than that, he just felt angry and alone. His wife had left and there was no one he could talk to about it.

In their bedroom, he turned in a slow circle. Nothing had changed—it still smelled the same, with his and June's inherent scents mingling into one, and the blankets were still twisted on the bed where they'd been thrown hours earlier—

yet the room looked utterly different. This used to be their haven, the place they'd come to at the end of the day and lie in bed, June's head on his chest, but now her leaving seemed to have scraped all the love out of it.

Ben rubbed his hands over his face, Officer Moretti's words echoing in his mind. *If you really want to find where your wife went, you might want to start by being honest with yourself about why she left in the first place.* But Ben honestly *didn't* know the why. He didn't have a clue about what he was missing.

He walked to June's bedside table and stared at the objects on it. They were all so unique to his wife, he had the absurd sensation that if he pressed them together, she'd somehow materialize out of them. There was the enormous bottle of cheap Jergens body lotion she was always slathering on her legs, the small piece of jade she scraped against her feet for some dance-related reason, the copy of *The Goldfinch* that had been there for months, her thick-frame reading glasses folded neatly on top. He placed the glasses to the side and picked up the novel, but then something else caught his eye beneath it: a thin black book. Frowning, Ben put *The Goldfinch* on the bed beside him and lifted the other, which was bound with a black elastic. A journal? Had June had been writing in this? Since when? He slid the elastic to the side and opened the front cover.

But rather than a page full of writing as he'd expected, he saw that the first fifty pages or so had been ripped out, their remnants like fringe on the spine. The rest of the journal was untouched and blank. Ben ran his thumb along the line of ragged edges, his mind racing. It couldn't be a coincidence— June's disappearance and these redacted pages—and Ben could think of only one reason why she would've torn them out. A dark fear lodged itself into his mind: What could she have written that she'd want to hide from her own husband?

# FIVE

———

*Monday, February 6*

Dear Mom,

We haven't spoken in a while and that's my fault. Ever since you kicked the bucket, I've let you off the hook in terms of getting in touch. Which is why I'm writing to you in this journal now—I'm taking things into my own hands.

I remember this one time in college, I got stoned with Theo Kowalski in my dorm room and we started talking— as all stoned college students do—about death. I'm not sure if Theo was a nihilist or enlightened, but his view on death was that we shouldn't be afraid of it because it's inevitable. I thought this was dumb. What did inevitability have to do with fear? So we began the playful arguing of two people who are both distinctly aware of the possibility of sex afterward. His arguments struck me as overly big-picture: dying was a part of life; people were destined to vanish into memory and then into nothingness; entire species had been wiped out before and this would happen again. To us humans, eventually.

And why were we all so worried about this fate? It happened to the dinosaurs and look where we are now.

As you've probably guessed, Mom, I wasn't handling this line of conversation well. I've never been particularly afraid of dying myself—well, okay, of course I am—but what I was even more afraid of was everyone around me dying. But on top of this, I was stoned! I remember breaking out into a full-body sweat. I told Theo that even though death is inevitable, it's still natural to fear the pain of grief.

"Well, sure," he admitted. "But do the dead ever really leave us? Can't we talk to them whenever we want? Don't they live on in our minds and isn't that where everything else lives anyway?"

I said it wasn't the same for someone to be *alive alive* and for someone to be alive in our minds. I told him, as an example, how I know you, Mom, better than anyone in the whole world and yet how often you still surprise me. I could rarely predict what you were going to say or do. My point being: you can talk to the dead, but they can't talk back.

I'm not sure what Theo said in response. At some point, we stopped talking and started making out. But thinking about it now, I wonder if maybe he was onto something: maybe it is just that easy to conjure up the dead. So I'm giving it a shot and talking to you because I have no one else to talk to.

*Why* don't I have anyone else to talk to, you ask? Take today for example. I woke up this morning feeling ambitious. There were three things I wanted to do: go to story time at the library, take a walk, go to the grocery store. I know, I know, stop the presses! What an ambitious day! But I have a three-month-old. I'd like to see you do any better.

I woke up to Mikey crying a little after five. I changed him, fed him, I even put him into his daytime clothes. I realize that he's three months old and daytime clothes are no different from pajamas, but it feels symbolic to change his outfit. It feels like we're telling the world we're ready for the day. I was still wearing yoga pants, mind you, but I had on my long black silk top, and at this point, yoga pants and a silk top is dressy casual. Ben left for work sometime in the middle of all this, and when I was done about an hour later, I was already exhausted. How bottle-feeding a crying infant feels like running a marathon is beyond me, but it does.

So I put Mikey on his play mat and sat on the couch—I wanted just a minute, just a second, to rest—but the moment I touched the couch, he started crying. I checked his diaper—clean. I'd just fed him, but offered him another bottle, only to be rejected. So I did the only thing that seems to calm him down. I picked him up, held him in that weird way he likes with his face all smooshed in my palm, and lightly bounced him. But he just cried and cried. I tried talking to him, singing to him, but he cried over it all. I tried once to reach for the TV remote, but that made him cry louder, so all I could do while he cried was watch the minutes tick by on the clock. Finally, mercifully, his crying grew softer. I tiptoed to the mirror in the entryway to look at his reflection and—yes!—his eyelids were drooping.

And then, finally, he was asleep. In his room, I lowered him into his crib, but the second he was on the mattress, his eyes popped open and he glared at me with such anger it took my breath away. *Why are you so bad at this?* he seemed to be saying with that look. He started crying again, which was when I started crying too. "Please," I said to him. "Please stop crying."

Later, I checked my phone. Somehow, magically, it was after eleven. We'd missed story time. Again.

The day passed in a loop. Mikey did finally fall asleep for a few minutes, and after his nap, when I finally got him fed, changed, and in a good mood again, I decided we could try to do the second thing on my list: take a walk. But just as I had buckled him into the stroller, I smelled something and by the time I got him out, he'd had a massive blowout. There was liquid baby poop everywhere. It took me an hour to get him and the stroller cleaned, and by then he was crying again. As I bounced him in my arms, I looked at the clock and was both surprised and not surprised at all to see it was after two.

When I put him down a second time, I called Moli. She sounded so awake, like she was wearing freshly washed jeans instead of yoga pants, like she had clean, dry hair and a happy baby. She sounded so far away from how I felt. I wanted to curl up inside her voice like a cat in a patch of sunlight. I drew my knees beneath my chin, closed my eyes, and listened as she described her day.

"Oh, June," she said at one point. "Fifteen months is such a fun age. Clementine is obsessed with walking. No. Running. I actually can't believe how fast she is. Like"—her voice grew incredulous—"she's faster than me. I'm a grown-ass woman and I literally can't keep up with her." She laughed and said, "So anyway, how're you?"

I opened my mouth, but nothing came out. It felt like I'd run into a verbal brick wall. I didn't want to tell her about how I cried today when Mikey wouldn't sleep, or about how, when I think about how afraid I am for his well-being, the intensity of my own fear scares me so much that the other day I got so worked up about the possibility of something happening to him, I literally threw up. These stories sounded too extreme, not right for a Tuesday afternoon chat after she'd just told me about how Clementine had said "doggie" for the first time. So I told her a more moderate story: how the other day, when Mikey wouldn't stop crying, I put fifty miles on the car driving him around because, once upon a time, that had calmed him down. This time when I did it though, he just cried and cried.

"Holy shit," Moli said. "What a nightmare." She laughed a sort of disbelieving laugh. "But isn't it crazy how little that stuff matters when you think about how obsessed we are with them?"

I tried to laugh, too, but my throat constricted so tightly it hurt.

When Ben came home and asked me how my day was, I couldn't tell him the truth. He'd been put on a big client's merger a month before Mikey was born, and he's been more stressed and overworked than ever. He immediately poured a glass of whiskey before he'd even kissed me hello. So I asked him how *his* day was and he said it was fine, he just had a little more work to do. It was 11:16 pm. I thought about how he'd left for the office early that morning and how he'd told me recently that the client he was currently negotiating a contract for was never happy, calling him at all hours of the day to yell at him about yet another piece of language he found unsatisfactory.

Suddenly, my own set of worries looked feeble next to his. Because really, what could I say? *I'm exhausted—just like you?* Or: *Our child—an* infant—*cries too much?* Or how about: *I'm so scared something's going to happen to Mikey that I vomited?* And because it was clear he'd had a rough day and hadn't complained about it, I felt as if he'd challenged me to a martyrdom contest: Who could suffer in silence the longest? So when Ben asked again how my day had been, I smiled tightly and, just like he had done, I said it had been fine.

Now look, Mom, it's not as if Moli and Ben are the only people in my life. I still have friends from the studio and the company, but none of them have kids. And I have my new neighborhood friends, too—Sydney, Reese, and Kirsten. But they're not the type of friends I call up individually. They're my Maplewood Mom group. I've only ever talked to each of them when I'm talking to all of them.

Plus, it's not the recipient of the news that I worry about so much as the news itself. How can you tell anyone that you're not sure this whole being-a-mom thing is right for you *after* you've already become one? Even the most empathetic person would put CPS on their speed dial just in case.

So that's why I've been reduced to taking the advice of stoned Theo Kowalski and talking to the dead through a little black journal. Because I can't talk to anyone else. I just wish you could talk back.

Love,
June

# SIX

———

*Seven years earlier*

After their spontaneous kiss in the hospital waiting room on New Year's Eve, June didn't think she'd ever see the good-natured, broken-handed stranger again. Even though he'd gotten her number before she'd been summoned to an examination room, she assumed that because he'd propositioned her—a complete stranger!—with a kiss, he was the type of man who did things like that often. It would take months for her to understand that Ben Gilmore wasn't frivolous when it came to women, and when he'd spotted her—red-nosed, bleary-eyed, and in her pajamas—he'd fallen. Just a little, but still. She didn't know that about him yet, though, so when he called a month and three days after they met, June was surprised.

"Took you long enough," she said after he explained who he was—*the guy who, well, tricked you into kissing him.*

"You did give me mono," he said. "I left my bed for the first time last week."

"How do you know *I* gave it to you? If you're the type to go kissing every girl you meet in hospital waiting rooms, I wouldn't be surprised if you were constantly coming down with something."

It was impossible for June to know that on the other end of the line Ben was smiling, but somehow, she did, and she tried to envision what that looked like, conjuring the stranger's face in her mind—light eyes, sandy-red hair, fair skin that flushed easily. She opened her mouth to add that she *had* warned him about her germs and also that she was genuinely sorry for the mono, but before she could, Ben had already moved on.

"So I was calling," he said, sounding suddenly breathless, "to see if you'd like to go to dinner with me?"

The invitation made June's stomach flip pleasantly, and even though a part of her felt she should say sorry but she had to focus on her career—just out of the undergraduate dance program at NYU, she was swamped with taking dance classes, teaching them, auditioning, and working the front desk at her mom's dance studio—a much larger part of her fluttered at the prospect of going on a date with him. She liked the way he hadn't tempered his invitation with an out for himself. Unlike so many guys, who always seemed to try and trick her into spending time with them, he hadn't built any plausible deniability of romance into his request. Plus, at the first sound of his voice on the phone, June's mind had flashed to that impromptu New Year's Eve kiss and she'd smiled helplessly. So what if she was busy? She could squeeze in a date with this Ben guy. She was twenty-three and in New York; she could do anything.

After dinner on their first official date, Ben and June walked slowly along the sidewalks of the East Village in the cold. Every now and then, one of them would sway slightly, the fabric of their coats brushing against each other, and they'd straighten their trajectory, all the while hoping it would happen again.

As they rounded the corner onto East Fifth Street, June inclined her head toward the end of the block. "My dance studio's up there."

Ben stuffed his hands into his pockets and turned to her, walking sideways. "You know, I've never seen a dance studio before."

"You could now if you want."

He stopped short. "You mean you have the keys?"

June, who'd been half joking, raised her eyebrows. "Well, yeah."

Even though she had done it a million times, slipping through the darkened doorway of the studio tonight felt clandestine and thrillingly forbidden. She and Ben were both still a little buzzy from their shared bottle of wine, and this detour had the distinct air of adventure. They tumbled onto the darkened landing, Ben's presence turning the familiar space into something new, something electric. As they bustled around blindly, June heard a thud against metal, the sound of a stubbed toe.

"Ow, fuck," Ben said under his breath.

June clapped a hand over her mouth to muffle her laughter.

"Oh, real nice," he whispered, which made her laugh harder.

They tiptoed up the narrow set of stairs to the second-floor studio, and June flipped on one of the lights, casting them in a dim, ghostly glow. Just as the darkness of the stairwell had blurred their edges, the light clarified the space between them and it seemed suddenly impossible to cross.

Ben took off his coat and draped it onto the ledge of the front desk, taking care not to knock anything out of its spot.

He stuffed his hands into his pants pockets and looked around. On the wall behind the front desk, sleek metal letters spelled out: Michelle Maxwell's School of Contemporary Dance. A thin, big-screen computer sat on top of the desk, cluttered with Post-it notes. The place smelled slightly of vanilla, rubber flooring, and feet.

"So this is a dance studio."

"Well, this is just the front desk." June walked toward the studio facing the street. "*This* is a dance studio."

As she passed him, Ben had the urge to hold out his arm and pull her toward him, but he found that he couldn't. He followed her instead, catching the scent of her shampoo—coconut—and, while he'd never really liked the taste or smell of coconut before, suddenly, it struck him as the most intoxicating thing in the world. Walking through the doorway, Ben gazed around the studio, at the soaring ceiling and the enormous floor-to-ceiling windows that let in the light of the city in matching panes on the black floor. June walked to the wooden bar lining one wall and Ben turned in a slow circle in the center of the room. She moved differently here, he noticed—she slowed down, her back straightened—and it made the space feel almost sacred.

"So you've always wanted to be a dancer?" he said. "From the time you were…four? Five! Two."

"Around there, yeah."

"But…" His voice faded as he tried to articulate the general confusion in his mind. They'd talked about the basics of both their jobs at dinner, but Ben hadn't begun to understand the details of June's daily life. "You're not, like, a ballerina. Are you? Or on that show? What's it called? *You Want to Dance?* Or *You Think You Want to Dance?* You know the one. My sister loves it."

June laughed. "I'm not a ballerina, no." She placed a gentle hand on the wooden bar and swept a pointed foot in front of her. "The goal is to be on a company for modern or contemporary dance. Martha Graham or Alvin Ailey or David Parsons or something, but companies are insanely competitive. Some people audition their entire careers and never get on one. Like my mom, for instance. And she was crazy talented. I mean, she still is—she runs this place—but she sorta aged out of the whole company scene a while ago. Anyway, I'll audition for Martha Graham this summer, so hopefully, I'll make that and, in the meantime, I teach classes here and work the front desk and audition for everything."

"What kinda stuff is there to audition for?"

"Well, just before I met you, I did a *Rockin' X-mas Eve* dance special. It was for a local TV station and I had to wear a very uninspired slutty Santa's helper outfit. But the pay was good." She let out a self-deprecating laugh. "And…let's see. I filmed a razor commercial a few months ago. I was mainly just a pair of dancing legs, but you know, it's money and a line on my résumé. And I'm doing some charity event next week for Eva Longoria. Although, that one's not so much dancing as just walking around dressed like a Vegas showgirl and taking pictures with the guests. I just cobble together anything I can get at this point."

"Wow," Ben said. "That sounds…tough. No, exciting. Both." He knew this was the reality of so many New Yorkers—the life of the starving artist—but it felt very far from his life as a law student, with student housing, a strict class schedule, and the promise of high-paying job offers when it was all over. "Do you like it as much as you thought you were going to?" he asked. "Like when you'd dream about it as a kid?"

June's eyes flitted around the studio. "I think I thought I'd be further along by now. I know that probably sounds naive or greedy or whatever—I mean I'm only twenty-three—but I've always had all these ideas in my head. Like, I walk around the streets, and I look at people, and I imagine telling their stories through dance. I see a man and he looks sad, and then I'll see a flash of myself on stage with my body sort of contracting, melting. I imagine the path his tears would take through his wrinkles and try to envision how I'd show that. Or I see a kid jumping over a puddle and I envision how I'd do it on stage. I'd do a grand jeté and sort of flap my hands around. Sometimes I think this makes me unique and that I'm destined to become the next big thing. And then sometimes I think I'm completely delusional because in reality most of my life is just getting squished inside the subway with my gross dance bag as I rush to yet another audition that takes five hours of my life and then doesn't hire me."

She sighed. "So I'm either God's gift to the world, or I'm chopped liver. There's rarely any in-between. But overall, I guess to answer your question, yes, I love it." She swept her foot out again, this time accompanied by her arm, rounded in front of her.

"Your mom must be proud of you," Ben said. "Following in her footsteps."

June hesitated. "Yeah. Anyway, I just want a big life," she continued, dropping her hands by her sides. "I want everything. I want to take over the fucking world."

He grinned. "I'm jealous."

"Of what?"

"Of your certainty. I've never been so sure of anything. Especially not of what I want. I have no idea what I want. Other than like a family and a house and stuff."

"How very quaint of you."

Ben ran a hand through his hair, a laughing, sheepish grin on his lips. "Oh, and what? You think being a dancer makes you Che Guevara?"

She laughed. "What about law school? You're not sure about that? About—what are you studying again?—mergers and acquisitions?"

"I'm definitely not sure about that. But I don't know what I'd want to do more." He hesitated and when he spoke next, June noticed that something had shifted slightly in his voice. It was as if he'd let something in his manner drop, as if he'd just become a little bit closer to the person he was inside. "That's sort of my biggest fear, actually."

"What d'you mean?"

"I'm scared that, like, my life will pass me by, you know? Sometimes I feel like my life just keeps happening *to* me instead of me choosing it, like I'm sleepwalking or something. Does that make sense?"

June nodded. "Of course."

"But the thing is, I don't know how to make choices when I don't know what I want." He sighed. "That's why I'm jealous. Because you do not strike me as the type of person who sleepwalks through life."

"That doesn't mean I don't have my own thing."

"Which is?"

She squished up her face. "Mmm—I don't know."

"Oh, come on. I told you mine."

She let out something halfway between a laugh and a sigh. "Fine. I, um… I try. Very hard. All the time." June had never put words so specifically to the aching knot inside her, and she found she couldn't quite do it.

Ben shook his head. "You try to do what?"

"Everything. I try all the time to do everything right. Like, to be the perfect dancer, the perfect friend, perfect daughter."

"But isn't that just another way of saying that you work hard for what you want?"

"It's more than that, though. I try to be the perfect thing for everybody at all times. Like I'm constantly molding who I am to the people around me so they'll like me." June flushed from her own vulnerability, but she found that she didn't want to stop. "Like—okay—right now? When I was doing those little dance moves? That wasn't like, subconscious or anything. I did it because I wanted you to think that dance is just so intrinsically part of me that I do it while I talk. I wanted to look pretty and interesting. I mean, I didn't articulate it exactly in my mind, but it wasn't mindless either." Her face suddenly burned so hot it hurt.

He studied her. "That sounds…exhausting."

She laughed. "I'm tired all the time."

They stood like that, across the room from each other, in silence for a long moment. Ben wanted to say something else, to tell her she didn't have to try that hard around him, but he thought it would be cliché or sound empty. Instead, he walked across the floor toward her, his heart beating hard against his ribs. How was it possible for one person to make him both so nervous and so bold at the same time?

When he was standing right in front of her, June lifted her face and, through the dim light of the night, Ben looked into her eyes and felt as if he could fall right into them. He reached a hand to her waist and pulled her close. Then, in the darkness, for the second time, they kissed.

# SEVEN

———

Tuesday, February 7

Dear Mom,

Everyone always told me that it would take time for the sting of your death to wear off—not exactly a silver lining, but for years I've really been looking forward to that numbness. As it turns out, though, all those people were full of shit. Because as I get older, I don't get numb to your absence, I just get more and more pissed about all the accumulating things I can't call you up on the phone to talk about. Like, today, for instance.

Today, Mikey and I went to Jitterbuggies. It was the first day of the new course of the mommy-and-me dance and music class that my Maplewood friend group—Sydney, Kirsten, and Reese—all claimed saved their lives as new moms. The three of them had signed up for the next six-week course and because Mikey, at three months, just reached eligibility, they insisted I did too. They had no idea how little convincing I needed. Before his birth, I was ambitious about Mikey's artistic and intellectual development, but now I'd sign us up for eating Play-Doh if it would force us out of the house.

And they were right; the class today was a godsend. By some miracle, Mikey and I made it there with only a few tears (him) and just a little pee (both of us). When we got there, it seemed Mikey was so pleased to be with other people who weren't me, he didn't cry once during the entire class. He's never been that content before and if I hadn't been so grateful for it, I might've resented his little demonstration. It was like taking a broken car to the mechanic only to have him tell you everything is fine. My own baby was gaslighting me.

There were more women in the class than I'd expected, probably ten other mom-and-baby couples, including, of course, Kirsten, Sydney, and Reese, looking almost offensively fresh and clean, I might add. Kirsten, with her wavy blond hair and her lithe little body in expensive athletic gear, looked like Sporty Barbie. Sydney at least had the decency to wear a ponytail, but her chestnut highlights were intact all the way to the roots and anyway, she's so tall and gorgeous she could wear a bag and make it look chic. At least Reese, with her practical chin-length bob and chunky sweater, looked like a normal human, but it still seemed as if she'd showered, which is more than I can say for myself.

The teacher introduced herself and had us go around and say our names, our babies' names, and how old they are. When it got to me, I said my name and Mikey's name, but then I forgot the last thing she'd asked for.

"Age," Reese called out from two spots over.

"Oh, right," I said. "I'm thirty."

It took me an embarrassingly long moment to realize why this made everyone laugh because I am stupid with sleep deprivation. When I finally figured it out, I laughed, too, but it felt hollow. It probably seemed like a silly, nothing sort of mistake to everyone else, but I knew the reality of it: my center of focus is still myself, not my baby. Narcissism isn't cute ever, but especially bad in combination with motherhood.

After I told them Mikey was three months old, the teacher led us through a nursery version of "Baby, It's Cold Outside." We ended by nuzzling our noses to our babies' noses and when I did, I looked into Mikey's eyes and tried to convey how sorry I am that he got stuck with me—selfish, unclean me.

After class, Sydney, Kirsten, Reese, and I went to lunch at Arturo's. We settled the babies in their carriers then sat on the bench seats. "Will any of you judge me if I get a glass of wine?" Reese asked, and instantly, it was as if we were playing hooky from our real lives.

Reese was a glass and a half in when she began the story of her baby Nina's constipation. "On the third day, when she still hadn't pooped," she said, "I took her to see Doctor Albright, who gave me some advice."

At this, Kirsten's wide blue eyes went even wider with sudden understanding. In her slight Southern accent, she said, "Oh, no."

Reese shot her a look. "Has Georgia seen Doctor Albright for constipation?"

Kirsten pressed her lips together, looking both horrified and on the verge of laughter. She nodded wordlessly.

"What?" Sydney interjected. "What did she say to do?"

"She told me," Reese continued, "to swipe Nina's butthole with a Q-tip."

Kirsten buried her face into her hands and groaned.

"And?" I asked. "Did it work?"

Reese's eyes shot to mine. She paused for effect. "Immediately."

We burst out laughing, but as it had at Jitterbuggies, my laughter died too quickly. It was as if I'd suddenly been transported back to my prebaby brain and was looking at the scene as a non-mom. I looked around at these three women, who are smart and funny and totally capable, and thought: here we are, day after day, using all of our brainpower and energy to solve someone else's constipation. It seemed like we'd all been reduced to who we are to someone else. We used to contribute to the world and now we tell stories about buttholes.

Nina started crying then and Reese had to settle her down, and by the time it was quiet enough for us to hear each other again, the laughter was gone.

Reese gazed down at Nina, now sleeping in her arms. Her baby was like a miniature version of her: olive skin, dark wavy hair, beautiful inky eyes. "Do you all, you know, ever think about what your lives would be like if you hadn't had them?" We all knew, of course, who *them* was and my armpits prickled with sweat. If only they knew how close that question hit home. Motherhood suits them all as if they'd written the manual on it. I glanced at Kirsten to find her looking—as I'd predicted—perfectly horrified, as if Reese had suggested we enter into a suicide pact.

"Oh, Kirsten," Reese said. "Don't look at me like that. I'm obviously obsessed with my daughter. But sometimes I think about my life before with some, you know...curiosity. It's like wondering about an alternate reality. Kirsten, stop it! That doesn't make me a monster."

Kirsten shook her head. "No—I... I didn't say it did."

Reese gave her a look. "You didn't have to."

Kirsten took a deep breath as if to say something, but then stayed quiet.

"Of course it doesn't make you a monster," Sydney interjected. "It makes you human. And yes, I love a good alternate-reality fantasy. Like, okay, here's one. In college, I studied abroad in Florence and I loooved it. For four months, I just studied art history and went to museums and ate gelato every afternoon and I never even gained weight because you walk everywhere. And the air there actually smells like flowers. So sometimes I fantasize about what my life would've been like if I'd moved back after college, if I went to graduate school there or worked in an art museum or something."

"Ooh, that's a good one," Reese said.

Sydney nodded. "If for no other reason than that gelato. But thank God I didn't because then I probably never would've met Jonathan and had Layla. What about you, Reese? What's your alternate reality?"

Reese placed Nina back into her carrier so gently Nina didn't even stir, then she wobbled her head, thinking about it. "Well, it's nothing as concrete as graduate school in Florence. It's more just like I think about what if I'd wanted something else. Because—you all know—all I've ever wanted was to be a mom. I used to think I wanted like, seven kids. That's insane, obviously, but even now I want like at least two…maybe three more? So I guess my alternate reality is if I didn't want kids at all." She frowned. "It's weird because I do. More than anything. But then I look at you two"—she looked at me and Sydney—"and you're both so ambitious and driven and your careers are amazing. Sometimes I think about if I had wanted something like that."

"I hardly have a career right now," I said.

"Well, yeah, not right *now*." Reese laughed. "You just had a baby. I mean in general."

"But you like staying home with Nina, don't you?" Kirsten asked. She was still barely masking her horror.

"Yes, of course. That's literally what I'm saying. It's just—sometimes I look at all of your lives and wonder. You know?

Come on, Kirsten. You've got to have some unlived life you sometimes fantasize about."

Kirsten frowned, but there was something else behind it.

"There is!" Reese said. "I can tell. Come on. What is it? You wanted to stay in Georgia and open a peach orchard?"

Sydney and I laughed. It was so spot-on. Kirsten named her daughter Georgia after her own birth state and lobbied hard for the middle name Peach until her husband, Liam, put his foot down. Sweet Kirsten with her bouncy blond hair would look perfect strolling the aisles of a peach orchard in overalls. But Kirsten seemed, if possible, even more disturbed at the suggestion.

"I—I can't do this. I love Georgia too much. I could never want her out of my life, *even* for a stupid fantasy."

Reese laughed and rolled her eyes. "All right, all right. You're a better mom than all of us—"

"I didn't mean—" Kirsten started to say, but Reese cut her off.

"I'm teasing you," Reese said, throwing an arm over her shoulders. "We love you and little Georgia Peach, and we wouldn't want you two anywhere but here." Then she looked at me. "What about you, June? Are you better than me and Sydney too?"

I hesitated. On the one hand, it was as if I'd been waiting to be asked this for months. And yet, I felt shitty just thinking about it, let alone verbalizing it. But they'd shared theirs and I was two glasses of wine in at that point, so I told them.

"Right before I found out I was pregnant with Mikey," I began, "I was offered a role in a ballet. At my company."

"Wait," Reese said. "A ballet? I thought you did modern dance."

"Well, it's a contemporary company, but each production is made up of ballets." They still looked confused, so I added,

"A ballet is basically just a show. Anyway, the—show had already been cast, but I'd been the understudy and unexpectedly, the girl who was originally cast broke her foot so I got the role. The thing was, she was a principal dancer and I was a chorus member."

Their faces didn't change, and understandably so. They didn't know the nuance of the Martha Graham hierarchy. Why would they? I could have elaborated; I was literally the lowest in the company, tapped to do one of the lead parts in our repertory. That *never* happened. It was nothing less than shooting the moon. But instead, I said simply, "It would've been a big deal for me, career wise. Anyway, the ballet was based on the Greek myth of *Medea*. The play by Euripides. And I was going to be Medea."

"Is she the one who has snakes for hair?" Reese asked and Kirsten said, "That's Medusa."

"Medea gets left by her husband for a princess," I said. "And then she gets revenge. So anyway, that's my alternate reality. That's what I fantasize about—what would've happened if I could've been Medea after all."

For a moment, no one said anything and I realized I hadn't played the game right. They could hear something in my voice that hadn't been in theirs. My alternate reality was too real, too close to my actual reality to be a fantasy. It sounded more like regret.

I wish more than anything I could've called you, Mom— you, who gave up all the same things I did in order to have a baby. I wanted to have you assure me that I made the right choice, to hear you tell me, despite how bad it all feels now, that everything is going to be okay.

Love,
June

# EIGHT

———

On the second morning of his wife's disappearance, Ben awoke in his clothes from the night before, his mouth tasting like whiskey, and immediately checked his phone. His heart hammered with desperation to see June's name at the top of a text explaining everything. At the very least, he was hopeful for an update from Officer Moretti, but other than an onslaught of work emails and a handful of texts from Moli, there was nothing new, and Ben felt his hope grow cold.

After he got Mikey situated with his mom, he told her he had to work all day, then he called in to his office to tell them he was still sick and would work from home again. But what he really did was take his laptop to a coffee shop where he ordered a cup of coffee and a turkey sandwich, settled at a little table by the window, and hacked into June's email account—his own Gmail login page had saved the password from long ago. He felt pathetic and maddeningly inert sitting there while June was getting farther and farther away, but after going to the police and calling all her friends, he was no closer to the truth. Now he had to dig deeper.

But even after going through weeks' worth of messages,

he didn't find anything to help him understand where she was or why she left. He heaved a frustrated sigh then logged into their bank account, scanning their credit card activity for anything out of the ordinary—the purchase of a plane ticket maybe, a hotel room, an Airbnb—but not a single line item stood out. How was it possible that June had disappeared without leaving a single piece of evidence behind? He flipped over to their online list of bank transactions, but before he could look at the first line item, a waitress arrived with his sandwich.

"Sorry this took so long," she said, sliding the plate onto the table.

Ben tore his eyes away from his screen to look at her. He'd completely forgotten that he'd ordered food. "It's fine, thanks."

"Is there anything else I can get you?"

Ben flicked his eyes from her to his screen then back again. She was obviously just doing her job, but he had the urge to shout at her to leave him the fuck alone so he could investigate his wife's disappearance in peace. "No, thanks."

"What about a refill on that coffee?"

"Really, I'm—" But he couldn't finish because something on his screen had finally caught his eye. He stared at the tiny line item and June's only giveaway: a cash withdrawal made three days earlier in the amount of five thousand dollars.

"Shit," he hissed, smacking a palm onto the table. Next to him, someone jumped and it was only then that Ben remembered the waitress. But when he lifted his head to tell her, yet again, that he was fine, thank you, he saw that she was already backing away.

Ben sank back in his chair, the screen swimming before his

eyes. Yes, he'd been furious at June for leaving, and yet, up until this moment, in some deep part of his brain, he'd still been harboring the hope that she had some forgivable reason to do so—she was overwhelmed with Mikey and sleep deprived; maybe she'd just wanted to spend a night alone in a hotel. But in reality, he now knew, she was walking around somewhere with enough money to start a new life. The extent of her betrayal was right there in front of him, in black-and-white, and his entire marriage suddenly felt like a sham. He had the urge to snap his laptop shut and drop the whole search. If she didn't want him and Mikey in her life, Ben wouldn't grovel to get her back in theirs.

But then he thought of June, not the June who'd torn out those mysterious pages from her journal or the one who'd made this withdrawal, but the real June, the one he'd been in love with. That love had not been a sham. No matter how devastating her actions were now, Ben knew that was true; he felt it deep inside him, like a thrumming chord. They were bound together, she and him. Ben wouldn't just let her go; he couldn't.

He looked again at that number, and this time it struck him differently. For as far as five thousand dollars could take her, it wasn't exactly vindictive. She hadn't been trying to gouge him; it seemed more like the amount you'd take to escape. Then he looked at the date of the transaction: three days earlier, the day after that party at Sydney and Jonathan's for their baby's first birthday. That fucking party.

Ben hadn't wanted to involve the guys from Clark & White or their wives in all this—he hadn't wanted to tell anyone the truth—but now he didn't see any other option. June had been acting off ever since that party. If something happened there that triggered her leaving, Ben was going to find out. Because if he were right and June had been trying to escape, the obvious next question was: What was she running from?

# NINE

—

*Seven years earlier*

June's love for Ben snuck up on her slowly, subtly, and then, in the middle of their first summer together, it hit her all at once. It happened on a Saturday evening, after the first day of her first audition for the Martha Graham Dance Company.

Ben had spent the start of the weekend in his new office at Clark & White. Upon his graduation from Columbia a month earlier, he'd received a handful of offers from local firms, but his old internship boss had wooed him better than any, with long, wine-dense dinners and promises of fast pay raises. Ben hadn't been able to muster much enthusiasm for the prospect of working in mergers and acquisitions for the rest of his life, but none of the other firms had particularly dazzled him either, and he'd had to remind himself that it wasn't as if accepting a position at age twenty-six was pigeonholing his entire future. He could work at Clark & White for a few years, sock away some money, and then decide what to do next.

He'd accepted and his life had transformed overnight. Within the course of a day, he was no longer a student, but a well-paid lawyer—pending his passing of the bar. He no longer lived in Columbia student housing surrounded by friends, but had moved to a spacious one-bedroom apartment on the Upper East Side to be closer to his new office in Midtown. Now, in the mornings, he put on a suit.

That Saturday night, standing in June's apartment after the first round of company auditions, June told Ben with a broad smile that she'd made it to callbacks the next day. He scooped her up in his arms, her dance bag still slung over her shoulder, and spun her in a half circle before depositing her down and kissing her full on the lips.

"Congratulations."

"Thank you. I'm freaking out." She heaved a sigh and let her bag fall to the floor. She walked to the sink, filled a glass with water, and drank it down. "Today was nuts."

"Why?"

June gave him a look. "They cut half of us after the very first across-the-floor. Literally all we did was walk across the stage and the next round"—she snapped—"half were gone."

"Holy shit," he said. "They're not messing around."

"No, they are not."

"Have you called your mom?"

"Yeah. She's excited. But I also think she sort of expected it. She made it to callbacks her first time, too. I really wanted to tell Moli—I thought she might be here—but I'll tell her tomorrow." They were clearly the only two in the apartment. Moli's and Emilio's doors were open and dark. "Anyway, let's go to my room. I need a bed." She tugged her dance bag onto her shoulder, but Ben grabbed it from her and pulled it onto his own.

"So," he said, when he'd clicked the bedroom door shut behind them. "What time do you go back tomorrow?"

June's face fell suddenly. "Oh, shit, I just got nervous thinking about it." She pressed two fingers to her neck like she was taking her own pulse then sank onto the bed.

"Hey," Ben said. "It's normal to be nervous. But you know how to do this. You've auditioned a million times."

"Not for Martha Graham."

"Martha Graham would be lucky to have you."

While Ben still knew very little about the actual dance part of the dancing world, he wasn't lying. At the first live performance of June's he had been to—a contemporary show at the Joyce Theater in Chelsea—he'd sat in the audience, a bouquet of yellow roses in his lap, transfixed and heart racing. He was biased, of course, but he thought she'd been the best one on stage that night. And that wasn't just because she could extend her leg straight up or that she could do what seemed like half a dozen turns without a trace of effort. It was her emotional performance that impressed him most. Ben had expected a show of smiling women in thick makeup, but June, in character, had hardly smiled once. In fact, she'd looked almost furious up there, desperate and yearning. He hadn't understood the plot—he'd been far too nervous for June to pay attention to that—but her face had told the story of pain and perseverance, and he'd wanted so badly for her character to get whatever it was that she was longing for.

Now, June scooched across the bed, leaned against the wall, and rubbed her eyes. "I really want this," she said, which, to her, felt like the understatement of a lifetime. She didn't just want this; her body thrummed with aching for it. "And I don't want my nerves to fuck it up."

Ben considered this then said, "Maybe you can trick your mind."

"What d'you mean?"

He began to pace the three-foot-wide space between her

bed and the walls. "Your body doesn't actually know the difference between nerves and excitement. Both release that same chemical, nora"—he snapped twice in slow succession—"norepinephrine! And that causes the same symptoms. Butterflies and all that."

June watched as he absently touched the bristles of her makeup brush with the backs of his fingers, and something warm bloomed unexpectedly in her chest.

"Think about the words," he continued. "*Nerve* means guts or courage, but then the plural, *nerves*, means nervous. They're very similar." He picked up a pencil and pushed the pad of his index finger into the lead. Then he put it down again. "So tomorrow, when you're stretching or whatever, just tell yourself that you're excited instead of nervous."

"Have you ever tried this?"

"Well. No. But that's why on *The Bachelor* they always have them do those weird, nerve-racking dates—like belaying down a skyscraper—because their bodies remember the norepinephrine, whether it was released from nerves or excitement. And excitement is so closely associated with love that they're literally tricked into thinking they love each other."

June bit back a smile, no longer nervous. In fact, she was no longer thinking about her audition at all, or even about what Ben was saying. She was trying to focus, but kept getting unexpectedly charmed. Amongst all her things, so feminine and small, Ben seemed solid and masculine. The dichotomy of his strong hand with its gentle grip made her feel strangely wobbly inside, and she had to rein her mind back to the conversation. "How d'you know what they do on *The Bachelor*?"

Ben gave her a look. "You know, June, you shouldn't be so narrow-minded. Men can watch *The Bachelor*."

She laughed. "I know men can watch it, but *you* don't watch it."

"No, that's true. But I've walked into the room a few times when my mom and sister were." He turned to the window. "And you can see the moment it happens. After the skyscraper, when the couple touches down on solid ground, they think they're in love. It's amazing, really. That a shared experience of fear can do that."

He picked up a swatch of fabric June didn't remember she had or why she had it. It was a bluish gray, the sky before a storm, stapled to a thick paper square labeled "swatch." He absently rubbed it against his stubbled jaw, and it was in that moment June realized the feeling that had been bubbling inside her was love. She loved him. It may have seemed like a nothing kind of moment to ignite an emotion as sweeping as love, but as she'd watched him move absentmindedly around the room, June felt she'd gotten a window into who Ben was when he wasn't trying to be anything at all. Up until this point, she'd known he was funny and smart, attractive and generous, but something about the way he rubbed the tiny swatch of fabric against his cheek made her understand that he was also kind and tender and good. Her chest felt as if it might explode—was it nerves or excitement or both?

"So…" she began, heart pounding. "I guess that means you should get me scared then. Take me skydiving or scuba diving or something."

Ben cocked his head to the side, gazing unseeing out the window. "Scuba diving?"

"I don't know. It could be scary. If we ran out of oxygen or something."

His hand holding the fabric swatch slowly returned it to its spot on her windowsill and then he stood like that, completely motionless, for so long June suspected he'd forgotten what they'd been talking about. Her chest flared. Had her indirect reference to love been too direct? Had it been too soon? But then, suddenly, Ben spun on the spot, arms out like a bear's and lunged toward her. "Roar!"

June shrieked with laughter as he tackled her to the bed. His body pressed against hers, his mouth and whiskers grazing her ear, goose bumps blooming on her neck. "Did that do it?" he asked, but June was too breathless with laughter to say anything at all.

# TEN

———

Monday, February 13

Dear Mom,

The list of things I wish I'd asked you when you were alive is an endless, growing thing. Some recently added items include: Did you ever fantasize about alternate realities? Did you ever think about what your life could've been if you'd made the Martha Graham Company? Or if you'd never met Dad and hadn't gotten pregnant and only had yourself to support? I mean, probably not, because nothing ever really got in your way. Here you were, this nineteen-year-old from nowhere Texas, with no money and no contacts and still you made a name for yourself as a dancer and business owner in New York City.

But if you did fantasize about some other life, I wouldn't have held it against you. Ever since that conversation yesterday at lunch, thinking about my alternate reality is all I can seem to do.

In it, I would have debuted in the Graham Company as Medea. I would've been on stage that first night of the tour in Philadelphia instead of having to take the train and sit in the audience, six months pregnant, tears falling onto my newly swollen belly as I watched Natalia Mikhailovich dancing my part. I've never actively rooted against another dancer before, but there was a part of me that wanted her to show some sign of weakness up there, some sign that I could've done better. Nothing career ending, just a little something for my ego.

It wasn't that I felt I deserved the role more than she did. After all, Natalia's a principal dancer; it made way more sense for her to be cast than me. But it was exactly that, the unlikelihood of every moment that led up to me getting the part: Hiromi walking in on me dancing our duet; Sasha breaking her foot; me being the only one in the entire company who knew the choreography. When Hiromi suggested I learn the role, I felt so unbelievably lucky, I worked harder at it than I had at anything else. I came to the studio early and stayed late, I researched Medea online, I read and reread the play every night before bed. By the time I officially auditioned, I didn't have to try to act like Medea; she was simply a part of me.

Even that night at the debut, as I watched another dancer portray her, I still felt like Medea. In my theater seat, my body twitched along with the choreography. I felt her anger, lived her story.

It starts when she falls in love with Jason. He's a mortal, she a sorceress, so their love is unlikely, but they're happy. They move to Corinth, start a family, and life is going well—they have two sons; they're madly in love—until Jason decides he wants to be a king and leaves Medea to marry the princess of Corinth. But that's just the beginning of his betrayal. After he cheats on her and leaves her, Jason claims to Medea that he did it *for* her, so their "sons could have the status and wealth of royalty." The level of his gaslighting is infuriating. And of course, as a white dude in antiquity, things turn out just fine for him. If Medea had cheated, she would've been banished or maybe even killed. Jason, on the other hand, is welcomed into the royal family with open arms.

Furious with her husband, furious with the society that allowed him to do what he did, Medea plots her revenge. She sends a poisoned crown to the princess, which makes all her skin melt off her body. Jason reacts, unsurprisingly, with self-righteous rage. He calls Medea bitter and crazy, claiming yet again that he was cheating on her for *her own sake*. Psychopath.

Throughout the play, you can tell that Euripides has sympathy for his main character. There is no redeeming quality in Jason, but it's obvious he empathizes with Medea. Even till the very end, through her last horrific act of revenge, Euripides is fighting for her. He doesn't kill her like so many writers from antiquity probably would; he lets her fly to Athens with Aegeus in a golden chariot of flames. It's my favorite part. He doesn't absolve her, but he gives her the chance at a new life.

On stage at the ballet's debut, Natalia moved through Medea's rage into her self-actualization, while I sat watching, burning, thinking about what my life would be like if everything hadn't happened the way it did.

When I went into Hiromi's office to tell her I couldn't accept the part—I'd be six months pregnant during the tour— I told her I wanted to come back as soon as I could. She very kindly outlined the parameters of the company's maternity leave, but I could tell she thought I wouldn't return after those six months. When most girls leave to have a baby, they don't come back.

The other day, as Mikey was napping, I made some tea, and as the water heated up, I started doing some warm-ups in the kitchen. I hadn't even realized I was doing this until, in the middle of some pliés and relevés, I noticed how good it felt to use my legs in that way again. So I started doing more: tendus, rond de jambes. But then I did a pas de chat and the moment I left the ground, I felt this enormous gush. I peed myself doing the simplest, smallest jump in the history of dance. And it wasn't just a little; I had to change my underwear *and* my pants. I thought about the look Hiromi had given me that day in her office, that almost piteous smile as I told her my plans, and I finally understood. Even if I do come back to the company after all this, my body will never be the same again.

It's not that I even want this alternate reality—in the theater that night I did, I admit it, but now I don't. If keeping Mikey safe and healthy required me to never dance again, like not even a slow dance at a wedding, I'd do it in a heartbeat. I guess I just wish for the alternate reality where I get to do it all, dance on stage as Medea, have Mikey as well as an intact vagina, and—since I'm wishing for things here—have a mom who didn't die and leave me to talk to her through this stupid fucking journal.

Oh, Mom, I'm a mess and I miss you.

Love,
June

# ELEVEN

———

It was early afternoon when Ben knocked on Sydney's door.

"Ben," she said after opening it, her voice lilting up at the end of his name like a question. She was dressed in a cream-colored sweater and tight jeans that accentuated how tall and thin she was. Her long brown hair fell over one shoulder like a smooth sheet. "Hi. Is everything okay?"

"Hey, Sydney, sorry to barge in on you at"—he checked his watch—"one fifteen on a Thursday. I would've called, but I realized I don't actually have your number."

"No, it's fine. What's—" She faltered. "Do you want to come in?"

"Thanks."

Sydney smiled, a polite mask over her obvious confusion. "Of course," she said, holding the door open for him to pass through.

As he walked through the foyer, he was reminded how nice her and Jonathan's house was. It looked like it belonged to a long-established couple with a lot of money and good taste, rather than young parents of a one-year-old. An ambassador could live here, he thought, or maybe a heart surgeon. Everything was impeccable. An enormous gold-framed mirror hung above a long, thin wooden table, both of which looked like they'd been custom-made to fit the space. Even though their kid's birthday party had only been four days earlier and had no doubt wrecked the place, their home looked flawless. Ben pictured his own smaller, older house and felt a knee-jerk sense of inferiority, but then it turned to irritation. He'd always been so disdainful of his parents' addiction to affluence, so when and how had he let himself get so preoccupied with it?

"Reese is here, by the way," Sydney said, leading him back into the house.

"Oh, good. I actually wanted to talk to her too."

Sydney turned, obviously taken aback by this. "Is everything okay? Is June okay?"

"She's fine," he said automatically, even though nothing could be further from the truth. "I mean, she's fine, physically speaking. I just wanted to ask you some questions."

A look of understanding passed over her face, and Ben wondered what exactly she thought she understood.

"Reese," she called as they walked into the living room. "Ben's here. June's Ben." At that, Ben felt a tugging beneath his sternum; he didn't feel like *June's Ben*, not anymore. "He wants to talk."

In the living room, Reese, dressed in a flannel shirt and jeans, sat cross-legged on the rug as two babies crawled around her. Ben vaguely recognized the babies as those of his colleagues but even if he didn't, it would've been easy to see who belonged to who; with her olive skin, wavy hair, and dark eyes, Reese and Will's daughter was a near carbon copy of her mom. As he stood in front of her and Sydney, Ben was struck with the oddness that these two women, whom he'd only been around a handful of times, played such a big role in June's life. When he and June lived in the city, they went out all the time with both sets of friends. He'd known Moli and others from the dance world enough at one point to call them his own friends. He had their numbers in his phone, texted them on birthdays. Now, even though Jonathan and Will and Liam were his closest friends at Clark & White, they spent so little time outside the office that their wives and children were little more than strangers to him.

Reese smiled, but she looked uncomfortable. Like Sydney, she had a glint of understanding in her eye. Why did these women suspect he was there? What did they know that he didn't?

"Why don't I get Margot to watch the girls while we talk?" Sydney suggested. "She's just in the other room working on something." She looked at Reese. "It's almost nap time anyway. What do you think? Just bump it up? Have Margot put them down?"

Ben knew from Jonathan that Sydney was so successful in her own right that she had a part-time assistant who helped with administrative work as well as with the baby.

"Have *another human* put Nina down?" Reese said as she grabbed her baby by the armpits and sat her in her lap. "Good Lord, what could be better?"

Once they'd settled the babies with Margot, they returned to the living room and the two women turned expectantly to Ben.

"So what's up?" Reese said.

His gaze darted into his lap. It was humiliating to have to utter any of what he was about to say. "First of all, I know you'll probably tell this to Jonathan and Will, but could you just ask them not to bring any of this up at work?" He couldn't stand the thought of walking into Clark & White while the minds of all his colleagues buzzed with speculation about what had happened between Ben Gilmore and his missing wife.

Reese nodded and Sydney said, "Of course."

"Thanks." Ben ran his hands over his face. "June is…missing. Well, actually no, she left."

Whatever had given the women the knowing look in their eyes, it wasn't this. Both their faces widened in shock. "Oh, my God," Sydney said.

"Where's Mikey?" Reese asked.

"He's with my mom. She drove down yesterday to help out until June gets back."

"Okay, that's good. So…wait. June *left*? What d'you mean? Do you know where she is?"

"No, that's why I'm here. I keep calling her, but her phone keeps going to voice mail. I've talked with her best friend—"

"Moli," Reese said.

Ben looked at her. "Yeah." For some reason, this made him feel territorial over his wife, as if he needed to prove that he knew June better than they did. But of course, that was exactly why he was here: because right now, he probably didn't. "And I've called her dance studio and her old company and they both said she hasn't been to either in months. I filed a request to locate with the police, but—"

Reese's eyebrows shot up. "You went to the police?"

"I didn't know what else to do. Not that *they* can even do anything. Because like I said, she's not technically missing."

Sydney nodded slowly, her brown eyes wide. "Okay. Wow. How can we help?"

"Well, I know you all see each other a lot, with that Jitterbuggy class and stuff, and I was just wondering… Did she mention anything to either of you about leaving?"

Reese and Sydney shared a glance. "No," Sydney said. Reese shook her head. "Sorry."

"Oh." Ben frowned. The way June had always talked about these women, he'd thought that they'd be able to tell him everything he needed to know. He hadn't planned for their ignorance on top of his. "Okay…well, did she mention *anything* out of the ordinary? Anything that struck you as odd or off or anything?"

Sydney fiddled with her wedding ring.

Reese shifted in her seat. "Well, there was that whole Greek mythology thing."

Ben stilled. He didn't know what he'd been expecting, but it certainly wasn't this. "What Greek mythology thing?"

"You know. June was reading a lot about that old Grecian story. It wasn't like, off or anything, but she talked about it more than I've ever talked about Greek mythology."

"What story?"

Reese frowned. "It wasn't Medusa… But I can't remember what it was." She looked at Sydney, who shook her head and said, "Me neither."

Ben buried his face in his palms, rubbing his fingers into his eyes. He had absolutely no idea what to do with this bizarre new information. "Okay, well, what about the party last Sunday? Did something happen that either of you know of? June was acting sort of weird when we got home. Sort of… distracted." He thought back to that afternoon, when she'd given Mikey his bath, then handed him off to Ben without even drying him off first.

Again, the two women shared a look, and again, Ben had the distinct sensation that he was missing something.

"Yeah…" Sydney started hesitantly. "I was sort of surprised to see you all there, actually."

"Why?"

"Well, just that—I mean, Ben, we haven't seen June in a while. I didn't expect her to come to the party because we hadn't heard from her in like, the two weeks leading up to it."

"But what about Jitterbuggy? I thought it was twice a week."

"It is." She gave him a confused look. "But June stopped going."

A vague memory of a past conversation with June formed in his mind. "Right. Yeah, she did mention that... But she stopped because of Mikey's sleep schedule. That doesn't ex-plain why she hasn't been around for other things. I know you all do wine nights and lunches and stuff."

Sydney narrowed her eyes at him.

"What?"

She shook her head. "No, nothing. I just didn't know about Mikey's sleep schedule. I thought she stopped going to Jitter-buggies because of the petition. And..." But then her voice faded, as if she'd changed her mind about something. "Well, anyway, after that, things just sort of got crazy."

Ben felt vaguely dizzy. "Petition?"

"You don't know about the petition?"

He took a deep breath. He wanted to say that he and June had just been busy recently, that they talked all the time, just not all the time *now*. Now, all he could do was work and all June could do was take care of Mikey. They were in survival mode. But it didn't mean they didn't communicate. It didn't mean they didn't love each other. "It's been a busy month. What petition?"

Sydney studied him as if she were trying to gauge some-thing, and Ben got the feeling they were finally coming around to whatever they'd been keeping from him. "Maybe you should talk to Kirsten about it," she said after a moment.

"We don't really know all the details, and she'll be able to tell you a lot more than we can."

"Kirsten, Liam's wife?"

She nodded.

"What does she have to do with it?"

Sydney looked down, her discomfort palpable. "Look, we don't really know or understand the full story, but something happened between Kirsten and June. About two weeks ago, they both sort of disappeared. They stopped responding to texts, stopped coming around to wine nights. It seemed like there was some sort of…bad blood between them."

Beside her, Reese shifted.

"And Kirsten told us some stuff about June," Sydney continued tentatively. "But honestly, we don't really know what to believe." Finally, she looked up and held Ben's gaze. "My point is, we'll do anything to help you find June and bring her back, but…if you're trying to understand what was going on with her and why she stopped coming around with us, you should talk to Kirsten."

# TWELVE

---

*Seven years earlier*

After dinner one night, six months into their relationship, June turned to Ben and said, "My mom's having one of her parties tonight. Do you wanna go?"

By this point, June had told Ben all about the parties of her youth, the famed and spontaneous Maxwell potlucks of the East Village. They started years ago, before June was even born. Whenever Michelle was hungry or bored, she would make a phone call or two and, for the rest of the evening, artists from all over the city would migrate to their tiny apartment bearing dishes—cured meats, hunks of cheeses, olive tapenade, chutneys, chicken satay—and they'd eat and drink until dawn.

When June and Ben arrived that night, they were met with a cacophony of voices, and June was immediately swallowed into a series of embraces. To Ben, the crowd seemed like a single organism, absorbing the newcomers into its body effortlessly. June was introducing him around when Michelle emerged through the throng. She was in head-to-toe black, the only color of the outfit a bright turquoise scarf with white polka dots tied like a bandanna around her head. She clutched an unadorned martini with slender fingers, smiling at June, her eyes wide in happy surprise.

"So Terry wasn't lying after all—my offspring *is* here." She pecked June's cheek then shifted her attention to Ben. "And that would make you Ben. It's so nice to finally meet you," she said, pulling him into a hug. "I want to know everything. But first"—she extricated herself from his arms and looked at June—"have you heard any news?"

Ben looked confusedly from Michelle to June, but June knew exactly what her mom was talking about. She'd gone out last week for *Come Fly with Me*, a Broadway musical with songs by Frank Sinatra and choreography by Twyla Tharp. It would've been the biggest line on her résumé to date, with relative job stability, prestige, even healthcare. But more than that, June wanted it because she was still stinging from the rejection of the Martha Graham Company the previous month. She'd made it far into that second day of auditions, but not far enough.

"Mom," she said. "I promise, if I book Broadway, you're not going to have to ask to hear about it. Plus, it was like three days ago. It'll probably be a while before I hear anything."

"Right. Sorry, chicken." Michelle grabbed the side of June's ear and rubbed it between her index finger and thumb. "That was stupid of me."

June swiveled her head away from her mom's grasp. "It's fine," she said, and when Michelle didn't immediately drop her ear, June playfully swatted a hand to the side of her head. "Get off me."

"Okay, okay." Michelle turned again to Ben. "So, Ben. June tells me you're a lawyer. You'll have to meet Frank, then. He's here somewhere."

Ben smiled politely. "Is he a lawyer too?"

"Oh, good Lord, no. But he *desperately* needs one."

Later, as Ben returned to the living room with a glass of wine for June and a beer for himself, a slender white man with stacks of turquoise rings caught his eye and grinned. "Ah, Ben, you're here. Good. I was about to tell the story of the first time I met June."

"Can't wait," Ben said with a grin, then leaned over the couch to hand the glass of wine to June, who gave him a look of amused embarrassment. He waggled his eyebrows.

"June couldn't have been a day over five," the man began, speaking to the room, "and you all remember—that's back when she hadn't grown into her eyes yet. She looked like an adorable fly—tiny body, huge eyes. So I'm sitting there, talking to Dee Dee"—he nodded toward a Black woman with braids piled atop her head—"when all of a sudden, I hear this blood-curdling scream. I turn to see little June standing on the coffee table, pickle in hand, yelling for her mom. Well, I thought she must be *bleeding* with a scream like that. And clearly, Michelle thought so, too, because I turn to see her tearing through the crowd. She shoves whatever drink she was holding into the closest set of hands, grabs June's wrists, and starts shouting *What? What is it?* June's squirming around, clearly trying to get out of her grip, so finally, Michelle lets her go, but instead of pointing to some unseen injury, June starts…*dancing*. Michelle was obviously confused—we all were—but then June gives her a very pointed look and says, *It's the mama-papa!*

"That's when we realized she was talking about the music. It was The Mamas & The Papas. That song 'Dedicated to the One I Love.' You know the one. And suddenly, five-year-old June is doing this whole complicated routine. At first, when the song starts off slow, she's doing all this beautiful modern work, and then when it picks up the pace, she starts these fan kicks followed by these fierce shoulder pops, and the whole time she's holding this pickle and giving her mom this incredulous look, like *Aren't you gonna join me?* Michelle had no choice. She joined in on the side of the coffee table, and it was immediately clear they had a whole choreographed duet together."

Ben laughed along with the rest of the room.

"But it gets better," the man continued. "We're watching, hysterical, and suddenly during the refrain right in the middle, Lawrence—a dancer—gasps and says *That's Graham choreography!* June was five! And she was already doing the moves of one of the most famous choreographers in New York. It was the cutest thing I've ever seen."

"That's because you haven't seen me do Twyla Tharp choreography," June said as the room laughed. "It's adorable."

"You know…" Ben heard a voice say. He scanned the crowd to see who was talking and his eyes landed on an Asian woman with hair to her waist, a large silver pendant around her neck. "I think Michelle probably still has that CD around here somewhere…"

All eyes swiveled to June and Michelle on opposite sides of the room like they were magnets. Mother and daughter locked eyes dramatically, aware of their audience, emoting a mixture of mock horror and real amusement.

Suddenly, Michelle shouted across the room. "Ben, June! Run!"

In the seconds following, as everyone thrust their heads back with laughter, Ben caught the smallest exchange between the two women, one that was meant just for them: across the crowded room, Michelle gave her daughter the briefest flicker .

of a wink. Then June was on her feet, her hand sliding into his, and she was dragging him through the crowd to the door. Even after they disappeared beyond it, he could hear the delighted shrieks of laughter of the people they'd left behind.

Out in the hallway of her childhood apartment building, June could tell Ben was both relieved and pleasantly surprised at how well his first introduction to her life had gone. He slung his arm around her neck and planted a kiss on the side of her head.

"Thank God we got out of there," he said. "They were for sure gonna try to rope me into that dance."

June laughed, but her mouth felt tight. Her mind was still back in her old apartment, snagging on that story of her dancing on the table, holding a pickle. She'd heard it many times over the course of her life, and it always used to make her swell with pride—what a cute, precocious kid she'd been—but tonight it was twisting into a knot in her stomach. Her mom had been grooming her for the dance world for years and, in the wake of her first rejection from Martha Graham and now maybe one from Broadway, too, June realized just how little she had to show for it.

June had grown up in the same 652-square-foot apartment Michelle had first leased when she got off the bus in Manhattan from Texas, and while she and her mom had always been comfortable, June had learned from an early age the limits of their money. They shopped exclusively at consignment stores because buying new clothes was "wasteful" and for the "creatively bankrupt." They had countless dinners of butter noodles with ill-fitting sides of whatever was in the house: yellow squash, tuna fish, artichoke hearts from a jar. And yet, because of the potlucks, June had also rubbed elbows, literally, with some of the most financially successful people in the art community.

So when she walked into the enormous colonial on the sprawling estate of Ben's childhood to meet his family for the first time, their affluence didn't make her uneasy. It did, however, put things into context.

Ben had never worn his wealth on his sleeve or scorned it like only people from money could, but as she walked beneath the two-tiered chandelier in the foyer of his family's house, she retroactively put the pieces together in her mind: how, even at nice restaurants, Ben would sometimes order an appetizer in addition to his entrée and drinks, based on his hunger or mood rather than the prices; how he had a different, perfect jacket for every type of weather; how, once when they went out for seafood, he'd known the names and flavors of the three sauces that came with their oysters.

That night in the colonial, June had been introduced to five smiling faces: Ben's dad, Robert, his mom, Kate, his younger brother, Charlie, and Charlie's girlfriend, Claire, and the youngest of the three siblings, Amy. Kate, Charlie, and Amy all had the exact same strawberry blond hair as Ben, although June could tell that his mother's was from long hours in a salon rather than the lasting color of her youth.

"So," Ben's dad said to June after they'd settled down to dinner. "Ben tells us you're going to be on Broadway."

The words felt like a slap across June's face, but before she could respond, Robert continued. "We want to hear all about it. And sorry ahead of time for any inane questions. We love a good Broadway show, but the Gilmores have always been decidedly ignorant when it comes to the arts."

"Dad—" Ben said, and although it came out sharp and

reproachful, his family clearly misinterpreted the reason behind it.

"Yes, *Robert*," Kate said with a mockingly scolding look to her husband. "You're making us look like plebeians, but we heard the show's going to be all Frank Sinatra music, which is something even us *artistically ignorant* can appreciate."

Robert laughed. "Well, that's true. Even I know about Ol' Blue Eyes."

June had the sensation of being in a conversational tornado, as if she were spinning around and around, unable to correct its trajectory. Beside her, she heard Ben start to say something, but Charlie spoke over him. "Dammit, June, why'd you have to be in a *Sinatra* musical? We're in serious danger right now of Dad breaking out into song."

Robert pointed his steak knife at his youngest son. "You should be so lucky." He looked to June and added, "I have an excellent singing voice," to which Charlie and Amy said in unison, "No, he doesn't."

"Dad," Ben snapped again, finally getting the attention of the table.

But June didn't want him to swoop in and save her. She cleared her throat and, keeping her tone as light and pleasant as she could, said, "I think there's been some miscommunication. I *auditioned* for a Sinatra musical on Broadway. I didn't *get* it."

The room fell quiet and June's body radiated with heat. She wanted to contract into herself.

Ben sighed. "I told you guys that." He hesitated. "Of course, she could still get it. She just hasn't heard yet."

June could have let it end there. She could have given them all the gift of optimism—so much easier to move on from with vague *good luck*s and *hope you hear soon*s—but something about the way they'd so casually brought up the whole thing, as if being on Broadway wasn't even something to be very proud of or excited about, had her hot with indignation. "Actually," she said, throwing a look at Ben, "I just heard it was cast. Apparently, one of Moli's friends made the ensemble. So… I guess I didn't get it after all." She forced out a laugh, but it sounded off in the stillness of the room. She could feel all the eyes of her boyfriend's family on her.

"Oh," Ben said, a concerned line between his brows. "I'm sorry."

But June couldn't look at him. She flapped a hand and looked around the table instead. "It's fine. Really! I didn't mean to bring everybody down." She laughed another unnatural laugh.

"Oh, I'm sorry," Kate said. "I must've misunderstood Ben on the phone. I just thought…" Her voice trailed off.

"Honestly," June said. "It's fine. There will be many more auditions."

"Actually," Ben added, "June's in rehearsals now for a show coming up next month. It's going to be at the Joyce Theater in Chelsea."

"Oh, that's wonderful," Kate chirped, but June registered the looks of polite incomprehension on every face there. No one knew what the Joyce Theater in Chelsea was. *Wait till they hear the name of the show*, she thought with bitter amusement: *Cassandra in the Flesh*—an original contemporary showcase where all the dancers wore nude leotards and where the musical motif was nothing but a heartbeat. That was sure to get them as excited as a Broadway musical scored by Ol' Blue Eyes. What she really wished was that she could say she was in the Martha Graham Company. She could've told them about

the tour schedule that spanned the world and had her performing on the biggest stages in Paris, San Francisco, Athens.

"Well, I think it's incredibly brave to try to make a living
by dancing," Robert said, laughing.

"Dad," Ben said.

"What? It is! Lord knows none of us could do it. We just
make a living sitting at a computer, using nothing but our
brains. How very old-fashioned we must seem."

June could have smiled and cut her New York strip, and
the conversation would have turned benignly away from their
guest's embarrassing career, but she couldn't. Maybe it was
because of the way Robert said the word *brave* tinged with
condescension or because he'd just made dancing sound so
disdainfully blue-collar. Or maybe it was because, sitting in
this absurdly big house, she wanted to prove that their son
wasn't padding her income with anything more than a few
dinners out.

"Actually," she said, looking at Robert, "I don't make a
living doing it. I teach ballet to five-year-olds and I answer
phones." Even before she'd finished saying it, she wished she
could take it back.

June registered the flash of pity and embarrassment in everyone's eyes before Robert cleared his throat. "Well, good
for you! Maybe your work ethic will start to rub off on Ben
here. As lazy as he is, he sure could use it!"

Everyone laughed and the conversation mercifully moved
on to Charlie, but just before it did, in the awkward moment
as everyone grabbed their wineglasses and shifted in their
seats, Ben slipped his arm beneath the table, grabbed June's
hand in his, and gave it one tight squeeze.

It wasn't until later that night, when they were getting ready
for bed in Ben's childhood bathroom, that June realized she

wasn't the only one who needed comforting after that dinner. Because while Robert had insulted her career, he'd belittled Ben's character. And wasn't that so much worse for no other reason than that it was directed at his own son?

As Ben brushed his teeth, June leaned back against the bathroom counter. "Is your dad…" But her voice faded, unsure how to finish.

Ben spit into the sink, then dropped his toothbrush into the holder. "Always like that?"

"Well. Yeah."

He pressed a washcloth to his mouth. "Sorry for all that shit he said at dinner."

"No, it's…whatever. But what about what he said to you?"

Ben frowned. "What did he say to me?"

"That you're lazy."

"Oh."

She made a face. "Ben, you're like the least lazy person I know."

He shrugged. "Yeah, well, my dad wouldn't really know that."

"What d'you mean?"

"Just that he doesn't really know anything about me. He was never around when I was growing up. Like, that stuff about his singing voice? I have no idea what Charlie and Amy were talking about. He might've started showing up more when they were still living here, but not when I was. So when he wants to make fun of me, it's like he's throwing spaghetti against the wall to see what sticks."

*Make fun* seemed too benign of words to June—his tone in general seemed too benign. "Have you ever, like, said anything to him?"

"Like what?"

"I don't know—that you don't want to be around someone who makes you feel bad?"

He laughed. "I'm not sure empty threats would work with my dad."

June hitched a shoulder. "They wouldn't have to be empty. I mean, *do* you want to be around someone who makes you feel bad?"

Ben gave her an odd look. "He's my family, June. He's my dad."

"Right. No, yeah. Sorry."

They finished getting ready in silence, then Ben pulled back the bed covers and they both slipped in. Later, as she lay awake in the darkness, June turned toward him, molding her body to fit his much bigger one. She wrapped her arm over him, pressed her lips to his bare back, and whispered, "I love you." She couldn't tell if he'd heard her or not or if he was awake at all; he just grabbed her arm and wrapped it tighter around himself.

# THIRTEEN

——

*Wednesday, February 15*

Dear Mom,

I just realized that Ben and I haven't seen each other since yesterday morning, almost thirty-six hours ago. This isn't exactly unusual—when I was apprenticing with the company, I occasionally went on tour, so Ben and I have spent many nights sleeping in different cities, many miles between us. What's unusual about *these* thirty-six hours apart is how close we are. I could've reached out a hand and touched him, but we never spoke a word.

He wasn't home by the time I went to sleep last night and he was gone when I got up this morning. The only reason I even know he came home at all was because when I got up in the middle of the night to soothe Mikey, I saw the form of his body under the blankets. So I guess to be more accurate, I've seen him and presumably he's seen me, but neither of us was conscious when the other was.

When I fall asleep these days, his absence feels so gaping it's like a vacuum. Which is strange because even when we used to fall asleep together, it wasn't usually *together together*, you know? I'd lie tucked next to him, my head on his chest, and we'd talk about our days, or we'd read side by side and, every so often, his hand would find mine or my toes would brush up against his calf. Sometimes this would lead to sex and sometimes it wouldn't, but even when it did, afterward, we'd kiss good night and turn to our sides of the bed to fall asleep alone. Considering that, it seems odd that what I miss most now is him lying next to me, a few feet apart, at the end of the day.

On another note, the girls and I had wine night tonight. Despite the fact that our home is a disaster—still-packed moving boxes line the hallway and baby stuff is everywhere— I hosted. Sydney and Reese came over around seven, after they'd settled their babies with their husbands and after I'd put Mikey down, and we expected Kirsten around the same time, but thirty minutes passed and then forty-five, and then we'd already finished our first glasses of wine and it was eight and she still hadn't made it. I was about to text her when she burst through the door, and it was immediately clear why she'd been late: her lips looked like someone had been biting them, her makeup was smudged, her normally styled blond hair was a mess. She was the picture of post-coital disarray.

"Sorry I'm late," she said, her Southern accent a bit more pronounced than usual. "I had to put Georgia down, then Liam got home late—surprise surprise—and he's leaving town tomorrow so we had a glass of wine together, and well, we got to talking and…it just took longer than I thought." Her cheeks flushed red.

"Don't worry about it," Reese said, biting back a smile.

"What?" Kirsten said, frowning as she looked from Reese to me and Sydney, all of us trying to keep a straight face. If this had been Moli or any of my friends from the studio, we would've already talked about it and moved on by now, but this was Kirsten. And the fact that she felt she had to hide her garden-variety marital sex from her friends made the whole thing absurd.

"What's so funny?" she asked.

"No, nothing," Sydney said, pressing her lips together.

Kirsten put a hand on her hip. "What?" She looked at each of us, then she scrunched up her face, dug a hand into the neck of her sweater, and said, "Is my sweater on backward?"

Reese let out a little snort of laughter and we lost it.

"What?" Kirsten said. "What's going on?"

Reese waved a hand in front of her face. "I'm sorry, I'm sorry. It's just that—well, you look very…sexed-up."

Kirsten looked momentarily confused. Then she seemed to gather herself. She straightened her back, lifted her chin. "I'm neither confirming nor denying it," she said, which of course made us laugh harder.

She rolled her eyes, pulled two bottles of wine from her bag, and announced, "My husband's leaving town and I'm sad. Now, who wants to drink with me?"

We drank and talked, the white noise from Mikey's baby monitor singing in the background, and after a while, Kirsten topped off her glass of wine, and said, "You know what I think we should do? We should play Confession."

I looked around. "What's Confession?"

Sydney laughed. "It's this game Reese came up with to… I don't know"—she looked at Reese—"torture us?"

"No, no," Reese said. "It's not torture. I came up with it years ago when we'd all just met and I was so sick of those meaningless conversations about Netflix and Nordstrom, so I said we should play a game where we say what we're really thinking. Talk about our deepest fears or worst thoughts or whatever."

Kirsten got up onto her knees. "We haven't played in forever! Sydney, you go first."

Sydney scoffed. "Why do I have to go first?" But then she laughed and said, "Okay, okay, I will." She sighed, thinking. "So lately I've been so into the business that I'm feeling like a bad mom."

A little background for you, Mom: Sydney started an interior design company a few years ago, and this past year it really started taking off. Her Instagram just blew up and now all these companies like West Elm and Pottery Barn have teamed up with her to showcase their stuff on her feed. It's not my personal style—everything's very white—but objectively, she's killing it.

"The thing is," she continued, "business is going so well that I'm having to spend more and more time on it and less and less time with Layla. My assistant-slash-nanny Margot is my favorite person right now. And I mean, intellectually, I know that it's okay, but there're some days when I'm so absorbed in work that for just a moment I'll forget about Layla. That sounds bad. What I mean is—you know how you think about your kid, like, all the time? Like even when you're not thinking about her, you still kind of are?"

I nodded. Mikey is like a tapeworm in my brain. I was thinking about him as Sydney talked, my eyes sliding over to the baby monitor to make sure I could see his chest rise and fall. I couldn't, and my heart nearly stopped, but then he twitched in his sleep and I relaxed.

"Well, some days," Sydney continued, "I'll be working and I'm so into what I'm doing, staging a house or editing photos or whatever, and my level of focus almost gives me a high, and then all of a sudden I'll remember Layla—my *baby*—and everything inside me will sort of drop with guilt because I forgot her. What kind of mother does that make me?"

I could tell by the way she was talking that she both believed and didn't believe what she was saying, like her guilt was real, but she knew it was unfounded. I could tell that while she felt bad for relying so much on her nanny/assistant, she was also proud of her work and happy when she came home to Layla. I could tell that her love for her daughter was both intense and uncomplicated, that if she actually, truly felt like a bad mom, she wouldn't have been talking about it so casually, if at all. I ached with jealousy. I would have given anything for her confession to be mine.

"That doesn't make you a bad mom, Syd," Reese said. "You're showing Layla firsthand to follow her dreams. You're showing her that when she grows up, she can have kids and a fulfilling career if that's what she wants. That makes you the opposite of a bad mom. It makes you a really, really good one."

"That's true," Kirsten said. "And at least this is a good problem to have. I mean, not that you feeling like a bad mom is a good problem. But it's a problem of riches! Your business, which you started from scratch, I remind you, is doing so well that you have to spend more time on it."

"Your problem," I said, adding on, "is that you're *too* much of a badass."

"You're just better at everything than everybody else," Reese said. "It's hard work being that good at everything."

Sydney started laughing. "Okay, okay! Enough!"

But then Kirsten joined in. "You're so good at being both an interior designer and a mom that Chip Gaines is going to divorce *Joanna* for you."

I frowned. "Who's Chip Gaines?" By now we were all laughing and when I said this, everybody laughed harder.

"Oh, June," Kirsten said. "You don't know anything, do you?"

Sydney flapped her hands. "We need to talk about someone else now. Please. Reese, you go."

Reese groaned. "No. I don't want to bring you guys down."

"What're you talking about?" Kirsten said. "The point of Confession is to share. You're not gonna bring us down." But then Reese gave her a meaningful look and her face changed. "Oh," she said. "Right."

I looked from her to Sydney to Reese. "What? What do you all know that I don't?"

Reese took a deep breath and explained that before they met me, before she'd gotten pregnant with Nina, she'd had four miscarriages. And while she wanted to get pregnant again—soon, maybe—she was scared because the slew of doctors she'd seen hadn't been able to diagnose anything wrong with her. "Apparently," she said, "the miscarriages had just been *unviable fetuses taking care of themselves* or something like that."

"Jesus," I said.

"Right? Anyway, you all know how much I want a big family, but I don't know if I can go through that again. It was just…too much."

We sat for a moment as this unsolvable problem swirled around us. It struck me that while my new friends' "confessions" were real and hard, they also seemed so wholesome compared to my own. As they struggle to achieve a work/life balance and grapple with how to expand their family, my problem is that I'm an inherently bad mom, self-centered and resentful of my own child. Because the truth is, I don't like my new job of being a mom yet. I liked my old job a whole hell of a lot more. Here I was, only feet away from these very nice women, and the distance between us felt like an uncrossable gulf.

Then Reese's bright voice brought me back. "See? I told you I'd bring you down."

The three of us made a murmur of protest, but she waved it away. "Let's move on. I don't want to talk about it anyway." She turned to Kirsten. "And besides, you're the one who inflicted this game on us. You should have to go."

It was clearly meant as a joke, but Kirsten burst into tears.

"Oh, my God," Reese said. "Kirsten, I'm sorry! I was just teasing you. I don't blame you for the game. I'm the idiot who made it up!"

Kirsten was shaking her head, her eyes closed tightly, as if to forcibly stop the tears from falling. "No, no," she finally managed to say. "It's not that. It's—it's—Liam!" Her husband's name came out as a wail.

I exchanged a glance with Reese as Sydney leaned over in her chair to rub a hand over Kirsten's back. "Kirsten, honey," she said. "What are you talking about? Are you and Liam having problems?" It was hard to imagine after she'd walked in here an hour ago looking like she'd just had really good sex.

"No, no," Kirsten said quickly. Her eyes skittered around the room. "It's just—he's leaving town tomorrow and leaving me alone with Georgia. Again. I mean, Georgia and I are great together, but his schedule is getting so bad, I'm honestly starting to feel like a single parent."

"Clark & White," Reese declared. "The number-one thief of husbands since 1976."

"Yeah," Sydney said with a sad little laugh. "We can definitely empathize with you there. But at least he's doing it for you and Georgia," she continued, and Reese nodded in agreement. "It's not like he has a gambling problem or a mistress or something. I mean, he's working to provide for you both."

Anger exploded in my chest so suddenly, it was like I'd been kicked. This was *Medea* all over again! But instead of another woman, Liam's Corinthian princess—what he's leaving his wife for—is his work. And society has said not only is it okay for him to disappear into his job, but it's honorable because he's doing it to "support his family." We've all swallowed this so many times, when Kirsten doubts it, she has her very best friends to force it down her throat. But the truth is, her husband is choosing status, money, and distraction over being home with his family. If that's not a modern-day Corinthian princess, I don't know what is.

And then, of course, I realized how blind I'd been. It wasn't just Kirsten's husband who was cheating on her with his work, it was mine too. It was all of ours.

I sat there, seething with quiet fury. It ricocheted through me, gaining speed and targets. I was mad at Sydney for saying what she'd said, I was mad at Liam for making Kirsten feel like a single parent, and I was mad at Kirsten for not being mad. More than all that, though, I was mad at Ben for being just like Liam, just like Jason from the play, for turning me into a real-life Medea.

Sydney and Reese continued to comfort Kirsten as I sat there in silence because I couldn't say any of this out loud. I couldn't criticize all our husbands in one fell swoop. And even as apt a metaphor as *Medea* is, I know that rambling on about a Greek tragedy isn't exactly normal. But more than all that was how utterly alone I suddenly felt. Was I the only one thinking this? Was I the only one who saw how unfair it was?

The sound of my name brought me out of my thoughts.

I looked up to see Sydney, Reese, and Kirsten all staring at me. "Sorry. What?"

Kirsten laughed, but I could see tears drying on her cheeks. "I said it's your turn for Confession."

"Oh. Right." I was still burning with indignation, but I tried to play along. "I guess mine would be that I just... I don't feel like I'm a very good mom." I honestly hadn't meant to say it; it was as if some third party had plucked the truth from deep inside me and spit it out of my mouth.

Sydney smiled empathetically. "I feel ya, sister."

I smiled back, but it felt flat and tired.

Reese took a sip of wine. "Come on, give us the details."

I racked my brain for something bad but not too bad. I felt the conflicting urge to both prove how terrible I am and have them exonerate me at the same time. "I didn't like breastfeeding," I said. "I stopped when Mikey was only eight weeks old."

Reese guffawed. "God, I hated breastfeeding. It hurt like a bitch. It felt like someone was sandpapering my nipples. That does *not* make you a bad mom."

That wasn't it though. For me, breastfeeding felt so intensely intimate that I cried every time I did it. Maybe that sounds sweet or something, but I hated it—it felt like I was an abused farm animal. Mom, do you remember that one time our elementary school went on a field trip to a farm upstate and I came back so upset because I thought the baby pigs were going to kill their mama pig because they drank from her so violently that it shook her entire body? And she just lay there with her eyes squeezed shut as her own babies ravaged her? Breastfeeding didn't just hurt; for me and probably the pig, it felt like psychological torture.

"Plus," Reese continued. "Not liking something is just a preference, a thought. And your thoughts don't make you a bad person. Especially not your thoughts as a new mom. And thank God, too. If you all could read my thoughts, you'd lock me up."

I tried to smile, but it felt tight. I couldn't make them see or maybe I didn't want them to see. It's not the bad thoughts I have about motherhood that scare me. It's how I feel about Mikey. It's that I'm numb to him. Or maybe it's that I love him but don't like him? Or that I'm obsessed with him but also don't care about him? I don't know how to put into words the strange contradiction inside me, but the horrible truth is that I don't feel about Mikey the way a mom should feel about her child.

I haven't told you that yet, Mom, because I keep thinking it will just sort of fix itself, but it keeps not fixing itself. And I'm doing everything I can think of. I talk to him, sing to him, I even have a routine to get skin-to-skin contact with him, because apparently, it releases some sort of hormone to facilitate an emotional bond. So this is what I do every day: I set a timer for ten minutes and rub Mikey's legs. I stare into his eyes for ten minutes and wait for affection to fill the hole in my heart, but it never does. And if Mikey likes it, it's lost on me. Sometimes he doesn't even seem to register anything. "We're bonding, Mikey," I tell him. Usually, he ends up crying.

But again, I can't say any of this to the girls. I'd sound like a sociopath. So I tried to think of something else. I kept envisioning Mikey lying on his back as my phone ticked away the minutes, my thumbs rubbing soft circles into his skin, the look in both of our eyes blank as sheets of paper. To the girls, I said, "I also accidentally skipped Mikey's latest vaccination appointment."

All three of them gasped and I instantly regretted saying it.

"Oh, God," Reese said. "You're not an anti-vaxxer, are you?"

"What? No. I just said I did it by accident, didn't I?"

Sydney was looking at me with wide eyes. "How did you miss it? What happened?"

So I told them. A few days ago, Mikey had been crying nonstop and I couldn't figure out why. I tried everything as usual—he'd been fed, burped; I held him like he likes with his face smooshed; his diaper was clean—nothing worked, and I was getting more and more flustered and he was getting more and more agitated. In the middle of all this, I apparently got a call from Doctor Albright's office that I didn't hear. When I listened to the voice mail hours later, I realized I'd completely forgotten about our appointment. So I called them back and rescheduled.

What I didn't tell them was that when Mikey was crying, he started sobbing so hard that he actually made himself throw up, which made me start to cry. I called Ben, but he didn't answer. He texted me back a few minutes later, saying he was in a meeting and was it an emergency? I told him no, then I went into the closet, put Mikey on the floor beside me, and pressed a scarf around my ears as he cried and cried.

"Oh, so you have him scheduled for another appointment?" Reese said with a little shrug after I'd finished telling them the partial, watered-down story. "You're taking care of it. You may be scatterbrained, but you're not the worst." She threw me a little wink.

I looked at the baby monitor, at the ghostly image of Mikey sleeping. *I'm sorry*, I said in my head. *I'm sorry. I'm sorry. I'm sorry.*

I guess I should say sorry to you, too, Mom, for not being

completely honest before. I will be from now on. Maybe then
you'll be able to cross the great divide and help me fix whatever it is inside me that feels so broken.

Love,
June

# FOURTEEN

———

Walking through his front door after talking with Sydney and Reese gave Ben the strange sensation of stepping into someone else's home. He suddenly felt separate from the trappings of the life he'd so arduously built for himself and his family, with their oversize house and mortgage payments, with the lawn they paid someone to cut, with the furniture, the style of which had seemed so important when they'd bought it. In the wake of June's disappearance, it amazed him that he'd once cared about any of it.

"Hey," he called as he walked inside, pulling off his coat and hat.

"In the living room!" his mom called back.

He walked in to find her and Mikey in the center of the floor on a quilt. His mom was holding a glass of white wine and there was music on low in the background.

"How was he?" Ben asked, grabbing Mikey up for a kiss, but just as he did, his phone buzzed from his pocket. It had rung so often these past two days that he'd developed an initial Pavlovian response of hope—Was it June? Was it Officer Moretti?—and then one of inevitable irritation because it was never June and it was never Officer Moretti. Ben hitched Mikey up on his hip, pulled out his phone to glance at the screen, and cringed to see that it was one of the other lawyers on his current merger case. He silenced the ring with his free hand.

"He was great," his mom said. "How's June? Have you talked to her?"

"She's fine," he said, but he felt so tired saying it.

"And her dad?"

"Yeah, he's gonna be okay. The hospital wants to keep him another night, but then they'll let him go home." It was dangerous to tell her that June's dad was leaving the hospital—she might start to expect June to plan her return trip—but he couldn't think of a reason why a hospital would keep a patient unless he was afflicted with something worse than his made-up diagnosis of a mild heart attack, and that would complicate the lie even more.

"Oh, good. Did they give him any medication? Or tell him to make any changes? A heart attack is pretty major. Even a mild one."

Ben exhaled a deep breath, trying to make it sound like it wasn't a sigh. His phone rang again and this time he didn't even check it before he silenced it. "I'm not sure. June was pretty flustered when I talked to her. She wants to stay with her dad for a while to make sure he's okay. So, sorry to ask, but would you be okay staying a few more days?"

A little wrinkle creased his mom's brow. "Oh, she's staying in California?"

Ben kissed Mikey's soft forehead then put him back onto the quilt. "Just for a few more days."

His mom reached over and scratched Mikey's tummy with

her manicured fingers. "It's just from what you said, it sounds like her dad's getting better."

"It's okay if you can't stay," Ben said, not meaning a word of it. Even with her help, he felt as if he were treading water, his mouth at the surface, gulping frantically for air. Mikey, as if sensing something wasn't quite right, tried to look at his dad, but he was facing the wrong way and smooshed his head against the quilt fruitlessly.

"Oh, honey," his mom said. "If she's decided to be with her dad, I'm more than happy to stay here with her baby."

Ben jerked his head back. Yesterday, when she'd said she worried about Mikey without June, he'd thought she'd been criticizing *him*, the floundering dad. But now he understood that her passive aggression was aimed at June, who she believed was helping her ailing father. What the fuck kind of logic was that? "Okay, great. Thanks." His voice was tight.

Once again, Mikey tried to catch sight of him, wiggling back and forth.

"So did June say when she *was* planning on coming home?"

"No. Mom. We talked for like a second."

Mikey, who was apparently getting desperate, tipped his head back, rocked, and then for the first time in his life, he flipped from his back to his stomach. Ben, who rarely got to witness Mikey's first anything, felt an unexpected soaring in his chest. Typically, in the event of a minor milestone, June would send a text and Ben would read from his desk, feeling simultaneously elated and guilty. He opened his mouth to say something, but shut it again, the swelling in his chest dropping like an anvil. Mikey hadn't had the audience of both his parents for one single thing, and in a moment when Ben should have felt pride and happiness, he just felt bereft.

"Oh, yeah," his mom said cheerfully. "You didn't tell me

he was rolling over from his tummy yet. He's been doing it all day."

Ben's shoulders slumped. He'd wanted to be a dad for so long, he just assumed he'd be a good one, and yet, here he was, missing so many moments of his son's life. "I didn't know."

His mom, who'd been gazing at Mikey, looked up at him. "Oh, don't worry about that. It doesn't mean anything. Your father missed every one of your firsts and he was still a great dad."

Ben stiffened, but before he could respond, his phone rang yet again, and he felt the last of his patience snap. He dug it out from his pocket, turned his back to his mom and son, and answered it with a quick glance at the screen, which showed a number he didn't recognize.

"Hello." His greeting came out hard.

"Oh," a woman said, and while the voice sounded vaguely familiar, with its soft, Southern drawl, he couldn't place it. "Ben, this is Kirsten Aimes, Liam's wife. Sydney just told me that June is, well, that she's missing, and I thought maybe we should talk."

At that, Sydney's words from earlier rang in Ben's head. *Bad blood*, she'd said of what was going on between Kirsten and June. He walked out of earshot of the living room. "Right. What's up?"

"Um. Actually, I think we should talk in person."

He closed his eyes. "You have me now. So why don't we talk now."

"Right. That makes sense. Sorry, I'm just a little—I don't know."

But Ben was sick of being polite and accommodating. His life was crashing down around him and he just wanted some goddam answers. "Kirsten? What do you have to tell me?"

"Well, this isn't exactly how I would've liked to do it," she said, "but here goes... Ben, June's been cheating on you. I know, because she's been cheating on you with my husband."

# FIFTEEN

——

*Six years earlier*

Throughout his life, Ben felt as though the path of his future had been predetermined, grooved out in front of him by his parents. He had memories of sitting idly by as his mom filled out his high school forms, selecting which electives he'd take—debate over creative writing, Latin over Spanish. For his higher education, his parents had told him he could go to undergrad and law school anywhere he wanted—so long as they were Ivy Leagues on the east coast. And then his father, who was friends with one of the firm's partners, had secured his summer internship at Clark & White, so upon graduation, his position there had seemed inevitable.

But over the first year of his and June's relationship, Ben felt his future expand with possibility in a way it never had before. It wasn't just that June was ambitious herself, although that was a big part of it. It was that, despite her being so far removed from everything he'd grown up learning would make him happy—a Connecticut colonial and a high-paid desk job—she was more passionate about her work and life than anyone he'd ever known.

He began to think of moving to another firm, maybe even another area of law, civil or environmental. He'd been mulling it over for months now, and the thought of doing something else terrified him, yes, but it was also the only thing that loosened the pressure that had begun to tighten around his chest every weekday morning when he woke.

He wouldn't walk away from a steady job without a plan in place, but he wanted to talk it over with June. The two of them had dinner plans that night and Ben would tell her then. The thought made him feel like he might levitate off his office floor.

It was four on Friday afternoon, hours before their dinner reservation, when he got the call from June, and the moment he heard her voice, he knew something was wrong.

"My mom has breast cancer," she told him. "Stage four."

For a flash of a moment as her words rang in his ears, Ben felt very far from reality, as if he were an actor performing a scene he hadn't prepared for. This wasn't how his and June's life together was supposed to unfold. They were supposed to have more time, time to travel, time for June to establish herself in the dance world, time for Ben to figure out what he wanted to do. They were supposed to go out tonight and talk about his career. Now it felt like everything was happening too fast and too wrong. Ben squeezed his eyes shut, his heart sinking to the pit of his stomach.

"Where are you?"

"My apartment," she said, and he was out of his office before she even finished the last word.

Michelle's treatment plan was aggressive, and in those first few months of chemo, everyone in her life rallied around her with the energy and optimism of an army fighting its first battle, everything referred to in terms of violence and war. People said how strong she was, how she'd crush this, how fucking cancer could go to fucking hell, how she was a trouper, a fighter. But of course, what no one said, was that she was also the battleground.

In those first few months, Michelle's apartment turned into a lively convalescence home with a revolving-door policy of visitors bearing gifts—boxes of takeout that went uneaten, boxes of books that went unread, baggies of medical-grade weed—as if they were visiting a shrine, and Michelle was their deity.

At her first chemo appointment, Ben and June sat with Michelle as the medicine coursed through her veins, and they spent the night in her apartment, lying side by side in the twin-size bed from June's childhood. The most common early side effect of chemo, they knew, was nausea, so June had prepared her mom's apartment appropriately. She'd stocked it with brightly colored plastic trash cans from Bed, Bath & Beyond, scattering them strategically. She put one by the bed, one by the couch, and a few lining the way to the bathroom in case her mom tried and failed to make it to the toilet in time. She'd asked her mom's friend Dee Dee, who'd delivered some ginger tea, for more of it, and Dee Dee had brought over an entire shopping bag full of tea boxes along with ginger capsules and peppermint oil you were supposed to rub onto your wrists and behind your ears. But Michelle hadn't needed any of it. She'd reacted so well, in fact, that she made plans for after her second appointment the following week.

"If you're staying over already," she told June, "we might as well make a night of it. Bring food and wine—not for me, June, for you and Ben. And Moli!—invite Moli. Oh, please, it's been so long since I've seen her." And so, even in the wake of her cancer treatment, the consummate host had planned a party.

"Moli, how's the studio?" Michelle asked from her spot

lying on the couch that Friday evening after her second chemo treatment.

As she'd requested, Ben, Moli, and June had come to keep her company, arms laden with provisions and trash bags full of pillows and blankets. They were circled around the coffee table scattered with plates, Thai food containers, and half-drunk glasses of wine.

"Things are going well," Moli said. Before Michelle's diagnosis, Moli had taught a handful of classes a week at the studio, along with working her survival job at a chocolatier in Midtown. But for the duration of her treatment, Michelle had taken time off from teaching and asked Moli to fill in the holes. "Everybody misses you."

Michelle laughed. "Well, of course they do. They're only human. And how are you? I feel like I haven't seen you in ages."

Moli leaned over the coffee table to grab a chopstick full of Pad Thai. "What d'you want to know?"

Michelle took a sip of the tea June had brewed. "How's your love life?"

"Actually," Moli said as she finished chewing, "I have met someone."

June's eyes widened and she snapped her head to look at her friend. Her chopsticks froze midair. "Who?"

"I met him a few weeks ago at the chocolate shop."

"What? Why don't I know about this?"

"June, your mom has *cancer*. You've been preoccupied."

"What's his name?" June asked at the same time Michelle was saying, "Tell us the story of how you met."

Moli looked at June. "His name is Ezra. Isn't that sort of an unsuspectingly hot name?" Then she turned to Michelle. "So he came in the store one day and he bought a box of chocolates. I honestly didn't even notice him really, because I had an audition later that day I was thinking about and he was cute, yeah, but he was buying chocolates, so I assumed they were for his girlfriend or wife or something. But then when he was checking out, he made this big deal about them being for his mom, who was visiting. Then two days later, he came back, and then he came again the next day. Every day he bought one chocolate and he'd always start up this whole big conversation around picking out this new chocolate, like he'd say he liked the texture of the last one, but he now wanted something less sweet, or whatever... Well, about two weeks into this was when—" She waved a hand in Michelle's direction.

"The tornado hit," Michelle offered.

Moli nodded. "When the tornado hit. And so I told him I was gonna be working at the dance studio and not the chocolate shop anymore and he said, *I wish the dance studio had something I could buy from you.* And I said, *You wish the dance studio had* chocolates *you could buy from me.* And then he gave me the cutest little smile and said, *I don't actually like chocolate.*"

Ben, June, and Michelle all laughed. "Of course he doesn't like chocolate, you idiot," June said, swatting Moli's upper arm. "I swear. Sometimes I think you're all beauty no brains."

"By the way," Michelle said, "what was your audition for? The one you had the day he first came in."

Moli smiled, then glanced at the floor. "Oh, yeah... It was for *Anything Goes.* And I, well, I booked it."

It was clear to Ben, from June's and Michelle's reactions, that he was the only one who didn't understand what that meant. He'd learned the word *booked* from June—it meant you'd gotten a job—but *Anything Goes* was lost on him. He looked at Michelle, whose eyes were wide, then at June, who'd frozen, her chopsticks midair, a clump of rice noodles hanging down like tentacles.

"You booked *Anything Goes*?" she said slowly, her face blank.

Moli pressed her lips together to stop herself from smiling and nodded.

In one rush of motion, June threw her chopsticks onto her plate, jumped up, and screamed. Moli hunched over in laughter, burying her face in her hands, watching June through her fingers. June wrapped her arms around her and kissed every part of her head she could get to. Ben grinned as he watched them and glanced at Michelle, who had sunk back into the couch, but was laughing softly. When June sat down again, Ben asked, "So what's *Anything Goes*?"

"Oh, Ben," Michelle said. "What could possibly fill your brain if not the full list of current Broadway shows?"

"It's Broadway," June said. "Broad. Way."

His smile flickered for just a fraction of a second. June had recently found out that she'd not booked yet another Broadway show, and he wondered if Moli's success stung at all. Yet, if June was reminded of her own failure, she was hiding it well.

"Oh, and it's perfect for you," Michelle said to Moli. "All that tap."

"That's the only reason I booked it."

"Do you know when it's gonna debut?"

Moli fiddled with her chopsticks. "I think they're hoping for April of next year, so like seven months?"

"I can't wait to see it," Michelle said.

Next to him, Ben felt June stiffen. "Be right back," she said, standing up. "I'm just gonna open another bottle of wine." As she walked away, she called over her shoulder, "I'm so happy for you, Moli!"

Meanwhile, Michelle was already asking another question about the show, so Ben stood up to go to the bathroom. But as he passed by the kitchen, he spotted June, her palms pressed into the counter so hard her fingers were white. Her face was contorted with a silent cry.

He frowned, crossing the few steps over to her. "June? What's going on?" Could she possibly be reacting like this because Moli was going to be on Broadway and she wasn't? He put his hand on the small of her back, which made June squinch her face even tighter.

He waited as she took a breath, then wiped both middle fingers beneath her wet eyes. "Seven months is a long time," she said finally.

Ben stared at her. He didn't know what she meant or what to say.

Before he could think of anything, she clarified, "I mean, in terms of cancer."

She bowed her head and Ben sighed. He pulled her into him and held her as she cried fat, silent tears onto his shoulder. He was an idiot. Here he'd thought she was upset because she wasn't going to be on Broadway next spring, when in reality she was upset because she didn't know whether or not her mom was going to live that long.

That evening, after Michelle had gone to bed, Moli went to sleep in June's old room and Ben and June made a pallet on the living room floor, two comforters beneath them and a quilt on top. They settled in, lying side by side, the lights of the city streaming in through the blinds. The sound of cars and plumbing and far-away shouting wove together, the comforting white noise of New York. Ben didn't know how long they'd been lying there when he felt June turn beside him.

"You awake?" she whispered.

"Mmm." He opened his eyes a fraction. In the darkness, he could just barely make out her face.

"D'you remember when I called you that day a few weeks ago…to tell you about my mom?"

"Mmm-hmm."

"Remember how we were supposed to get sushi that night?"

"Yeah."

"You said you wanted to talk."

Suddenly, Ben's heart beat fast. He closed his eyes, pretending like he was trying to remember. What he'd wanted to talk about of course was quitting his steady, exorbitantly high-paying job to search for his passion, but that was no longer an option. He knew that June was worried about what this cancer would do to her mom's finances, and he thought she should be. He didn't know the cost of all this treatment, and he knew that the apartment he was lying on the floor of now was rent stabilized, but the fact remained that June and her mom were dancers. June was already taking off time from teaching, sacrificing part of her paycheck to be here.

Ben didn't think they would let him pay for any medical expenses outright, but there were ways he could help. He could buy groceries, pay for dinners, maybe even ask June to move in and tell her not to worry about rent for a while. He didn't want to come across as patronizing, but he didn't think there should be anything wrong with a person helping someone they loved.

But he knew if June suspected how unhappy he was at Clark & White, there was no way she'd want him to stay there just so he could help her and her mom. Plus, he couldn't lay this petty gripe about work at her feet now. She didn't have the bandwidth for anyone else's problems. Ben would stick it out for another year or two, help June in whatever way he could, and quit just a little later than expected.

"Hmm?" he said. "I wanted to talk? I don't know. I don't really remember."

Next to him, June hesitated. "Oh," she said after a moment, and Ben couldn't tell whether or not she believed him. "Okay… Night." Then she turned onto her back and they lay in silence until they fell asleep.

# SIXTEEN

———

*Thursday, February 16*

Dear Mom,

I took Mikey to the library today so I could do some research on *Medea*, and I read through all the different translations of the text I could find, which led me to a new version of the first line I hadn't seen before: "If only the swift Argo never had swooped in between the cobalt Clashing Rocks to reach the Colchians' realm..." It's the same sentiment as in other translations; Medea's nurse is bemoaning the fact that Jason ever met her mistress. But it's those first two words of this translation that really get me. "If only..." What two words could possibly be more haunting?

Here's my question for Medea: knowing what you know now, would you have made different choices, and if so, when? If you were given the option to look at the timeline of your life, to what point would you have turned back the clock? To the time before you sought revenge upon your cheating husband? Before you moved to Corinth? Before you met Jason, the man you once desperately loved? Would you give up years of happiness because you knew it would end in pain and horror? What about you, Mom? Was there anything in your life that was good until it wasn't? And would you have wanted to change it, if you could?

All of this was jangling around my head when I left the library to get to wine night with the girls, and I guess I was distracted because as I was leaving, I walked straight into someone.

"Oh, my God, I'm so sorry," I said, taking a step back and checking on Mikey in his carrier. Miraculously, the jolt hadn't even woken him.

"No, I'm sorry," said a familiar voice and when I looked up, I realized the person I'd run into was Kirsten's husband, Liam. Underneath his coat, I could tell he was still dressed for work in an expensive-looking suit. His wavy brown hair was combed, his square jaw shaved.

"Liam? Hi. What're you doing here?"

He dipped his chin toward an armful of children's books. "Replenishing Georgia's stash."

I stared at the books in dismay. He and Kirsten were already reading to Georgia? Georgia, who was only a month or two older than Mikey? Georgia, who wouldn't understand the meaning of words for months? Georgia, who could only eat, sleep, and go to the bathroom like every other baby in the world? I deflated with inadequacy. Before Mikey was born, I read literary novels aloud to my belly, so eager to impart knowledge; now I couldn't even get him to stop crying long enough to open a board book. How far my standard of motherhood has fallen.

"Looks like your reading material is a little more highbrow than ours," Liam was saying, nodding toward the stack of *Medea* translations in my hand. "You a big—what is that?—Greek mythology fan?"

I forced a laugh. "Oh, no. I, um, I'm just doing some research. You know how I used to dance with the Martha Graham Company, right?"

"Of course," he said. "Which is amazing, by the way."

"Oh, thanks. Anyway, they have a ballet inspired by *Medea*"—I held up the books—"and I just got curious."

"Oh, cool. What's it about?"

So I told him, and to my surprise, he seemed genuinely interested. Talking about the play got us talking about the ballet adaptation, then about dance in general, then about auditioning. At one point, he told me a story of when he auditioned for his sixth-grade class's reprisal of *Fiddler on the Roof*—everyone had to audition—and he'd been so scared that, in the middle of singing "If I Were a Rich Man," his voice cracked and he ran out of the room. He had me laughing so hard, I peed a little. I realize that's not saying much these days, but still. At one point, I noticed a dull ache in my heels from standing for so long, but I was absorbed in the conversation and I didn't care.

"Well," he said after a while. "I should probably get going. The library's about to close and I wouldn't want my six-month-old to go a night without fresh reading material."

I balked. "The library's about to close? What time is it?" I checked my phone and saw that I was almost an hour late for wine night. On my screen was text after text from the girls, asking where I was. "Shit," I said, typing out a quick apology. "I'm so late."

"Oh, yeah," said Liam. "Shouldn't you be with the girls right now? Kirsten left like an hour ago."

"I am, yeah—" But I stopped. I'd just remembered Kirsten's "confession" the other night, about Liam leaving her alone with Georgia. "Hey, aren't you supposed to be out of town?"

He gave me a confused look. "Out of town? No?"

"I thought—" I began, but decided to drop it. His plans had probably just changed and I was already so late as it was. "Never mind. This has been really nice. I'm glad I ran into you."

He grinned. "No, I'm glad I ran into *you*. I was destined for a night at home alone with my paperwork and a glass of scotch. You saved me."

When we hugged goodbye, I remembered how good it felt to be held—even briefly—by a man. My physical relationship with Ben has been relegated to perfunctory kisses, brushes of skin against skin as we sleep. We're just too busy for anything else; we hardly see each other. As I picked up Mikey's carrier and walked to the car, I felt light and happy.

Afterward, though, when I finally made it to Reese's for wine night, I felt off. I tried to start a conversation about books and then I mentioned something about *Medea*, but everything I said just fell flat as the three of them circled back to babies and motherhood. I felt like they were advertising their happiness and competency as moms, and my lack of it shined more acutely by comparison. I smiled hollowly through their mock complaints about motherhood as they stroked the cheeks of their happy, sleeping babies.

I felt bad about losing track of time and coming so late, but if I could look back on the timeline of my day today and change it, I don't think I would. When I got back to my own house after wine night, it was dark and cold. Ben was still at work. And standing outside the library with Liam today was the least lonely I've felt in a very long time.

Are you getting any of this, Mom? Or am I just, as I suspect, shouting into the void?

Love,
June

# SEVENTEEN

———

Kirsten opened her front door before Ben even finished knocking.

"Ben," she said, sounding pleasantly surprised, as if he'd just popped by to say hello, as if they hadn't planned this visit expressly to discuss the topic of their spouses cheating on them, with each other.

The previous evening, after Kirsten had dropped that bomb, they'd arranged to meet the next day. Ben had pushed for the morning, but she'd wanted to meet when she could get a sitter to take Georgia out of the house, so they'd settled on late afternoon instead. Now, as he stood on her front doorstep, he found that he couldn't stop staring at her. Despite her preppy outfit of blue jeans, a soft-looking coral sweater, and diamond stud earrings he could never imagine June wearing, there was something about her that reminded him a little of his wife. They shared a similar build, thin and petite, and their faces weren't wholly unalike, both with fine features and round eyes, but as he looked at Kirsten, he decided it wasn't so much her physical appearance as something in her expression that reminded him of June. And yet, what exactly that was, he couldn't say.

"Hi, Kirsten."

She opened the door wide for him to pass through. "Well, come on in. I'm sorry for the mess, by the way. I just haven't had any time."

Ben gazed around as he followed her through the house, feeling confused by her apology. He and June had only been in Maplewood for about six months now and this was the first time he'd ever been to Kirsten and Liam's place. It was almost preternaturally bright and clean, the surfaces gleaming with incoming sunlight. There wasn't an errant baby toy or piece of junk mail anywhere. His own house flashed in his mind with its usual clutter of baby things and the sink full of dirty dishes. This house made theirs feel downright putrid.

Kirsten waved a hand, gesturing around vaguely. "It's hard to keep up with a baby, but I'm sure you know that. And sorry about me, too. I'm a disaster."

Ben frowned. Compared to June's rumpled clothes and unwashed hair, Kirsten, with her fresh-looking outfit and bouncy blond waves, looked like she'd just gotten back from a health resort. He'd never say anything to June about the lapse in her physical maintenance, nor did he really think it meant anything—she'd just given birth and was taking care of their baby—but it did make him wonder if Kirsten thought, for some reason, that it was polite to apologize or if she was just delusional.

She led him to the living room and they sat opposite each other, Ben on the couch, she in a large wingback chair, a coffee table between them.

"So," Ben started. "How do you know June and Liam are…" His voice faded. He couldn't muster any small talk right now—he needed to hear what she knew—but he couldn't quite finish the question either.

Kirsten stared at him a long moment before ducking her head to tuck her hair behind her ears. "You know, I really thought I could do this, but I think I need a drink. Do you want anything?"

"Oh. Um." Ben had the urge to take her by the shoulders and shout *Tell me what you know!* But if playing along with her delusion that this was some carefree social visit got her talking, then that was what he'd do. Plus, he had to admit, a drink sounded deeply good to him right now. "Sure. Thanks."

She stood up and went to the kitchen, grabbing glasses, a bottle of wine. "Hope you like Pinot Noir," she said as she walked back over and handed Ben a very full glass. She set the open bottle on the table between them.

"So," Ben tried again. "Why do you think June and Liam are seeing each other?"

Across from him, Kirsten took a deep breath as if she'd only now resigned herself to the fact that she'd have to actually talk about what they were here to talk about. "At first, it was just Liam I suspected," she began slowly. "After Georgia was born, things were a little…rocky. But I mean, we'd just had a baby! We were both exhausted and I was hormonal, so I just thought it was normal new-baby stuff. Then things at Liam's work picked up. But well—you work there, you know—working a lot is sort of part of the deal. So I didn't think much of it, plus, I was still so preoccupied with Georgia. She wasn't sleeping through the night and in general she's a really fussy baby. But then one day, I looked up and realized I hadn't seen Liam in two days. I was up during the night and he was gone early in the morning and didn't get home until late." She shook her head, laughing, but it came out broken and bitter. "I can't believe I still didn't see it then, but like I said, I was just so tired."

Ben frowned. Her story was hauntingly familiar—it mirrored his and June's life to a tee. He thought about all his late nights at Clark & White and tried to remember if Liam had been there with him, but he couldn't.

"It took me seeing the two of them together to suspect June at all," Kirsten continued. "I drove past the library one night and I saw them outside talking. Of course, I didn't suspect anything right away because, you know, June's my friend. But well, I sort of stayed there for a while watching them, and they just seemed like they were in their own little world. They were laughing and talking for *so* long. And when they hugged, it felt—I don't know—like they loved each other or something."

Her words struck Ben like a slap across the face and it took him a long moment to remind himself this wasn't proof of anything; this was one unhappy woman's perspective. "But, Kirsten, that's not exactly hard evidence."

"No"—she shook her head—"it's not."

It was the way she said it, more than anything else, that made Ben afraid of what was to come.

"But that's not all," she continued. "I began—" But she stopped herself, as if changing her mind about something. "I saw them at the party last weekend. At Layla's birthday. They were in the garage together."

"The garage? What were they doing?"

"Well, I walked in to get more champagne and I saw them in each other's arms. The moment I opened the door, they jumped back from each other. That's when I knew, with absolute certainty, they were seeing each other. The look in their eyes was so…guilty. So I told June to…" She hesitated. "Well, I told her to leave."

Ben could feel his brain trying to rectify this new information with the June he knew. Would she really have a clandestine meeting with a lover in someone else's garage during a baby's birthday party? It was cruel. And yet, hadn't he suspected that something had changed for June that day? Hadn't he just been asking Sydney and Reese about what had happened at that party? And he didn't believe Kirsten was lying. Her pain was real and raw. "Have you talked to Liam about all this?"

She swallowed hard. "Not yet. I didn't even know if I should tell you, but when I heard June had left, I just thought you should know."

"Yeah. No. Thank you." Ben's mind was scattered and racing. Did this explain why June had disappeared? Obviously, she hadn't left Ben to be with Liam—Liam hadn't gone anywhere—but was it possible she'd fled because of guilt, because she was trying to break things off with Liam before she got in too deep? He ran his hands down his face. "Is there anything else?"

Kirsten let out a little scoff. "Isn't that enough? They were—God, you should have seen their faces when I walked in on them."

Ben winced. "Okay, you're right. I'm just trying to understand." He paused. "So there's nothing else you have to tell me?"

Kirsten hesitated briefly, her eyes darting to the rug.

"*Is* there something?" he pressed.

Her gaze leaped to his. "No. That's everything."

Ben studied her, but it seemed that moment of indecision had passed. He took one last long drink of wine, then placed his glass too hard on the table between them, the dregs leaping up the edges. "I should go. I need to get home to Mikey." But the truth was he just needed to get out of there. He could feel his insides popping with anger and resentment and confusion, as if he were plugged into something electric, and he didn't think he could maintain this semblance of calm for much longer. He wanted a glass of whiskey. He wanted to smash something.

"Oh," Kirsten said, and Ben thought she sounded slightly disappointed. "Right. Of course. Georgia and the sitter will be home soon anyway."

He was at the front door when he suddenly turned back to face her. He'd been so upset he'd completely forgotten that she was going through the same thing he was, and he thought he realized now why she'd tried to treat the conversation like a friendly visit—grief was isolating and she'd been alone in hers for too long.

"Hey," he said. "If Liam really did cheat on you, he's a fucking asshole."

Kirsten smiled a sad, wobbly smile. And then, without preamble, she lifted up on her toes and pecked him on the lips. When she sank down again, she touched her fingertips to her mouth. "Oh," she said, looking confused as if she weren't entirely sure what she'd just done. "Sorry. I shouldn't have done that."

Ben felt something warm travel through him. It wasn't lust or love or even like. It was the golden sensation of being needed and desired, something he hadn't felt in a very long time. He swayed slightly on the spot as if his brain and his body couldn't come to terms with what they wanted. If he could somehow know, with absolute certainty, that June and Liam had done what Kirsten said they'd done, Ben would've grabbed this woman's waist, pulled her to him, and kissed her on the mouth. And he would've done it for no reason other than to make them both feel desired, even if only for a moment. But he wasn't letting go of hope, not yet.

"I have to go," he said thickly.

He pulled open the door and walked into the biting air of the encroaching night. As he made his way down their front path, Ben realized through the lingering fog of the kiss, that he'd been so absorbed in Kirsten's story of the affair that he'd forgotten to ask her about both the Greek myth June had been obsessing over and the petition Sydney had told him about. But in that moment, he didn't care. His wife had apparently been kissing someone else and now, apparently, so was he. That was enough.

In his car, he sank his face into his hands and for the first time in a very long time, he wept.

# EIGHTEEN

———

*Five Years Earlier*

It was the start of 2013, after Michelle's second round of chemo, after the lumps in her breasts multiplied into lumps in her lungs, when her army of friends finally lost its optimism. The violence of their previous words—*fight, win, survivor*—morphed into words of complacency. *How're you doing?* they'd ask. *Are you comfortable? Is there anything we can do to make it easier?* What no one said outright was that the *it* everyone was referring to was *dying.* They wanted to know how they could make it easier for her to die.

Leading up to Michelle's diagnosis, Ben and June spent many nights together in the same apartment but just as many nights apart in their respective ones. After, without announcement or acknowledgment, they began to sleep side by side each night of the week, usually in the king-size bed in Ben's apartment on the Upper East Side.

One night in the middle of a cold January, Ben woke to find himself alone in bed. In the darkness, he felt June's absence rather than saw it, the air in the room somehow empty.

He reached out a tentative hand to her side, but rather than falling upon a body, all he touched was the cold sheet.

He lay like that for a moment, wondering where June was, feeling like he should probably check on her, but even with his eyes closed, they burned with exhaustion. He'd been put on the new acquisition case for one of Clark & White's biggest clients last week and he'd been working long hours ever since. While he was good at what he did, he was still one of the new guys at a competitive company. He needed to prove he was worth his salary and he couldn't do that when he was sleep deprived. He turned away from her empty spot and went back to sleep.

The next morning, after his alarm went off at 6:30, Ben pulled on sweatpants and a sweatshirt and padded out of the bedroom. It was only when he saw June, sitting at the kitchen table, working on her laptop, that he remembered that moment from the night before.

"Morning." His voice came out as a croak.

June turned to look at him. "Morning." She sounded very much awake.

"You made coffee yet?"

"No."

Ben got the coffee going and leaned against the kitchen counter, rubbing his face. "What're you up to?"

She glanced up briefly. "Submitting to auditions."

"Find any good ones?"

She let out a tired exhalation of bitter laughter. "No."

It was obvious to Ben that something was off, but he didn't know what it was and he wasn't entirely sure he wanted to. He felt like an asshole for even thinking it, but since Michelle's diagnosis, he was always having to talk June off some cliff. He would continue to do it as many times as she needed, but it never failed to make him feel like he wasn't enough, that he was pathetically ill-equipped to help her with something as momentous as losing a parent.

Looking at June now, he could see the toll it had taken on her. Her long brown hair, which was piled messily on top of her head, looked kind of dirty. Behind her reading glasses, she had dark circles under her eyes, and he could make out the protrusion of her collarbones through the fabric of her old Lauren Hill T-shirt. He thought back to the times they'd had sex recently and how her hipbones had been sharp against his fingertips. It was no wonder why she looked like this— she'd been taking care of her mom, teaching the handful of classes Moli hadn't taken over, and still had been going on auditions like her life depended on it. Sometimes she had two, three a day. And to his knowledge, she hadn't booked anything in months.

"It seems like you've been auditioning more recently," he said hesitantly.

"I have."

Ben waited for more, but she offered nothing, so he turned to grab a mug from the cabinet. "You want some coffee?"

June sighed, and it sounded slightly irritable, but when she spoke, her voice was normal. "Yes. Thank you."

He poured coffee for them both, adding milk to hers, and placed it in front of her on the kitchen table. "I'm gonna get ready for work," he said.

But as he was walking away, June turned to face him. "I want my mom to see me in something. That's why I've been so crazy about auditions lately. I'm just—I just wish there was something good out there for me to do."

Finally, everything clicked into place. What she meant, Ben knew, was: *I want my mom to see me in something before she dies.* He took a deep breath and surreptitiously glanced at the stovetop clock. He had to be at work in an hour. He had a meeting at eight with the acquisition team and it was one he could absolutely not miss or be late for. "June, your mom's seen you in so many cool things."

Tears formed and fell swiftly down her face. "Not big things though. She's seen me in a stupid razor commercial, dancing while I shaved my legs. She's seen me in a lot of shows in a hundred-person theater. I want her to see me in something big. I want her to see me on Broadway, like Moli. Or in the Graham Company. But their next round of auditions is in like six months."

Ben hesitated. "Your mom is proud of you. I know you know that."

"I don't know that. I know she loves me, but I don't actually know if she's proud of me. How could she be when I'll probably never do anything quite as good as she did? I mean, everything was so easy for her."

Ben frowned. Had June forgotten the details of her own mother's life? That she'd arrived in New York from a little town in Texas, with one suitcase and almost no money? That she'd gotten pregnant at twenty-four with a man whose ambition overshadowed his paternal instincts? "Not really. Your mom's gone through a lot of tough things in her life."

June bugged her eyes. "That's exactly what I mean. She had so many hurdles to get over and still she was this amazing artist, who somehow had time to be on Broadway and host parties and be a mom and open a fucking dance studio by the time she was thirty, and here I am with everything literally given to me and I'm nowhere near as successful as she was at my age. I just… I just want to give her a *reason* to be proud of me." She wiped the tears off her jawline aggressively and

Ben snuck another look at the clock. "And believe me, I realize how unbelievably narcissistic this makes me sound. My mom is dying and here I am talking about my stupid fucking dance career. But… I can't stand the idea of her dying, thinking she wished I'd done more."

"Oh, June." He walked over and pulled her into him. "I'm sorry." He held her like that until finally the stove clock ticked over to 7:15. "Shit," he said. "I'm really sorry, but I have to get to work. I have this meeting and Clark's gonna be there—"

June dropped her arms and leaned away from him. "No, yeah, of course. Go."

"I love you."

She nodded. "Love you too."

But as it turned out, it didn't matter how many auditions June went on. The last time Michelle would see her daughter dance was just a few weeks later in her own living room. Ben and June had come over for the evening like they had so many other times during her treatment and they sat around the coffee table, Michelle on the couch, talking and eating and listening to music.

June was midsentence when suddenly Michelle's eyes widened. "Turn it up."

It took Ben and June a moment to understand what she meant, but when they did, Ben went over to her old-fashioned stereo with the five-disc CD player and turned up the volume. It was "Dedicated to the One I Love" by The Mamas & The Papas.

"June," Michelle said, her voice thin and reedy. "Do our duet. Ben hasn't seen it yet, have you, Ben?"

"And we should keep it that way," June said.

Ben gave her a look. "You have to do it. I've heard about

this duet for over a year. Now the song is on and you have an audience and you have a stage." He nodded to the living room floor where they were sitting.

"Yes," Michelle added. "And I have cancer."

June rolled her eyes, trying to treat it as a joke like her mom had, but her throat felt tight. "Fine." She stood up and glared at her mom. "But I'm gonna hold you responsible when Ben breaks up with me after."

"You're underestimating the charm of the dance, chicken," her mom responded.

June laughed one sarcastic "Ha!" but still, she did the dance. Just as she had when she was a little girl, she did the opening Graham choreography that morphed into the jazz, rolling her hips and clapping to the beat. At one point, she did a turn that faced her to the back, and Ben glanced over at Michelle, expecting to see her watching happily. But what he saw instead almost knocked the breath out of him. Her hollowed face looked bereft, her eyes sharp as they followed her daughter's every movement. It was as though she believed, if she could just watch hard enough, she'd be able to turn the moment into something solid that she could slip into her pocket and take to wherever she was going. Ben realized then that all this time she'd been acting so stoic about her prognosis had been exactly that—acting. It had been just another one of her performances, for her friends, maybe even for herself, but especially for June. Ben looked away, and a few moments later, when he glanced back, her face had reconfigured itself. She looked like Michelle again, smiling and unflappable.

Toward the end of the song, when June hopped onto the coffee table, she bonked her head against the fan. Ben burst out laughing and Michelle joined in half a second later. Without pausing, June shook her head. "Such assholes," she called over the music. They both laughed harder and this time, Michelle's was full and immediate. Then, it turned into a cough.

When June finished, they applauded. She did a loose little curtsy and pecked Ben on the lips, still shaking her head in exasperated laughter.

Michelle, looking as bright and amused as her wrecked body would allow, gave Ben a pointed look. "Told you."

He nodded. "You did."

Then she turned her gaze to June, all her edges seemed to soften, and she gave her daughter a wink, so faint it almost wasn't there at all.

And though none of them knew it at that moment, by that point, Michelle only had a few days left. Maybe, if they'd known, they would've done things differently. Maybe June would've danced just a little more full-out, or she would've smiled a bit brighter, or she would've kissed her mom on the cheek instead of Ben. Maybe they would have somehow tried to make the moment *more*. But they didn't know, and anyway, it wouldn't have changed anything. When the time came, Michelle was on the living room couch, holding her daughter's hand.

# NINETEEN

———

*Saturday, February 18*

Dear Mom,

Sometimes, even after all these years, when something happens I want to tell you about, for a moment I'll forget that you're gone and I'll grab my phone to call you. Sometimes I'll go as far as to pull up the app before I remember, and then my heart sinks. Maybe it seems odd, but out of everything, what I miss the most about you being alive is talking on the phone. And I used to think this was just because of how fun you were to talk to. But now I think it's because of the way you made me feel about myself. No matter what, you always thought I was funny and creative, an artist with a full life. And when I talked to you, I felt I was all those things, too.

Now no one sees that side of me. Moli probably sees me as scattered and stressed. The Maplewood girls see me as just another mom. Ben doesn't see me at all. Which is why today, when someone *did* see another side of me, it felt so unbelievably good.

It's Saturday and even though he usually still goes into the office on Saturdays, today Ben worked from home. So when I put Mikey down for his afternoon nap, I gave Ben the baby monitor and slipped out of the house. With this small, precious window of time to myself, I decided to go for a walk. Recently, I've had the feeling of being underwater, as if the world around me is just above the surface and everything that's happening in it is muddied and muffled. But the moment I stepped outside, my head felt clearer. The air was cold and without Mikey, I felt unencumbered. As much as I love him, sometimes that baby can feel like a straitjacket.

I was walking around the neighborhood when suddenly, I heard my name. I looked up and saw—wouldn't you know it—Liam. He looked far more casual, in boots, jeans, and a hoodie, than when I saw him the other day at the library, and the change suited him. His dark, wavy hair wasn't combed and looked infinitely better than when it had been. His face was smoother, more relaxed.

"Oh. Hi, Liam," I said and realized I was smiling. I was happy to see him.

"Thank God you're here," he said as if he'd been expecting me. "I've been working and I'm so bored. I'm so bored I'm literally checking the mail, hoping someone would distract me. And here you are, come to answer my prayers."

That was when I realized we were standing outside his and Kirsten's house—I hadn't been paying attention to where I was going.

"Would you, um, would you wanna come inside for a bit?" he continued. "If I have to stare at this merger contract for one more second, I might drop dead."

I hesitated.

"No pressure. Here you are trying to go for a walk and I'm the overeager neighbor luring you into our house. Not to mention, Kirsten's out with Georgia, so I only have my own mediocre company to offer you."

"No, no. I want to." And I couldn't believe how true it was. I was so lonely. The only reason I'd been hesitating was because I hadn't particularly wanted to see Kirsten. I mean, I love the girl, but she's just so fucking perfect all the time, so smiley and clean, such a good mom. Sometimes she makes me feel like a different species.

Inside, we walked to the kitchen where I slid onto a barstool and Liam stood, leaning back against the island across from me. He offered me a drink and I asked for red wine because I felt like I was on a little vacation from my life. He opened a bottle and poured two glasses.

"So," he said, taking a sip. "How's your *Medea* research going?"

I couldn't believe he remembered, title and all. Whenever I brought it up to the girls, they always forgot I wasn't, in fact, talking about Medusa. "Fine. Although the story's pretty fucked up."

"Right. Doesn't she murder the woman her husband's sleeping with?"

I nodded. It gets so much worse, but I couldn't bring myself to tell him what happens after that. "I think I might have too much empathy for her. Like, does it make me a monster to be rooting for a murderer?"

Liam shrugged. "That's not all she is, though, is it?"

"You don't think murder's the type of thing to take over your identity? To swallow you whole?"

He let out a little laugh. "Maybe, yeah." He took a sip of wine. "But I don't know. I think it's hard to see people clearly. To fully understand someone outside yourself... What about you? Do you think it's possible for anyone to fully know you?"

Unexpectedly, my mind flashed to the first time Ben and I had sex after I gave birth.

The first time Ben broached the possibility, we'd been in bed, long after Mikey was asleep. I'd had my head on his chest and his hand began to wander from my hip to that sensitive spot just inside it. I flinched unintentionally at his touch and suddenly, I was awash in a machine-gun-fast series of emotions. First, my body felt entirely revolting. My waist was fat and loose and overly mobile. Like, I could grab big handfuls of it and shake it around. And then there was my vagina— gaping and flappy. It all seemed entirely undesirable and I felt wrapped up in that. I was angry at him for touching me when it was so obvious I shouldn't be touched, then I felt guilty for my misplaced anger. And with all of these emotions ricocheting through me, all I could do was lie there, stiff and unmoving.

"June?" Ben said and the sound of my name on his lips made me start to cry.

"Sorry. I just feel weird. I haven't felt sexual in so long."

"Hey." His hand jumped from my hip to my forehead and he ran his dry, warm palm over it and into my hair. "You don't have to apologize. It's totally fine if you're not ready."

At his words and their mercifully casual tone, I felt an invisible hand around my neck loosen. "Okay. Thank you." I'd gone from zero to sixty and back to zero all in the blink of an eye. I settled my body back against his and we turned on the TV.

We enacted a much less dramatic version of this scene probably four or five times after that. On the rare night we saw each other, we'd cuddle or kiss, and Ben's kiss would get longer, deeper, or he'd tighten his fingers on my waist and I'd sigh and say I still wasn't ready and he'd say of course, it was fine. I knew he wasn't mad or frustrated or anything, but I also knew he really wanted to have sex. And I really wanted *to want* to have sex.

So the next time he touched me, I leaned into it instead of pulling away. I willed my body to relax. I ran my hands over his shoulders and tried to focus on how much bigger and stronger he is than I am. I did everything I could—I even envisioned Ramy Youssef taking me from behind. I still felt tense and sort of outside my own body, but I was willing myself to want sex. But when he tried to put himself in me, I was too dry and so he used some lube, but suddenly, I felt ashamed and frustrated and he was pumping inside me and physically it felt good, but mentally I was freaking out.

And yet, I was paralyzed. I didn't want to make Ben feel bad for having sex with me when I'd so clearly cosigned the idea. I knew if I asked him to stop in the middle, he'd feel really guilty and it would be so awkward and he'd keep asking me what had happened and I wouldn't know what to say. Also, it's not like every time I've had sex, I've been one hundred percent into it. Sometimes I get distracted and think about a piece of choreography I'm working on or daydream about pasta. And even when my brain is off somewhere else, I can usually get back into it and eventually I come and then of course, I'm happy we had sex. So I thought I could do that this time.

But once I felt off, I couldn't come back from it. Afterward, I got up quickly and took a shower and when I got back into bed, his kissed me on the lips and said "I love you," and I could tell he had no idea that during that whole time, I hadn't been there in the room with him, and all I could think was *How could you not see me?*

I looked at Liam now. Did I think it was possible for any-one to fully know me? "No," I said. "Do you?"

Liam did a jerky little shrug. "Sometimes I catch Kirsten looking at me and I can just tell that she's seeing someone who doesn't exist, like the person in her head just doesn't quite match up with who I actually am. I shouldn't be saying this." He shook his head, but almost immediately continued. "Maybe that's just what marriage is. Just constantly over- and underestimating your partner, seeing them through your own gaze, never quite seeing them for who they really are."

I took a sip of wine and so did he, and for a while we just sat there together, not talking. In the moment, I agreed with him, but now I think it could be more complicated than that. Perhaps it's possible to be fully seen in your life, but not al-ways by the same person. Perhaps your spouse sees a part of the real you and your mom sees another part and your hus-band's coworker sees another, and if you put all those pieces together, you'd be able to make a full person.

Sorry for all the sex talk, Mom.

Love,
June

# TWENTY

Ben managed to drive half a block from Kirsten's house before he pulled over, his hands shaking on the steering wheel. It was impossible for him not to envision all the things that might've happened between Liam and June. Was that afternoon outside the library the first time they'd seen each other as anything other than friendly acquaintances? If so, how had it all started? Had June touched his arm and let it linger? Had Liam pictured her naked when they hugged? Or had it begun earlier than Kirsten knew? Her words about that day sliced inside him like a knife. *When they hugged, it felt—I don't know—like they loved each other.* It seemed impossible and yet the suspicion crept into his head like a specter, its blackness billowing and growing.

Just as it began to take root in his mind, Ben saw it: a black BMW SUV driving slowly past with Liam Aimes in the driver's seat. Without thinking, Ben opened his car door and jumped out. He shoved his hands into his pockets and started walking down the sidewalk, back the same way he'd come. His heart collided painfully against his rib cage and his breath formed white clouds that disappeared quickly into the night. He reached the house just as the car was pulling into the driveway. Liam caught sight of Ben through his window, turned off the car, and opened the door.

"Ben? Hey," he said, stepping onto the driveway. "What're you doing here?"

"Hi, Liam." His name stuck in Ben's throat.

There was a pause as Liam waited for Ben to say something more, but when he didn't, Liam continued. "What's up?" He slammed the car door behind him.

Ben took a step closer. "I talked to Kirsten earlier."

"Kirsten? What about?"

"She was telling me about you and June."

Liam's smile faltered. "Oh."

It was all the confirmation Ben needed. "Yeah," he said, and then he punched Liam in the face. Pain shot through his hand to his armpit. "Fuck!" He hadn't punched anything since the night he'd met June so many years ago and he'd forgotten how badly it hurt. He thought he might've broken something.

Liam collapsed backward onto the driveway. He clapped a hand to his face and Ben saw blood spill through his fingers.

"Jesus!" Liam shouted in a strangled voice. The blood must've been filling his mouth because he spluttered and coughed. He took his hand away and spit out a mouthful of blood. A red string of saliva clung to his bottom lip. "What the fuck, man!" he shouted at him from the ground, the blood rounding his words. "What was that for?"

"I—Goddammit, Liam, what the hell was I supposed to do?"

"Supposed to do about *what*?"

"Your affair with June, you asshole. Do you know where she is? Are you in touch with her?"

Before Liam could respond, Ben heard a car door slam

behind him. He whirled around to see a cop car, its lights off, parked along the curb. From the driver's side emerged a female officer. It was dark out now, the nearby streetlight their only source of light, but Ben could just make out the woman's outline.

"Officer Moretti?"

The woman's gait faltered. "Mr. Gilmore?"

From the direction of Kirsten and Liam's house, Ben heard a door open and Kirsten call, "Liam?"

From the ground, bloodied-up Liam said, "Hey, Kirsten."

The two women approached from opposite sides, little Georgia on Kirsten's hip. When she got close enough to see Liam on the ground, she gasped.

Moretti looked from Kirsten to Liam to Ben and sighed. "I'm here because a neighbor called in a suspicious man in a car. Said he'd just been sitting there for a while, that he seemed a bit agitated." She looked at Ben. "Sounds like you might've been waiting for this man to come home."

"No, actually," Ben said as Liam yelled, "Yeah, he ambushed me!"

Ben whirled around. "You're having an affair! With my wife!"

Kirsten yelped. Liam wrinkled his brow. "What are you talking about?"

"Oh, God. Give it up. I know. Kirsten knows. Officer Moretti's been here for a fucking second and *she* knows! You're having an affair with June."

Liam leaned forward, shifting his weight onto his feet. He tried to stand, but he couldn't get enough momentum and he fell backward again, wincing. Kirsten took an automatic step toward him to help, but then, as if remembering why he was on the ground in the first place, stepped away, uncertain, adjusting Georgia on her hip. Liam tried again to stand and this time he made it.

"I am not having an affair," he said adamantly.

"Kirsten saw you two. At the library. And then at Jonathan and Sydney's party. You were—in *each other's arms!*"

"Yeah," Liam said. He looked from Ben to Kirsten and back to Ben. "I've run into June a few times. And do you know what we always talk about? How miserable she is. So yeah, I wasn't an asshole. I hugged her. Sue me!" He spat the last out with an accidental wad of blood. It landed between the two men in a slick glob.

Ben didn't think he could feel any worse, but suddenly, he did. The idea that June had turned to Liam when she was upset made him sick. Ben wanted to punch him again, to turn that face into pulp.

Moretti must have seen the look in his eyes, however, because she stepped forward, an arm flung out in front of him. "Woah, woah, woah. Right now, I can chock this up to a simple domestic dispute that worked itself out. A misunderstanding. If, that is"—she stared at Ben—"this ends now. And of course, if Mr.—" She looked at Liam.

"Aimes."

"If Mr. Aimes decides not to press charges."

Liam rolled his eyes, but didn't say anything. He looked so indignant, so self-righteously wronged. Could he be telling the truth? Ben glanced at Kirsten and she, too, was staring at her husband with confusion, absentmindedly rubbing Georgia's back. But she'd just told Ben that she'd seen June and Liam kissing in the garage, hadn't she? She had no reason to fabricate it and Ben had seen the truth in her eyes. But obviously, she and Liam couldn't both be telling the truth, so what the hell was going on?

"My advice to the two of you," Moretti continued, "is to go to the hospital and get yourselves checked out. Then, when you aren't being such idiots, you could have a real, adult conversation." She looked over at Kirsten. "Mrs. Aimes, do you think you could drive your husband to the hospital?"

Kirsten's head snapped to look at Moretti. She looked alarmed, but nodded.

"Good. Mr. Gilmore, why don't I give you a ride? I'd suggest you'd both go with Mrs. Aimes, but I doubt you two could handle it and you can't drive anywhere with that hand."

"Okay," Ben said, feeling like a chastened schoolboy. "Thank you." He looked away from Liam and took a step toward the squad car, but stopped short. Moretti wouldn't make him ride in the back like a felon, would she? "Can I, uh, sit in the front?"

Moretti rolled her eyes. "You're not under arrest, Ben. Shotgun's all yours."

# TWENTY-ONE

---

*Four years earlier*

Late one Tuesday night, a year after her mom's death, June walked into Ben's apartment and dropped her dance bag on the floor with a heavy thud.

Ben looked up from the contract he'd been reviewing at the kitchen table. From where he sat, he was slightly hidden by a wall, so he could see her, but she hadn't yet seen him. He noticed she had on her audition makeup, bright red lipstick and those fake eyelashes that made her eyes look enormous. She reached up a hand to massage her neck and he saw how sharp her collarbones looked.

"Hello!" she called too loudly for how close he was. "Ben? You home?"

"Hi."

June stepped around the partial wall that divided them. "Oh. Hi. I didn't see you."

"You just now getting back from an audition?"

June's obsession with auditioning had, to Ben's surprise, only intensified after her mom's death, and recently she'd been pushing herself harder than ever. But the role she'd most coveted—a spot in the Martha Graham Company—had yet again been denied her. Only this time around, Ben hadn't really been surprised by the news. And, not that he'd ever tell June this, but he'd been relieved when she'd come back that day with another no. Because on top of pushing herself to audition for what seemed like every dance role in Manhattan, in the wake of her mom's death, she'd lost more weight, as if grief had sucked it from her bones. Ben didn't think it was a good idea for her to join a company with such an intense rehearsal and performance schedule when she seemed to be at her weakest, both physically and emotionally.

"I'm just now getting back from an audition that started nine hours ago," she said.

"Jesus."

"I know. And it was terrible. *I* was terrible." She walked into the kitchen and leaned against the counter. "Recently, I've been feeling like the harder I work for this, the more I mess it up. It's like I'm holding my dance career so tightly in my hands that I'm choking all the life out of it."

She turned to fill a glass with water, but really, she just didn't want Ben to see her face. She hadn't been planning to articulate what had been percolating inside her for months, but now that she had, she felt it tightening her throat.

"It's called the yips, I think," Ben said.

June took a sip of water, swallowed, then looked over at him. "What?"

"The yips. It's when you get in your own head about your sport and instead of just playing, you overfocus."

"Okay. So there's a name for it." She heard the edge of irritation in her own voice and took a deep breath. "And do we know how to get rid of it?"

"I think you have to try less."

June let out one short laugh. "Great. The thing I've wanted my entire life, the thing I've been working for since I was like six, I just have to try less to get it."

Ben hesitated and it seemed to June like he was deciding whether or not to say what he was thinking. "D'you want a glass of wine?" he asked, then swallowed the last sip of his own.

"Sure."

Ben stood and walked to the counter, where the open bottle of wine sat uncorked. He poured her a glass, then re-filled his own. June leaned off the counter to grab hers and as she did, she met his eyes. "Hi," she said, smiling tiredly. "How're you?"

Ben smiled back. "I'm fine."

She craned her neck and they kissed.

"So what was the audition for?" he asked.

"That's the worst part. It was for a thirty-second commercial for some fruit company. We were gonna dance with bundles of fruit on our heads like Carmen Miranda. And we were gonna do it for like…nothing. I think the pay was two hundred dollars for a day of work and no royalties for airings. Not that I know the actual amount because I didn't book it. After nine hours of dancing, they lined us all up and then pointed at the ones they wanted to leave."

Ben balked. "What?"

"Yeah." But June hadn't even told him the worst part. As she'd stood in the line with the four other remaining dancers, the director of the commercial had pointed at her and told the casting director that he liked her look, but didn't think she had the "star quality" you apparently needed for a thirty-second fruit ad. His stage whisper had carried throughout the entire room, and June had been able to physically feel the pitying sideways glances of the other dancers. Heat had crept up her chest like a rash. Later, on the train home, that mortification turned to outrage.

"I mean, it's fine," she said now. "I just wanted the money. Which is ironic because I had to get my classes covered to go, so I actually *lost* money going to the audition."

But just as she said this, she wished she could take it back. June used to be more open about money at the beginning of her and Ben's relationship, but she'd begun to notice that whenever she brought it up, he would always try to help her out, to pay for a dinner she'd said was on her, or to wave her away when she asked how much she owed for a subway pass he'd bought for her. It wasn't that she didn't appreciate his generosity, but she didn't want him to feel as if she *needed* that from him. She rushed to change the subject.

"By the way, *Anything Goes* is closing."

Ben frowned. *"Anything Goes?"*

"Yeah, you know the Broadway musical Moli has been in for a year?"

"Oh, shit. Right. How's she taking it?"

June shrugged. "Surprisingly well, actually. I think she's pretty focused on the wedding anyway." Ezra, the man who'd eaten all that chocolate just to get to know the woman behind the counter, had proposed a few months previous. Moli's mom was insisting on a traditional Indian wedding, and Ezra's dad was insisting on a traditional Jewish one, so they were doing both, and the festivities were scheduled to span the course of four days. "But the other thing is, since the show's ending and since our lease is up soon, Moli's moving in with Ezra next month."

"What? Before they get married? Do her parents know she'll be living in sin?"

June smiled, but it felt thin.

"So what are you and Emilio thinking?" Ben asked. After all these years, the three original roommates—June, Moli, and Emilio—still lived together.

She took a sip of wine. "I don't know."

"Do you want to move here? You basically live here anyway."

June froze.

"What?" he said. "What's wrong?"

But she didn't know what to say. How could she explain that she felt guilty about how much she'd accepted from him over the past few years? She'd cried on him, fallen asleep in his arms, and he was right—she practically lived in his apartment. If she were being honest with herself, she *did* want to move in with Ben. She wanted to marry him someday. He was the nicest person she'd ever met and she loved him more than anything in the world, even her own independence. But she hadn't made it on her own yet, not really, and she didn't want to be the type of woman who relied on a man.

In the wake of that horrible audition, and that horrible man pointing at her and saying she wasn't enough, and all those pitying sideways looks from those other dancers, June felt too scattered and emotionally wobbly to articulate what she was feeling, so when she did, what came out of her mouth sounded all wrong. "I don't want your pity, Ben."

Ben was silent and when she looked up at him, he looked like she'd spat in his face. "Pity? June. We've been together for almost three years. I know our lives sort of stagnated there for a bit," he said, talking around the death of her mom like he did when he didn't want to upset her. "But doesn't this sort of feel inevitable? I mean, we're adults and we love each other. Do you think me asking you to move in is *pity*?"

"I—no, of course not. I just—I don't want you to feel like you have to support me. You shouldn't have to do that."

"Technically, you moving in here would actually be saving me money. I'm not saying you never have to pay rent again. I mean, of course if you need me to pay it, I'm happy to, but I'm not, like, offering to be your sugar daddy. We're a team. We help each other out."

"Yeah, but so far it's *always* you helping me. Our relationship feels so lopsided and I don't want you to wake up in five years and resent me for that."

Ben hesitated and the moment twisted in June's stomach. She so badly hadn't wanted that to hit home. But when he spoke again, his voice was clear and firm.

"June, I love you. You know that, right? You may think our relationship is lopsided, but if you do, you just don't see it properly. You don't see how you help me. You make me feel good about myself and you help me to be better and I want to live with you because of that. I want to live with you because being with you, for me, is better than not being with you." He grinned slowly. "Well, except for right now."

She laughed.

"And unless I'm completely delusional about what we have here," he continued, "I think you sorta feel the same way too."

June studied him, searching for any sign of that hesitation she'd seen earlier, but it was gone. In its place was Ben, whom she really loved and really liked, and who seemed so sure of what he was asking. Finally, she smiled and it was big and wide and happy. "I do."

Ben grinned. "Okay, then. Good. Now stop being an idiot and move in with me."

So they decided to live together and then, only a few days after, they decided to live together for the rest of their lives.

When June accepted his proposal—in bed on a cold Sunday morning, her mom's old ruby ring in his outstretched hand—Ben, who was so filled with elation he could feel it in his fingertips, resolved to stick it out at Clark & White for just a little bit longer. The idea of quitting had begun to infiltrate his mind yet again over the past year, but now he would have a wife to support and he wanted to ensure their security blanket before he did anything rash. And this time, because he'd already done it before, pushing that dream aside was just a little bit easier.

# TWENTY-TWO

———

*Tuesday, February 21*

Dear Mom,

I've missed you every day since you died, but some days that missing feels like something else. Some days it feels like a hole in my chest and the only thing that seems to fill it is anger: anger that you died before I got married and didn't get to go to my wedding; anger that you never saw me perform with the Graham Company; anger that you didn't get to meet your own grandchild; anger that you left me here to go through my life motherless. Some days your absence just feels like a stab in my heart and today was one of those days, so thanks a lot.

It all started at Jitterbuggies. The moment I walked in, I could tell something was off. Instead of the usual happy welcome from Reese, Sydney, and Kirsten, all I heard from the circle of women was the hum of hushed voices. I tried to catch someone's eye and Sydney gave me the smallest flash of a smile, but Reese and Kirsten were both too preoccupied with their babies to look up.

Our teacher sat down cross-legged at the head of the studio as usual and everyone quieted down. "Before we get started," she began, "I'd like to make a little announcement. You may see a clipboard floating around class today..." I looked around and spotted it in one of the other mom's hands. She was staring at it with a concerned frown. Whatever was on that paper had to be the source of Reese, Kirsten, and Sydney's awkwardness and I sighed out a breath of relief; I had thought they were being weird specifically to me, but they were just being weird in general. So what was on that piece of paper?

"It's a petition," our teacher continued tersely, as if she were both annoyed by and wary of the whole thing. I watched as the clipboard passed from one set of hands to another. Lily, one of the younger moms, studied it, then glanced both ways before sliding the pen out from behind the clip and quickly signing her name.

"You can look over it now if you'd like or after class," our teacher said, "but I'm gonna get us going so we don't waste any time. There are also some pamphlets behind the petition to provide more information if you're interested."

But I was no longer listening. The clipboard had finally made it into my hands and I was staring at the paper in front of me, my face burning. The words at the top read, *All Jitterbuggies participants must be vaccinated.* Beneath the title was a paragraph, presumably outlining the dangers of not vaccinating your children, but I couldn't read it. The words swam in my vision. All I could think was *How do they know?* And then it hit me. Mikey's missed vaccination appointment had been my "confession" at wine night, which meant that this petition had come from one of my own friends.

I flipped up the page to reveal a neat little stack of pamphlets beneath. On the cover were the words: *The Choice Not to Vaccinate Doesn't Only Affect You!* Beneath, was the picture of a mom with a baby in her arms. The woman's eyes had been cropped by the frame; the baby was wailing.

My stomach felt tight. I am that bad mother in the photo whose identity had been removed, an anonymous monster jeopardizing the health of all the babies in the room. Everybody knows you have to stay up-to-date with your child's vaccinations. It isn't something you let slip simply because you couldn't get your baby to stop crying one day. Which is why I've already scheduled his makeup appointment— it's in two fucking days—and obviously, I was not going to forget it this time. But I'd already told the girls all of that at wine night. This clearly wasn't about a vaccine; this was a vendetta.

I stared at all those signatures on the page, scanning the list to find Reese's name or Sydney's or Kirsten's, but I couldn't seem to focus. I wondered if anyone was watching me and I tried to work out what to do. It would be absurd to sign it, of course. And yet, not signing it would implicate me. I picked up the pen, fiddled with it, slid it back into its slot and handed the clipboard to the woman next to me. Then I scooped Mikey up and ran.

Ben came home early tonight—9 pm, long after I'd set the timer to bond with Mikey, and long after it went off ten minutes later with nothing inside me but a deep, racking sense of guilt. When Ben walked through the door, I wanted to throw my arms around his neck like he was a soldier come home from war, but I was so filled with shame, it weighed me down where I stood.

"Hi," I said as he walked into the kitchen, where I was leaning against the counter, holding a glass of wine. I wanted so badly for him to intuit my feelings, to sweep me into a hug and ask what was wrong.

He tossed his phone and keys onto the counter, but just as he opened his mouth to say something, his phone dinged with a notification. He picked it up, glanced at the screen, and sighed heavily. He typed something out, flipped his phone facedown, and finally looked up at me. I noticed dark circles under his eyes. "Hi," he said, leaning over for a perfunctory kiss. "I need a drink."

"I just opened a bottle of red."

"Mmm," he said, but his gaze slid over it and he walked to the cabinet where we kept the liquor I never bought but we always seemed to have. He pulled out a bottle of whiskey and poured two fingers, then flicked on the sink tap and darted his glass underneath. The way he did all of it struck me as practiced, which was weird because Ben doesn't really drink that much.

"How was work?" I asked.

He opened his mouth, but then sighed, smiling grudgingly. "I'd tell you, but—God, it's so boring. I'd much rather hear about your day with Mikey."

I looked at my own drink and thought about it. I thought about the petition, my chest so tight it hurt. I thought of the way Sydney's eyes had darted away from mine. I thought of myself as a dancer in the company, touring from city to city and stage to stage. And then I thought of myself today, withered by guilt and incompetency, struggling just to keep up with the basics of my baby's health. My life thoroughly mirrored Medea's now: from powerful sorceress to nothing more than a jaded, housebound mother and wife.

I wanted to talk to Ben, I really did. But if I told him about the petition, I'd have to tell him about missing Mikey's vaccination appointment, which I knew would freak him out. And how could I mention all these petty complaints when whatever was going on at work was obviously wrecking him? And on top of all of this, there was a tiny angry voice inside me that wanted to keep things even between us. *Fine,* I thought bitterly. *If you're not going to talk to me about what's going on with you, I'm not going to tell you what's going on with me.* It felt like the only way to hold on to my dwindling dignity. And no matter how dismal things got for Medea, she always held on to that.

I settled on the simplest thing I could say. "I decided not to go to Jitterbuggies anymore." Obviously, in two days' time, when Mikey was fully vaccinated, there'd be nothing they could do to stop me. But there was no way I was walking back in there, not now.

For a moment, Ben looked at me blankly. "Jitterbuggies…"

"You know, the mommy-and-me class I go to with the girls?"

He shook his head. "Oh, right. How come? Is everything okay?"

I hitched a shoulder and took a sip of wine. "It's not really working with Mikey's sleep schedule." It was a lie and an obvious one if Ben knew anything about our son's sleeping patterns, but he just nodded.

He stared into his drink for a long moment before lifting his head and looking me in the eyes. "I love you, June," he said and it sounded like the first completely true thing he'd said that night.

"I love you too." And yet, the words that sprung unbidden and unspoken in my mind were: *But love isn't enough. Not when you're drowning.*

Love you, too, Mom. Talk soon,
June

# TWENTY-THREE

———

On the morning after his driveway brawl, Ben sat in bed, gazing down at his throbbing hand, swollen and bound in a black Velcro splint. In the emergency room the night before, the doctor had taken an X-ray, diagnosed a fracture of the fifth metacarpal—the exact injury that had first led him to June all those years ago—and prescribed him the splint and a week's supply of codeine. But worse than the physical pain was the dread gripping his insides. What the hell had he been thinking, punching his friend, his *colleague*? What horrible rumors and HR nightmares would unfold if their co-workers found out?

He swallowed down a wave of nausea and was reminded of the whiskey he'd had the previous night. He knew he shouldn't have drunk while taking painkillers, but he felt as if he were stuck in some horrible loop, knowing he shouldn't drink, and drinking anyway. Plus, his mom had been up when he'd gotten home from the hospital, and to explain the splint, he'd had to fabricate yet another story: he'd been dropping paperwork off at a colleague's and the colleague had accidentally slammed Ben's hand in the car door. All these lies had him craving numbness.

But the thing that haunted him most was that he still didn't know the truth about June and Liam. Now that the events of the night before had had time to percolate, his anger had cooled, leaving confusion in its wake. The more he thought about it, something about the alleged affair struck him as off, and yet, June *had* been harboring some sort of secret—of that, he was sure.

He got out of bed and walked around to June's side. He'd dreamt last night about that little black journal with all those pages ripped out and had awoken desperate to find out what was in them. What had she been hiding? Ben grabbed the journal, opened it, and his heart sank. He'd been idiotically hoping that something would be different this time, but of course, nothing was. There was still the spine of torn edges, the unmarked pages behind. He thumbed through them, but again they came up blank. He flipped to the back, to the very last page, but again there was nothing there.

He let out a frustrated groan then hurled the journal to the floor. It bounced, pages fluttering, and as it came to a stop, Ben saw something inside it shift—a ripped slip of paper, thinner than his pinky finger. He frowned. There was something written on it. He reached down, slid it out from where it had been lodged between the frayed edges, and read the ending of some incomplete line: *the one who needs to die.*

Ben stared at the words written in June's messy handwriting, his heart thumping. What had she been talking about? Who needed to die? When his phone rang, he jumped. He pulled it out of his sweatpants pocket, his hand shaking slightly, his eyes not leaving that scrap of paper.

"Hello?"

"Ben. Hi." It was Kirsten. "Is everything okay? You sound weird."

But Ben couldn't think. "I'm fine. What's up, Kirsten?"

He heard her take a deep breath, but even so, when she spoke next, it was in an urgent rush. "I, uh, I think I was wrong. About Liam and June. I wasn't lying to you when you came over—I *did* believe what I said—but Liam and I talked at the hospital last night and he told me he wasn't seeing June, and, well, I believe him."

But her words felt as if they were coming from very far away, as if Ben were at the bottom of some deep well, and by the time they got to him, they'd lost all meaning. The only thing he had space for in his head was that line from June's journal: *the one who needs to die.* He rubbed a hand down his face. "Okay, Kirsten, thanks for calling, but I gotta go."

"Wait! Ben. That's not the reason I called. We need to talk—in person."

Ben closed his eyes. "Why?"

"It's about June. It's…" For a moment, her voice sounded almost ashamed, but then it faded and when she finished, her tone was forceful and resolute, nothing more. "It's important."

With those words, Ben filled with a profound heaviness. He thought of the concerned look his mom had given him the night before when he'd walked in the door with a splint on his hand and a lie on his lips. He thought of all the lies he'd have to continue to tell her, about work and the injury and June. He thought of how he needed to get Mikey breakfast and how Moli had called for an update, as had Dee Dee, as had almost every other lawyer who was on his current case. He thought about the four hundred unopened emails he had from work and how badly he wanted to just take a codeine,

throw the blanket over his head, and fall into the nothingness of sleep.

But he looked again at that unnerving line: *the one who
needs to die.*

"Okay," he said into the phone. "Give me ten minutes."

# TWENTY-FOUR

———

*Two years earlier*

June hadn't realized how much she'd missed Moli until she spotted her sitting at a tall table at the edge of the dimly lit restaurant and a small firework exploded inside her chest. They were both married now—Moli living in Brooklyn with Ezra, and June with Ben on the Upper East Side—and for the first time in their friendship, they had to work to see each other.

They hugged and to June's surprise, when they pulled apart, Moli's eyes were shining. "Moli, are you crying?"

"What? No." Moli pressed her middle fingers into her eyes and inspected them. "Maybe just a little. What? Can't a girl miss her friend?"

June laughed. "I miss you too."

After they'd settled in, the waiter came and took their drink orders—a Cabernet for June, sparkling water for Moli. When he disappeared, Moli touched a hand to her neck to feel her glands. "I'd kill for a glass of wine, but I think I'm coming down with something. And you know how alcohol always takes me from head cold to pneumonia in like a minute."

But the moment her friend had said the words *sparkling*

*water*, June had understood—Moli was pregnant. The certainty of this knowledge felt like a stone falling through water; it had shape and heft. And it was clear from her feigned sickness that Moli wasn't ready yet to share the news, so June would just have to pretend right along with her.

"Oh, totally. I hate that," she said in what she hoped was a light tone, but as she did, a sudden sadness welled up inside her. She and Moli never waited to tell each other big news. During the days of her mom's sickness, June knew Moli had held back about certain things, but that had been out of compassion, not secrecy.

Although, June had to admit, this did give her time to prepare the correct response. She'd gasp excitedly, clap a hand over a broad smile, maybe even cry a little. And it wouldn't be fake—she really *was* happy for her friend—but it would be...selective. Because a baby changed things. You could say it wouldn't, you could say they'd still see each other all the time, and maybe they even would, but a baby changed everything.

"Sorry you're not feeling well," she said, but didn't ask for details. She didn't want to force Moli into any more of a charade. "How's everything else going?"

Moli smiled so brightly that June's heart clenched. She wished Moli would just tell her. "Good," Moli said. "Really, really good. But I want to hear about you. And Ben. How's he doing? I got the feeling last time we talked that he's been...stressed."

June didn't remember what exactly she'd said about Ben during their last conversation, but Moli's reaction to it didn't surprise her. "He's fine. It's just— You know I sort of thought that after the wedding, he might look for another job. I mean, I think he likes it at Clark & White, but the longer he stays there, the more time he spends at the office. We haven't gone out together in months. Although that's partially my fault. Be-cause of the company." She waved a hand. "So I guess we're both just in a busy phase."

Moli clapped her hands together. "Okay, so I'm sorry that you and your husband are too busy for your marriage and all, but I still can't believe you're in the Martha Graham Company."

June laughed. That summer, she had auditioned for the company for the sixth year in a row. Like she had every other time, she'd made it through to the second day, to the last dozen dancers. But at the point when she was usually sent home, this time she wasn't. At the end, on Sunday afternoon, it had been down to her and three other dancers, two guys and another girl. June had stood there in the center of the studio, back straight, chin lifted, heart fluttering in her chest, chanting the silent prayer: *pick me, pick me, pick me.*

"Okay," the longtime artistic director Hiromi Kimura had said as she appraised them. "We'd like to speak with each of you individually. Please go wait in the hallway until some-one comes to get you."

June had swelled with sudden emotion—a mixture of des-perate hope and terror. A private meeting with the artistic director was no guarantee of an offer of apprenticeship. Some-times, she knew, Hiromi talked to the last few dancers sim-ply to encourage them to come back next year. She might even tell them to work on something—their feet flexibility or their arm strength. She might talk to all four dancers today and offer none of them a position.

It had happened to her mom. On the fourth and final time Michelle had auditioned, the company's artistic director had sat with her mom and told her that she'd really enjoyed Mi-chelle's performances over the past two days, that she'd remembered her from the past few years. While she was clearly a talented dancer, the director had gone on, the company just didn't have a spot for her body type at the moment. Maybe next year, the director had said, but by then, Michelle had opened the studio and her career had been set.

And if her mom hadn't made it, what were the chances that June would?

When her name had been called, June had stood and followed the woman back into the studio where they'd auditioned. Hiromi Kimura and the rehearsal director, Silvi Brawnish, had been sitting in two flimsy plastic chairs in the center of the floor.

"June," Silvi had said, gesturing to the empty chair across from them. "Sit."

June had sat.

"This is your"—Silvi had glanced at a piece of paper on her lap—"sixth year to audition for the Graham Company, correct?"

"Yes, ma'am."

Hiromi, June had noticed, had been gazing at her, her slender hands clasped gently in her lap, her face utterly blank.

"Well, then," Silvi had continued. "You've waited long enough for your news. We won't beat around the bush." She'd turned to look at Hiromi, who had held June with her steady, piercing gaze and said simply, "We're offering you an apprenticeship in the company, June. Congratulations."

An apprenticeship was the first position of every dancer in the company. It meant you were the lowest in the hierarchy, but a part of the company nonetheless. After six years of auditioning for it, twenty-five of dreaming of it, and even longer of hearing about it from her mom, June was finally a member of the Martha Graham Dance Company.

"It's amazing," she said now to Moli. "I mean, I'm exhausted all the time, which kind of makes you worry about the prospect of being a principal dancer, but it's what I've always wanted."

On top of that, her new full-time position as a proper dancer meant June had finally been able to leave her position at the studio's front desk. She was no longer answering phones to supplement her income. Nor was she still teaching classes, which, she'd realized with a bit of surprise, she actually missed. She realized she liked being the one to set the pace and create the choreography. At Martha Graham, she always felt just one step behind everyone else. But that was normal, she told herself. Along with one of the male dancers she'd auditioned with, she was the newest member of the most prestigious contemporary dance company in the country. A little learning curve was to be expected.

Still, she thought back to her classes at the studio with the smallest of aches. She loved her adult contemporary class and how much they all laughed together. And she missed the music video class she'd created a few years previous, inspired by her and her mom's duet to The Mamas & The Papas. It was silly and really more of a dance workout than anything else, but each month June would create choreography for one song—usually Lizzo or Beyoncé, but sometimes something more obscure—and then she'd teach it to her students.

But she didn't want to say any of that aloud, partly because it was absurd to miss teaching in a small-time studio when she was getting to perform with the company she'd always dreamed of, but also because the person who'd taken over her front desk position was Moli. It seemed that as June's career was finally taking off, Moli's was winding down. But the odd thing was that it struck June as mostly self-imposed.

She never heard Moli talk about auditions anymore—neither to say she'd been to one or to say she missed going on them.

"I'm so happy for you," Moli said. "You deserve it. I mean you deserved it years ago, but I'm glad the dance world finally got its head on straight and recognized what an amazing talent you are."

June smiled. "We should really do dinner more often. This is a great boost to my ego."

Moli laughed, but there was a flash of something else in her face, too, something that looked strangely like sadness. But then it disappeared, leaving June to wonder if she'd really seen it in the first place. "So," Moli continued. "How's the show coming along?"

The company was currently in rehearsals for a new ballet titled *Black Heart* by a visiting choreographer. It was both their first show of the season and June's debut with the company. While most of their performance schedule was outside Manhattan, *Black Heart* was going to debut in the New York City Center. "It's a little overwhelming how fast it's coming up, to be honest," June said. "I have, like, three weeks to stop sucking so much. But I can't wait for you to see it."

Moli smiled, but that flash of what June had seen before was back. This time there was no denying it. Moli looked sad and unusually reticent. "That's actually what I wanted to talk to you about…"

June took a breath. This was it. The pregnancy announcement. Of course Moli was satisfied with her life—she was about to be a mom. "What's up?" June said, eyes wide with what she hoped looked like unsuspecting curiosity.

"Well… Obviously, I'm gonna come to the show. I wouldn't miss it for the world, but… I'm gonna have to take the train to get there."

June let out a faltering laugh. "Moli, did you just now realize you live in Brooklyn?"

Moli laughed, too, but it faded fast. "I'm gonna have to take the train because… Ezra just got a job in DC. We're moving in two weeks."

June felt everything inside her drop. This, she hadn't been expecting. A baby would've changed things, yes, but it wouldn't have changed the fact that the two of them could still be together in the same room whenever they wanted. She looked into Moli's face, so tentative and apologetic, and June realized she needed to be the one convincing her friend this was going to be okay, not the other way around. She tried to muster the same bright response she'd prepared for very different news, but before she could even open her mouth, Moli spoke again.

"Oh," she added as happy tears welled in her eyes. "And I'm pregnant."

# TWENTY-FIVE

———

*Wednesday, February 22*

Dear Mom,

This will be hard to ask without sounding completely crazy, but were you at Whole Foods today?

In the months after you died, I saw you everywhere. The first time it happened, I saw you in the face of a woman on the train. She had your forehead, the shape of it, and the same straight dark hair. I couldn't see her face properly because she was looking down, reading a book, and when I glanced over at her, my heart leaped into my throat. Here I thought you'd been dead, but actually you were just riding the subway, reading a book! But then you moved—you lifted your face to glance out the window—and suddenly, you were a stranger. It felt like I'd been standing on a bucket and someone had kicked it out from under me.

It happened all the time after that. I'd see you in the flash of a woman's coat as she darted into a store, or I'd spot you walking in front of me on the sidewalk. As the years passed, those types of sightings got fewer and farther between, but even now, every once in a while, I'll see a flash of you in a stranger.

But that's not what happened today in Whole Foods. Today, I saw *you*. You had your hair down and you were wearing your oversize sunglasses; you even had your turquoise scarf with the white polka dots around your head. It was the same scarf you were wearing in that photo with me as a baby in your arms, and the same one that was around your head twenty-five years later as you got chemo in the hospital. The one you were wearing today was threadbare and faded and absolutely one hundred percent yours.

But what made me so sure that it was you, even more than the scarf, was that you were looking back at me. Those other yous never noticed me, but today you were looking at me first. It almost seemed as if you'd been watching me. You were wearing those sunglasses and peering over the edge of a giant sunflower, like you didn't want me to see you. I froze, standing still in the middle of a walkway until someone bumped into me. Mikey, who was in his carrier on my chest, started crying and I looked down to check on him. When I looked up again, you'd vanished.

After that first time on the train, when I saw the you that turned out not to be you, I followed that woman with the book. I wanted to see if I could find you again in her face. I followed her out of the subway and up onto the street, weaving through all the people on the sidewalk, my eyes on the back of her head the entire time. When she finally turned a corner and I caught sight of her profile, she was still only her, so I let her go.

I wanted to follow you today. I wanted to see that moment when you turned into a stranger, but you'd disappeared. I stood there, staring at the spot where you'd been. And then it hit me: *I have that scarf.* A few days after you died, Ben and I went to your apartment to pack up your things. Your scarf was on the coffee table by the couch and I picked it up and tied it around my wrist. I remember Ben stopping short when he saw me in it. I remember the way his eyes flicked to my wrist, the way he stood so still as he took it in. Sometimes I forget how close he was to you too.

Anyway, your scarf was around my wrist that day until, after all your stuff had been packed, I slipped it into one of the boxes. I remember it so clearly. I didn't even open the cardboard flaps. I just tucked it into the little square hole, a tiny puff of turquoise sticking out. I took the boxes to my apartment and put them in the back of my closet. Then later, when I moved in with Ben, I took them to his place, putting them into the back of another closet. And again, years later when we left the city for Maplewood, we moved them to the hallway by the downstairs bathroom. And in all those years, I've never opened that box. In all those years, each time I moved it, I saw the tiny square of turquoise sticking out of that little hole.

I raced home. I don't know how anything in the afterlife works, but I felt sure that that scarf couldn't be both around your head and inside a box in our house. There were three boxes of your things among a few of our own that we have yet to unpack, and I checked them all. The scarf was gone.

Mom, the truth is, I want you back more than anything, obviously. But this—you rising from the dead, wearing your old scarf that was in a cardboard box for years—is not the return I'd hoped for. And it raises the question—okay, it raises many questions—why now? All of this rattled around in my brain as I stared at the wreckage around me. In my hunt for the scarf, I'd upended every box, dug in every corner. I slid down the wall to sit heavy on the floor, surrounded by all your things. When Mikey started to cry, I touched his little feet and told him everything was going to be okay.

But I'm not so sure. I don't understand what's happening to me.

June

# TWENTY-SIX

---

Liam and Kirsten's front door swung open and Ben tried to hide his look of shock at the sight of Liam's face. His busted, bandaged nose had bloomed into two black eyes, and the marbled, purple bruising was far more jarring than the bright blood of the night before. Beneath his injuries, Liam looked stiff and stoic, but Ben thought he saw a twinge of satisfaction as Liam glanced down at Ben's swollen hand in its black Velcro splint. Perhaps it wasn't as bad as a broken face, but at least Ben was also in pain.

"I'm not sleeping with June," Liam said without preamble. "I'd never do that to Kirsten, *especially* six months after she had our first kid. I'd never even do that to *you* and I care about you a whole lot less."

Despite himself, Ben let out a small, surprised laugh.

"And anyway," Liam continued, "work has me..." He looked down for a second as if to regain himself. "Jesus, Ben, I don't have the fucking bandwidth for an affair."

Ben studied his face for a long moment until finally, all the conflicting thoughts that had been swirling in his mind for two days coalesced into a single clear one: June and Liam hadn't been seeing each other—he could see the truth of that in the other man's eyes. And if Ben were being honest, he didn't think he'd ever completely believed Kirsten's story, not really, not deep down. He'd just been so angry with June that he'd seized upon an opportunity to justify it.

He cleared his throat and forced himself to look Liam in the eye. "Well, then… I'm sorry I punched you in the face."

Liam did a twitchy sort of shrug. "Kirsten told me what she told you. I'm not exonerating you or anything—you were an asshole and my face hurts like a bitch—but you had your reasons." He hesitated. "To be honest, I'm not wholly innocent in all this, either…but I'm getting ahead of myself. Kirsten will explain everything." He stepped back to let Ben in. "She's in the living room."

Kirsten was sitting in the large wingback armchair, their baby crawling on the rug by her feet. She looked stiff as she stared at a spot on the floor, her blond hair flat, her eyes unfocused.

"I'll take Georgia to her room," Liam said, moving to pick up their daughter.

Kirsten blinked and looked at her husband as if she'd forgotten he was there. "Oh. Thank you, Liam."

Liam and the baby disappeared down the hallway and Ben settled onto the couch across from Kirsten, the same place he'd sat the day before, a hundred years ago. He gazed across at her. Her skin looked pale and also pink as if she'd just scrubbed it clean.

"We just got home from the doctor," she said.

Ben's stomach sank. *That's* what this was about? Liam's face? On the phone, Kirsten had said she needed to talk to him about June, but a doctor's visit could only mean one thing. At the hospital last night, Ben had called Kirsten and tenta-

tively asked her to relay Liam's diagnosis. By some miracle—
or probably just because of Ben's inherent feebleness—Liam's
nose wasn't broken after all. According to their doctor, Kirsten
had said, he'd have two good shiners for a while, but with
meds to manage the pain, his recovery wouldn't be too bad.

And yet, if Liam and Kirsten had gone back to the doctor
and then called Ben to talk, it couldn't be good news. Were
they going to press charges? The thought made his heart
hammer in his chest. That, on top of everything else right
now, would flatten him. He chose his next words carefully.
"I thought the doctor at the hospital said Liam was going to
be fine."

Kirsten stared blankly at him for a moment before frowning. "What—oh, that, no. We went to the doctor for me."

As much as this didn't clear anything up, relief flooded
through him like the loosening of a noose around his neck.
"Oh. Okay… Wait, what?"

"In the hospital last night," Kirsten continued, "I told Liam
about everything that's been going on, about how I suspected
he was having an affair with June. But there were other things
too. The petition, for one. And…" Her voice faded and she
seemed to change her mind about something.

"About that," Ben said, seizing the opportunity. "What
was the petition for?"

Across from him, Kirsten deflated. "You mean you don't
know?"

Ben bristled. He needed some sort of white flag printed
with the words *I don't know anything about my wife* that he could
raise each time someone asked about her. But he took a deep
breath and simply shook his head. Kirsten went on to tell him
about the Jitterbuggies petition she created to get June kicked
out of class when she first suspected the affair. The story made

Ben pulse with anger—it was so petty and cruel—but it also made his head spin with panicked confusion. June had forgotten Mikey's vaccination appointment? He rubbed his face with his good hand and added calling their pediatrician to his long mental list of things to do.

"But, Ben," Kirsten continued, "you need to listen to me. This is important. Last night, in the hospital, after I told Liam about everything, he asked me why I was doing all of it, and it took me a long time to find the answer. I finally said that I think I've been feeling like, since Georgia was born, I can't control anything anymore. My life sort of feels like it's spinning away from me. I think that's why I've been so obsessed with cleaning lately." Ben's mind flashed to that moment the day before when she'd apologized for her immaculate house. "And I think that's why I focused so much energy on June," she continued. "Because I thought she was sleeping with Liam"—her voice cracked and she swiped at a tear that had spilled over—"and so I tried to control her because I couldn't control him."

Liam walked back into the room then and he settled onto the couch next to Kirsten, placing a hand on her shoulder. The touch was tentative, somehow both supportive and reproachful. "Georgia just went down," he said. "Did you tell him?"

Kirsten angled her face toward her husband, but didn't look him in the eye. "Almost. Anyway," she continued, "I kept saying that being a mom is harder than I thought it was going to be and that I feel different from how I thought I was going to feel. And apparently Liam's nurse overheard everything I was saying and she kept looking at me and finally, she told me basically that what I was saying wasn't normal. Well, I got pretty upset because I already didn't feel normal and I didn't need a strange lady telling me so, but then she said, *What you're describing sounds like postpartum anxiety.*"

With those words, something deep inside Ben cracked open and out seeped both grief and understanding. Because he knew now why Kirsten had called him. He should have known a long time ago. He hadn't seen June much these past few months, but he hadn't missed the change that had taken place inside her. She seemed both emptier and more frantic somehow, as if her essence, whatever it was that made her June, had been scraped out and replaced with swarming bees.

"I feel like an asshole for not seeing it earlier," Liam said. "I knew something was off, but... Anyway, the nurse suggested we go to the doctor first thing. So we did. And she said the same thing the nurse did. Kirsten definitely has it."

Kirsten looked at Ben, determined and fierce. "June has it too." She stared at Ben as if she could force understanding into him with just a look. But she didn't need to. Ben sank his head into his hands as Kirsten continued to talk. "I think I knew during our wine night at y'all's place. She said something about, well, about feeling like a bad mom, and it felt like it came right out of my own brain. But then I saw her outside the library, laughing with Liam, and it swept everything else from my mind. Now that I've been thinking about it, though, there were other things. She seemed sort of preoccupied with bizarre stuff, like this show she was going to be in at her old company... Not Medusa..."

Ben looked up from his hands. The Greek myth was a Martha Graham ballet? And then it hit him. "*Medea.*"

"Yes!" Kirsten said. "That's the one. And then," she continued, "the other day, I ran into her at the store and she was really upset. She was a little...hysterical, actually. Her head was bleeding and she was yelling at the cashier."

Ben jerked his head back. "June was bleeding? From her head?"

"Just a little bit, but yes." Kirsten hesitated. "And my doctor said it can cause moms to think they're not good enough for their own baby or prevent them from bonding." As she talked, Ben thought back to the time days ago when he'd seen his own mother with Mikey and how something about the way they were together seemed off. Now he realized it was because, as she'd kissed his toes and tickled his sides, she had looked more comfortable with their son than June ever had.

"We thought you should know," Liam said, "because, well, we know June is…away. And untreated, postpartum can get dangerous. Here." He pulled out a folded brochure from his back pocket and handed it over. Ben smoothed out the creases and read the pamphlet's title: "What You Need to Know about Postpartum Depression and Anxiety." "I grabbed an extra one for you."

Ben almost laughed, but fear and panic were pulling at him from every direction, like an onslaught of hands, grabbing and tugging at his clothes, hair, skin. June was sick and alone, God only knew where. He absently flipped open the brochure and a line caught his eye like it'd been magnetized: *If untreated, postpartum depression and/or anxiety can turn into postpartum psychosis. This may lead to life-threatening behavior and is considered a medical emergency.*

With those words, the ones from June's journal resurrected themselves in Ben's mind and his palms broke into a sweat: *the one who needs to die.*

# TWENTY-SEVEN

——

*One year earlier*

June was an apprentice in the Martha Graham Company for nine long months before she was offered to sign on as a chorus member. During her apprenticeship, she had felt like a full-time dancer, working harder than she ever had before, but this rise in rank meant that now she officially was one. She'd travel with the company for every tour stop rather than just a few and her year-long contract included benefits and a raise. In every sense of the word and in every aspect of her career, it was *more*.

It also meant that, on top of learning the upcoming year's scheduled ballets, she also had to independently learn every chorus position in every ballet of the company's repertory. She'd started getting to the studio hours before their daily rehearsal, and when that wasn't enough, she'd also stay late. Soon, she had shin splints and bloody toes, bruised arms and legs, muscle fatigue and an unfamiliar throbbing band around her lower ribs, as if she'd been cracked in half and then put back together.

It was all this collective pain she was pushing through late one Thursday night, alone in the dark studio. For the ninth time in a row, June rose onto the balls of her feet and began to bend over backward slowly, shifting each vertebra one by one. Her knees jutted sharply out in front of her, her arms reaching into the blackness behind; she pulled herself in opposite directions. Just before she got parallel with the floor, she felt her spine grind in on itself as it had every time before. Rather than lowering gracefully, spiraling at the last minute to catch herself with her hands, she collapsed.

"Dammit!" She smacked the floor with her palm, then stood up fast, lifted her heels, and began again. And again, she fell, her knees popping painfully as she spun at the last minute. She scrunched up her face into a tearless sob. She was so tired. But she had to get this. Her back flexibility wasn't where it needed to be; she wasn't strong enough. She stood again, bent her back, and threw her head behind her. But she used too much force, tipping herself off balance, and she fell hard. Her bones knocked like pieces of porcelain against the floor, her jaw and cheekbone clattering. Her teeth clamped down on her tongue and the coppery taste of blood filled her mouth.

"Why can't I fucking do this?" Her voice bounced off the bare walls and in that moment, her mind flashed to her mom. June had wanted so badly to show her mom that she could be in this company; all her life, she'd dreamed of calling her mom with the news that she'd been accepted. But even now that she had, she still felt undeserving of it, not quite good enough.

A firework of anger burst inside her. *Fuck this*, she thought. Fuck this move that made her spine feel broken. Fuck this ballet that she would never be in, but still had to learn. She just wanted to dance in a way that made her feel good and talented, and almost without thinking, she began doing the duet her mom had taught her all those years ago.

The Mamas & The Papas sang in her mind and June did the choreography at the beginning of the song before it turns fast, the pieces her mom had taken from Martha Graham herself, the parts with the flexed feet and extended arms. Because she knew the choreography so well, it was her swirling emotion rather than her mind that propelled her across the floor, and she was able to simply let go. Just as the choreography shifted genres, June flung herself to the floor with a dull thud. She lay there, chest heaving, her cheek pressed into the studio floor as blood continued to seep slowly onto her tongue. Her reflection in the mirror was unrecognizable; it looked desperate and hopeless, a specter of herself, her eye sockets dark and deep.

"You're putting too much anger into it."

June sat up, her eyes flashing from her own reflection to the darkened doorway, toward the source of the voice. A figure was there, but shrouded in the darkness, June couldn't make out its edges. Then it shifted, catching the light.

"Hiromi," she said, clapping a hand over her chest. "I didn't see you there."

June's boss stepped through the doorway and into the dim glow of the moonlit studio. Her long black hair fell in a sheet over her flat chest. "Hello, June."

"I'm sorry, what did you say? I have too much anger?"

Hiromi shook her head. "You were doing *Cave of the Heart*, no? The story of Medea? I thought I recognized some of the Nurse's choreography."

"I..." But her voice faded. June had always assumed her mom had cobbled together bits and pieces of Graham choreography she liked, not taken them whole from an existing ballet. And because *Cave of the Heart* didn't have any chorus members in it, it hadn't been on her list to learn, but she supposed Hiromi would know. June felt a small pulse of pride for having learned a real Graham ballet at the age of five. It made her feel for the first time like maybe she belonged here after all.

"*Cave of the Heart*, right," she said. "I know it's not actually a ballet a chorus member can even be in, but it's just so…" She tried to put a word to how she felt when she danced her and her mom's duet, but her brain was dulled from exhaustion and she couldn't find the right one. She waved a hand vaguely.

Hiromi smiled. "It is indeed. Medea's story is one of my favorites." She cocked her head sideways and June had the unnerving sensation of the woman stripping away her physical form to study something unseeable underneath. "May I ask you what you were thinking in that moment?"

June almost lied. She almost said she'd been thinking about what the dancer is supposed to be thinking at that point in the ballet, about the story, about her character. But she knew only vaguely what Medea's story was and she'd been trying so hard for so long. She shrugged. "I was thinking about my mom."

Hiromi nodded, seemingly interested, but not surprised. "It's too much for the Nurse. She is supposed to be torn. She sympathizes with her lady, Medea, but she is also appalled by what Medea has planned to do. The Nurse is wise and magnanimous and upset, yes, but she's not angry."

June nodded dully. She felt chastened and so, so tired.

"Try Medea's part instead."

"Sorry?"

"Do you happen to know any of Medea's choreography?"

"I don't think so. No."

So Hiromi described some of Medea's choreography and when she was done and June didn't move, she added, "Would you like to try it?"

June's eyebrows shot up. "Now?"

"Now."

Her heart pounded. It was a rare thing to have a private audience with the artistic director in an empty studio, but June shoved the thought away. From her position on the floor, she slowly lifted herself once again to her knees. In her mind, she heard the opening notes of "Dedicated to the One I Love," but rather than let it make her sad or happy like it usually did, June let it make her angry.

She gazed at her own hollowed-out face in the mirror and made it someone else's. She let all her frustration and insecurity bubble up inside her and this time she didn't try to tamp it down. Her body took over, improvising off Hiromi's instructions. Her knees beat back and forth, carrying June across the studio floor. They accidentally knocked together once and she let the pain fuel her anger. She moved from her knees all the way to the floor, swimming across it, pouring then pressing her fingers into its surface. She rolled onto her back and arched her chest, a marionette on a string, a hand reaching into the empty space above her. Then, when she couldn't think of anything more to do, she dropped. She lay there, chest heaving for a moment, and as she did, she noticed her eyes were wet, tears pooling in the grooves beneath.

She turned to the doorway to find Hiromi smiling softly. "There," she said, her voice warm. "It was a bit out of control, but *that's* where your anger goes. Into Medea. You simply cast yourself in the wrong part."

June swiped her fingers brusquely under her eyes. "Thank you."

"Not at all. After fifteen years of this, you get rather good at casting." She studied June for a moment. "You could learn the role of Medea if you wanted. We are doing *Cave of the Heart* this season, you know. Of course, we already have the cast in mind and as a chorus member, you wouldn't be considered yet, but it could be possible for you to understudy. It would be a solid trajectory within the company."

June's eyes widened. "Oh. Wow. That would be... I would love that."

"No guarantees, of course. But it could be a good role for you, one day. Swing by my office on your way out. I'll give you copies of all the versions we've done."

"I... Thank you. I will."

"Like I said, no guarantees." She turned to leave, but after a few steps through the darkened doorway, she turned back. "And, June?"

June, who could barely see her now, raised her eyebrows.

"Don't try to be another woman's Medea. Be that angry, desperate one you were just now."

Later that night, June lay in bed, staring at the ceiling, thinking back to the moment earlier when Hiromi had first seen her from the doorway. In that moment, and then again lying in bed now, June's head swirled with a memory she hadn't thought about in years.

It was of the time she'd first learned what she now knew was the choreography from *Cave of the Heart*, what she still thought of as the choreography to her and her mom's duet. It had started as something silly and fun. Her mom had been paying bills at their little coffee table and June had asked to watch TV, but her mom had put on music and told her to dance instead. When that song by The Mamas & The Papas had come on, June had started doing ballet moves from her dance class and her mom had looked up and smiled.

She'd watched June for a moment before standing up and starting the song over. "Do that again," she'd said and so June had. "You know what could go in that spot instead?

You could do this." She'd done a bit of choreography and June had repeated it.

Pretty soon, they'd had the whole song choreographed and had been practicing it for what had seemed to June like hours. It was getting late and she remembered that she'd asked her mom if she could stop and color. For the briefest of moments, her mom's face had dropped, and that second had stuck inside June like a barb through her ribs. She'd intuited, though she wouldn't have the language to articulate it for many years to come, that when she danced, she made her mom happy and when she stopped, she made her mom sad.

"Hey, chickadee," her mom had said, "you can do whatever you want. I just wish, when I was young, I'd pushed myself a little bit harder." She'd placed a palm on top of June's head and squeezed twice in quick succession. "I'm gonna get back to these bills."

June, who'd felt heavier from the interaction without understanding exactly why, had gone into her bedroom with the intention of coloring. But instead, she'd practiced that duet well past her bedtime, so that the next morning she could show her mom the whole thing.

Lying in bed now, the memory churning in her mind, June spoke silently to her dead mom. *Look*, she said. *I did everything you wanted.*

# TWENTY-EIGHT

———

*Thursday (I think), February something*

Dear Mom,

I saw you again today, this time just outside the house. And yet again, I wasn't able to do anything but stand there, para-lyzed. I guess I've gotten used to the idea of you being dead, and once you get used to someone being dead, it's hard to process when that changes.

It happened as I was trying to get me and Mikey out of the house. We had to go back to the grocery store because seeing you there yesterday threw me off so much, I forgot to actually buy any food. Which meant that by 3 pm today, I'd eaten nothing but our last egg and I was starving. As we were about to walk out the door, I caught my reflection in the mirror and yikes. My hair was dirty; my eyes were dark and swollen. Since the petition incident at Jitterbuggies, Mikey's been fussy, and every time I've tried to get in the shower, he's started to cry, so I haven't properly bathed in a while. And after seeing *you* yesterday, Mom, sleep last night was impos-sible. A bad combination: filth and sleep deprivation.

Suddenly, a movement caught my eye. Just beyond our front window, there you were, on the sidewalk, in the same clothes you were wearing yesterday in the store: a camel coat over all black, big sunglasses covering your face, and that turquoise scarf tied around your head. It must've been thirty degrees out and all you had on your head was that flimsy scarf. Is it because your resurrected body is immune to the cold? Or are you more like a ghost, impervious to physical influences? If I'd had the courage to walk out the front door, would I have been able to pass right through you? I mean, I don't think so; you seemed so completely *real*.

Under my blankets now, with the lamp on beside me, I realize that I should have gone outside and asked you why you were there, what you wanted to tell me, but I was frozen with fear. I squeezed my eyes shut and tried to breathe. When I opened them again, you were gone.

That was when the swallowing started. I swallowed hard, and then right after, I had to swallow again, and then again. And suddenly, I was swallowing, already thinking about needing to swallow again. I slid down the wall and put my head between my knees. Mikey started to cry, but I couldn't comfort him. I was having some sort of swallowing fit. I reached a hand out, grabbed his little foot, and ran my thumb in circles over his ankle. I don't know how long exactly I stayed like that, but eventually both Mikey and I calmed down. I kept staring out the window at the place you had stood—wishing you'd materialize again or praying you wouldn't, I don't know.

And then it hit me: *Medea*! Your arrival could be explained by *Medea*. It makes perfect sense. The first time you appeared to me was just as I put together the link between my life and Medea's—a role I've been working toward my entire life. You laid the foundation of this when you taught me the choreography to Medea's ballet all those years ago. Then the foundation was solidified when I was cast as Medea in the Martha Graham version. Now I've completed my transformation: after moving to Corinth (Maplewood), my husband left me and my son for his Corinthian princess (Clark & White), and I promise if you asked him, he'd say he's doing it for me—just like Medea's husband "did it for her."

And if I am Medea, that means you are a character from *Medea* too.

As I was putting all this together, Mikey had cried himself to sleep and was drowsing in his carrier, so I took him upstairs with me to his room. I got all the library books I'd checked out about Medea and while Mikey slept, I sat on the floor and tried to understand which character you are. If I could just figure that out, I knew, I would understand why you're here and what you want to tell me.

And finally, *I did*.

After Medea is betrayed by Jason, she plots her revenge—to kill the Corinthian princess who has stolen her husband—but before she can do it, the king, the princess's father, comes to banish her because he's afraid of what Medea might do. This is perhaps the most infuriating of all developments: up until this point, Medea has done nothing wrong. She's been a devoted wife, a loving mother, and now when her husband commits adultery, the king banishes *her*? Sure, she's planning on murdering the princess, but they don't know that. Medea pleads for one day to settle her affairs and the king says okay, fine.

This is when, out of nowhere, Medea's friend, Aegeus, enters the story. He comes to Medea because he can't have children—which I think is code for he's having trouble with his penis—and he believes Medea, as a sorceress, can fix it. In exchange for her help, Medea asks Aegeus for a safe haven in his hometown of Athens after she's banished and he agrees.

This is the part of the story I'd been previously—idiotically—ignoring. Because it's like, the third act, and here Euripides is introducing a completely new character with a new problem for Medea to solve. It seems random, but it's not because only Aegeus gives Medea the assurance that she will have a safe place to go after her revenge. Without the promise of Athens, her plan is impossible. Without Athens, she cannot escape on a chariot of fire. Without Athens, she has nowhere to go.

And so it occurred to me that you are my Aegeus. And just as Aegeus did, you've come to me in the moment of my crisis. Medea was banished by the king and I have been banished from Jitterbuggies by my so-called friends. Which means you, Mom, have appeared to bring me to my Athens—my escape, my salvation. While all that is clear to me now, I don't know where, or what, my Athens is. Nevertheless, thank you for coming for me. I can't wait to see you again.

Love,
June

# CORINTH

# TWENTY-NINE

———

Ben came home from Kirsten and Liam's, popping with fear. He'd been so angry at June for abandoning him and Mikey, and then he'd been so angry at the idea that she'd cheated on him, that his initial worry for her had been swallowed by it. But now that worry had returned and it was so all-consuming, so fierce, he suspected it had simply been lying dormant, beneath everything else, all along.

He made his way up to his and June's bedroom, grateful his mom had taken Mikey on some errands that morning. He closed the door behind him hard, but then stood motionless, aimless, because what could he do? While he now understood that June was sick, he still had no idea where she was. He walked to her side of the bed and sat in the place she slept, as if somehow that could summon her to him. He stared at a spot on the floor until the snapping energy inside him reached a fever pitch.

"Fuck!" he shouted into the still air of their room. "Fuck, fuck, fuck!"

He grabbed one of June's pillows and hurled it against the wall, then he grabbed the second one and did the same. He dropped his elbows onto his knees and sank his head into his hands, but just as he did, something on the floor caught his eye. From inside one of the pillowcases, he spotted the corner of a piece of paper. He stood up, walked over, and fished the paper out. It wasn't a single sheet, he saw now, but a whole stack of them, and with one look at his wife's messy hand-writing scrawled across them, Ben understood that he'd finally uncovered her missing journal entries. How had he not found them before? He'd looked for them in every drawer in the house, under the bed, in her closet, but it turned out he'd been sleeping mere inches from them all along.

Pages in hand, he sank back onto the bed and for two hours he stayed like that, unmoving, poring over June's words in a feverish stupor. Each subsequent entry made him feel guiltier and blinder and more willfully negligent than the last. Although he'd believed Liam today when he'd said he hadn't been sleeping with June, with these pages, Ben now understood just how off base that accusation had been in the first place. June hadn't been having an affair; she'd been halluci-nating her dead mom and getting her own life confused with that of a fictional Greek sorceress. *I don't have the fucking band-width for an affair*, Liam had said earlier and that was clearly true of June too. But not only did she not have the bandwidth for an affair, she didn't have the bandwidth for reality either.

The sound of the front door opening brought him out of his tornado of thoughts.

"Hello!" his mom called. "Ben, we're home!"

He stared down at the last unread pages in his hand. He had yet to find the place in the journal that went along with that torn scrap of paper—*the one who needs to die*—and he had the urge to ignore his mom and just get through the last of it. But he couldn't. He needed to track June down. He folded the pages up, stuffed them into his pocket, and ran down the stairs.

With one look at Mikey in his carrier, Ben's chest swelled with sorrow. For the first four months of his son's life, Mikey had spent day after day with a mom who set a timer in order to bond with him. Had he intuited the purpose of those ten minutes? Had he somehow understood, each time the buzzer went off, that instead of love, his own mother still only felt a hole inside her? Ben bent over to grab the carrier from his mom, hastily unbuckled Mikey, and pulled him into his arms.

"Hey, buddy." He kissed Mikey's soft, little cheek and perched him on his hip.

"Is everything all right?" his mom asked.

"No, actually. I'm sorry to ask this on top of everything you've already done, but I think I'm gonna have to leave town for a few days." Of course, at this point, he had no idea where he was going to go, but he knew he had to leave.

"Oh, no," she said. "Is June's dad okay?"

"Yeah. He's fine. But there's something I haven't told you." He took a deep breath. "June has postpartum anxiety. I need to go be with her for a bit."

To his surprise, his mom, whose concern had been etched into the lines on her face, seemed to relax at his news rather than startle at it. She clapped a hand lightly over her chest. "Oh. Gosh, Ben, you had me worried for a second."

He frowned. "What d'you mean?"

"Well, that certainly seems to be a serious diagnosis these days, but when I was having children, we just sort of got over it."

"Okay, well. June's not really getting over it."

"Oh, honey, I'm not trying to minimize it. Having a baby is the hardest thing you can do. But you're *so* busy right now.

I'm just not sure June's baby blues warrant a trip to California when you're clearly swamped with work. You're providing for your family as it is."

Ben jerked his head back, feeling as though someone had just upended the snow globe that was his life. Did his mom really believe his sole obligation as a father and husband was to make money? At that thought, a creeping sense of hypocrisy climbed up his chest, but he pushed it aside. He opened his mouth, then closed it again. He didn't have the energy for some self-righteous argument right now. "Mom, would you mind taking Mikey for a few days if I left?"

"Of course, Ben. You don't even have to ask. Just—try not to be so hard on yourself. I know you want to help June, but you also need to take care of yourself."

Ben pressed his lips together. "Right. Thanks." He kissed Mikey one more time then handed him back over. "I have to go run some errands. I'm not sure when I'll be back."

It looked as if his mom were going to protest, but then she just sighed. "Take your time."

Outside, Ben tugged his phone out of his pocket and dialed Kirsten's number.

"Ben?" Her Southern accent was tinged with worry. "Is everything all right?"

"I have to go to the police station," he said, his hand drawn to the folded journal pages in his pocket as if by a magnet. "And I want you to go with me."

# THIRTY

---

*One year earlier*

June danced the role of Medea in *Cave of the Heart* for the first time one month after that late-night conversation with Hiromi. The Friday afternoon rehearsal wasn't technically an audition—no one was calling it that—but with the artistic director's rare presence in the studio, everyone knew that it was. The ballet had already been cast weeks earlier and to no one's surprise, the role had been given to Sasha, a principal dancer. But Sasha had left rehearsals the day before with an injury, something to do with her foot; no one knew the details yet. And because Hiromi and Silvi hadn't cast an official understudy at that point, June, still the newest chorus member and the only one who'd been studying the part, was the closest thing.

June performed the last moves of the ballet so lost in her role, she barely registered when Silvi turned to Hiromi, nodded at something unintelligible the other woman murmured, and then turned back. "June," Silvi said, and June's gaze snapped to meet her rehearsal director's. "Come down to Hiromi's office in a few minutes, all right?"

June nodded, still catching her breath. "Yes, ma'am."

Hiromi's office door was open when she got there five minutes later. From behind her desk, the company's artistic director smiled her usual, temperate smile. She raised a slender hand, gesturing June inside and then to the open chair next to Silvi. "Please, take a seat."

June sat.

"So, June," Hiromi began. "You came to us last year with more of a…commercial background, I'd say. How do you think you've adapted to the aesthetic of the company thus far?"

June tried not to feel stung by the assessment of her career up until this point because after all, it was no more than the truth. Her career had been commercial in the sense that she'd actually done commercials—for razors, for jeans, for bras. She'd done artistic performances, too, of course, but nothing on the scale of what they did at the Graham Company.

"I've…" Her voice cut out and she swallowed. Just being in Hiromi's presence still made her nervous and, if she were being completely honest, the company aesthetic didn't always feel natural in her body the way her own choreography did. Sometimes she felt her brain just wasn't wired in the same way Martha Graham's had been. And yet, being on this company, surrounded by the creative powerhouses of Hiromi Kimura and Silvi Brawnish, was the closest she'd ever come to what she'd envisioned for herself. She took a breath, trying to calm her fluttering heart. "This past year has been the best year of my career. I've grown more as a dancer here than I did in the ten years leading up to it. I've been challenged to improve in ways I hadn't known were possible and I'm very grateful for everything I've learned."

Hiromi studied her evenly. "I agree that you've been challenged and you've grown remarkably. However, as you know,

Graham dancers are both athletes and actors. As I mentioned the other week, you have great emotional depth. It's honest and demonstrative, but your Graham technique isn't where it should be."

June felt her breath kick out of her lungs. After everything she'd put into her apprenticeship, then into her new position and into learning Medea's part, it still wasn't enough. She wasn't enough.

"It isn't where it should be for a lead role in a Graham ballet, that is," Hiromi continued.

She studied June as if waiting for a response, but June remained silent. She didn't know what Hiromi wanted to hear and she didn't know what she wanted to say. She was fighting just to hold the other woman's gaze. It felt as if her boss's words were creeping up her neck and weaving their way under her skin.

"The reason I'm telling you this is because we'd like to offer you the role of Medea, but you're going to need to work. Hard."

"You—" June shook her head. "Wait. You are?" She felt whiplashed from the news, dizzy with it. "What about Sasha?"

"We spoke with Sasha this morning," Silvi said. "Her foot is broken. She won't be able to dance for a while."

"Oh, God." While the other woman's loss was quite literally her gain, June wouldn't have wished a broken foot on any dancer. Sasha's career was almost certainly over because of it. June felt breathlessly sorry for her colleague and also some other emotion she couldn't quite put her finger on.

"We're counting on you to fill her place as seamlessly as possible," Hiromi said.

"Right..." June said, trying to focus. "Thank you. I'll work so hard for this. I promise."

Hiromi looked evenly at her, but it was Silvi who spoke next. "We'll start rehearsals Monday. Like Hiromi said, it's going to be a lot of work." But she said it with a smile. "Is Ben going to be excited?" As the rehearsal director, Silvi had spent far more time with June than Hiromi had and she knew the details of all her dancers' personal lives.

"He'll be excited," June said. She'd already been formulating the story of this very meeting in her head to tell him over the phone the moment she walked out of the building. "He'll freak out." She smiled, but as she did, she realized the person she wanted to tell even more than Ben was her mom—her mom, who'd inspired her to audition for Martha Graham in the first place; her mom, who'd taught her the choreography to this very ballet all those years ago. For the first time in her career, June felt as if, if she could somehow relay the news to her, her mom would finally be proud.

She walked out of Hiromi's office, her nerves from the meeting finally starting to subside, and as they did, June realized that what she'd thought was the need to nervous pee was really just the need to regular pee, which made her think back to the rehearsal earlier. There had been a moment toward the end of the ballet, during an abrupt stop that swayed her body, when she had felt a small gush onto the fabric triangle of her tights between her legs, and thought *Oh, my period.*

But now, when she went to the bathroom, tampon in hand, she saw that it wasn't her period. Or it wasn't like any other period she'd ever had. In her tights were spots of pink rather than the familiar deep-red, clotted blood. She frowned, a nebulous suspicion forming in her mind. When was the last time she'd gotten her period? Like so many other dancers, her period was sporadic and, with her busy new rehearsal schedule, she couldn't remember. But suddenly, her body felt different, heavier, and with that, a terrifying suspicion took shape. June glanced in the mirror above the sink and locked eyes with her reflection. "Oh, shit."

# THIRTY-ONE

——

*February, I don't know the day*

Dear Mom,

Since my revelation yesterday that you're the Aegeus to my
Medea, I've been looking for you everywhere. I stayed up
all night waiting for your arrival, staring at the spot on the
street where you so recently stood. I paced the house, looking out every window. I was certain you'd come for me, but
after hours of waiting, I realized it was almost light out and
I'd waited the whole night for a thing that had never been
coming after all. I felt like a fool, not like Medea for once,
but like the stupid, entitled Corinthian princess who accepts
Medea's poisoned crown. Suddenly, the urge to shower was
overwhelming—I wanted to purge that poison and turn into
Medea once again.

As Ben and Mikey slept, I took a shower and I scrubbed
and scrubbed. But then halfway through, I couldn't remember if I'd washed my hair yet, so I did it again—or for the
first time, I'm not sure. But I couldn't stop envisioning that
poisoned crown, so I washed it yet again and this time I did

it right. I dug my fingers into my scalp and rubbed until the princess finally got out of my head.

It felt good to be clean after so many days without showering. That, and the fact that I'd figured out why you were here, had me invigorated. I could tell Ben was surprised when he woke to find me showered and dressed. Despite getting no sleep, I had more energy than I'd had in weeks and when he walked into the kitchen to find me in real clothes with a full pot of coffee already made, he laughed out loud, a happy smile spreading across his face. I jumped up to kiss him and he laughed again and pulled me close, pushing his face into my clean hair. I felt time-warped to some moment earlier in our relationship, when our happiness was simple.

After he'd left for work and after I'd done Mikey's morning routine, I decided to go to Whole Foods. I realized part of why I hadn't been able to sleep was probably because I'd been so hungry; I still hadn't eaten anything since that one egg yesterday morning, twenty-four hours ago.

The excursion started so well. Mikey was strapped to my chest and for once, he seemed happy to be out and about, or at least he wasn't crying. I had one of the big carts and was filling it with everything: fresh fruit and nice cheeses, frozen lasagnas for Ben when I'm gone, and steaks in case I had time to cook. I felt almost high with the knowledge that you were coming to bring me my Athens. I'd been scared before, but now you were like a light at the end of a very long and very dark tunnel.

But then, just as Mikey and I were finishing our first real successful shopping trip together, I heard it.

We were waiting in line to check out when our song came on—"Dedicated to the One I Love." My shoulders almost involuntarily began to roll, doing our opening choreography.

I marked out the dance there in the middle of the grocery store, Mikey strapped to my chest, moving with me. I leaned over to glance at him. He had an open-mouth smile on his face, drool on his chin. I wiped it with the hook of my index finger and pressed my lips to his head.

But then I remembered: this was also the last song we ever listened to together, Mom. Remember that? When Ben and I came over and our song came on and you asked me to dance? Standing in the line at Whole Foods, I remembered the coffee table littered with pill bottles and the way your turquoise scarf was tied taut over your bald head. I remembered how tired you looked.

"Turn that off," I heard myself say to the cashier as he scanned a tomato.

"Pardon?"

I laughed lightly, trying to sound normal. "Sorry, but is there any way you could change the song?"

He paused, tomato in hand, one ear cocked upward. "Is this Janis Joplin?"

"The Mamas & The Papas."

"Ah, yeah, 'California Dreamin'.' What, you don't like 'em?"

"Could you just—" I took a breath and started again. "Could you change it please?"

He chuckled and shook his head, punching in the code for my sweet potatoes. "Sorry. I don't have control of the music. But I totally know how you feel. Sometimes a song comes on and it drives me nuts and the only thing you can do is just bare your teeth and take it."

I inhaled slowly. "I actually really like this song," I said, opening my wallet.

The cashier smiled a wary smile, glanced at the still-long line of groceries he had left to scan, and picked up the pace.

I leaned over to make sure Mikey was okay and he looked fine. Even so, I gently grabbed his little leg, rubbing a circle on his calf.

Although the music was soft, it was all I could hear. It was at the part where, in our choreography, I would turn in circles. Once again, I thought back to that last time, when I jumped onto the coffee table—a move I hadn't done in years—and bumped my head against the fan. You and Ben burst out laughing, but then your laughter turned into a cough. You grabbed a tissue and coughed into it and I could see that you'd hacked up something thick and dark. You pretended like you hadn't, folding the tissue discreetly into your hand and tucking it beneath your pillow.

Standing in the grocery store, I began scratching at my head. Despite all those washes or maybe because of them, my scalp was itchy and I dug my fingernails into it. When I brought my hand down again, I noticed blood on my fingers. My breath grew heavy, frantic. How had the blood gotten there? Was it because I'd bonked my head on the fan? Was it from Medea's poisoned crown of thorns?

I didn't mean to, but I slammed my palms onto the little signing counter. "Could you please change the goddamn song?"

Well, that got the cashier's attention. He looked up slowly as if his exaggerated calm could offset my agitation. "Ma'am, I told you I don't control the music."

At this point, I noticed people shooting glances in our direction. Suddenly, a woman was next to the cashier, as if she'd materialized out of thin air. She smiled, glancing between me and him.

"Hi," she said. I suspected she was the manager. "Can I help with anything?"

"Sorry," I said, tucking my hair behind my ears, and then, out of the corner of my eye, I saw a flash of turquoise—your scarf! As if the song were your siren call, you'd come for me, all the way from Athens to Corinth, to beckon me home. I turned my head fast to look, but it wasn't your scarf after all; it was just the light blue of a small girl's puffy jacket, not even really the right color. "It's this fucking song," I said to the woman, my voice much louder than I'd intended.

The woman squinted her eyes at me—it wasn't unfriendly, just questioning. She looked at Mikey then back to me and nodded. "Music can be tricky." She turned to the cashier and said, "Brian, would you grab Dashiell over there and ask him to help us bag for a second? Then why don't you go to the back and see what you can do about this music, yeah? I'll finish up here." She darted her fingers over the keypad and before I understood what she was doing, she was bagging up my food alongside this Dashiell without ringing them up. "Don't worry about the groceries," she said when she saw my worried face. "They're on me."

"I'm so sorry," I said, scratching my scalp again. "I wasn't trying to—"

But the woman cut me off, inclining her head toward Mikey. "When they're that young," she said softly, "it can be so hard, we don't even know why we do some of the things we do." She threw me the smallest of winks and loaded a frozen meal into a paper bag. "This is just a favor from one mom to another. I'm sure you'll be able to pass it on one day."

And before I could protest again or even thank her, she was ushering me out of the store with a cart full of unpaid-for groceries.

That was when I heard my name.

"June!" the voice called again. I turned and all the softness that I'd felt from the interaction with the store manager hardened in a moment. It was Kirsten. Over the past few days, I'd come to the conclusion that it had to have been Kirsten who created the petition—I couldn't see either Sydney or Reese doing it—and I couldn't believe she had the gall to approach me now.

I stood still, watching her hurry over. She looked pristine as ever, her blond hair in artful waves, clean clothes, Georgia strapped to her chest, an adorable fox-eared hat over her curls. "June, hey." She was panting slightly and there was a hardness in her gaze I'd never seen before. "You were walking so fast! Where're you two headed?" The look she gave me and Mikey was suspicious, as if my three-and-a-half-month-old baby and I were planning a heist.

Before I could say anything, she continued. "How've you been?" Her tone was somehow both cold and sweet. I wondered why she was even talking to me. "How's Ben? Seems like a busy time at the office. Liam's been working like crazy." Her eyes darted over my face as if she were trying to decipher a code.

"Kirsten? I'm sorry, but I have to go."

"Really?" she said, her eyebrows high. "Where do you have to be in such a hurry?"

The last of my nice reserves evaporated. "Nowhere," I snapped. "I don't have to be anywhere. I'm just thinking of Georgia. You made it pretty clear that you don't think it's safe for her to be around my kid."

Kirsten's chin jutted back. "I might have made that petition, June, but you're the one who missed your own baby's vaccination appointment. It's literally the least you can do to take care of your child. I may be an overprotective mom, but at least I'm not a negligent one."

For the record, I took Mikey to his rescheduled vaccination appointment a few days ago, so by the time I was having this conversation, he was fully up-to-date, but that isn't the point. What Kirsten had said was the meanest thing anyone could've said to me. She had wiggled a fingernail into a wound and pressed down hard.

I took a few steps toward her and without thinking, I grabbed a bushel of bananas from the top of one of her bags in the shopping cart, held it over the frozen asphalt of the parking lot, and dropped it. "Stay away from me and my baby."

I turned to go, but I miscalculated the two babies strapped to our chests and they bonked against each other. Both Georgia and Mikey burst into tears. "Shit," I said. "I didn't mean— I'm so sorry—"

"No," Kirsten snapped. "*You* stay away from *me and my baby.*"

Are you going to come back for me, Mom? I think it's almost time for me to leave.


Love,
June

# THIRTY-TWO

———

At the police station, Ben couldn't stand still. The woman at the front desk—Cheryl, he remembered—was looking up at him in alarm as though he'd announced he was robbing the place. All he'd said was that he wanted to speak to Officer Moretti and that it was urgent, and she'd held her hands up as if this were a holdup.

"Calm down, sir. Let me just see if Officer Moretti is in." She lifted the phone from its receiver, her eyes still on Ben, then slowly lowered her gaze to dial. Ben turned to pace the small lobby. On one of his loops, he saw Kirsten watching him, a small wrinkle between her eyebrows. When they caught eyes, she nodded. He'd asked her to meet him there so she could vouch for his story and help him explain the risks of postpartum anxiety to Moretti, and he was glad that he had. She seemed far calmer than he was and he could use all the calm he could get.

"Mr. Gilmore?"

Ben turned to find Officer Moretti standing in the doorway that separated the public space from the offices beyond.

"Jesus," she said. "You look—How're you doing?"

Frowning, Ben glanced down at himself and realized, beneath his coat, he was still in the same clothes he'd worn to the hospital the previous evening. They were rumpled and slightly damp with two days' worth of sweat. He spotted a smattering of small red dots at the hemline of his old college sweatshirt and wondered if they were from his hand or Liam's face. He ran his fingers through his hair and a few strands caught on the Velcro of his splint, tugging his scalp.

"Officer Moretti. Hi. You remember Kirsten." He glanced at Kirsten beside him and Moretti followed his gaze.

Kirsten smiled a small, tight smile.

Moretti nodded. "I remember you, Mrs. Aimes. Nice to see you again. How's your husband's nose?"

In the small amount of skin above the collar of Kirsten's coat, Ben saw her neck turn pink. "Fine. Thank you."

"Officer Moretti, I need your help." The words tumbled out of Ben's mouth. "I know you might not completely trust me yet and then I went and punched a guy, which probably didn't help things, but June's in trouble." He jerked his head toward Kirsten. "Kirsten is June's friend, or"—his mind flashed to the last journal entry he'd read, the one where June had smashed Kirsten's bananas on the ground—"actually, they sort of hate each other—"

Kirsten snapped her head to look at Ben. "I don't hate June."

He glanced over at her. "Oh, okay." He looked back to Moretti. "Anyway, Kirsten was just diagnosed with postpartum depression—"

"Anxiety," Kirsten interrupted.

"Anxiety," Ben corrected. "And she thinks June has it too. And look." Ben handed Moretti the brochure Liam had given him. He pointed a shaky finger at the terrifyingly long list of symptoms that started on one page and wrapped around all the way to the next. He tapped his finger to the last item on the list. "Hallucinations. I've been reading June's journal and, well, she's been seeing her mom."

Officer Moretti looked at him with a blank, uncomprehending expression.

"Her mom's dead," Ben explained. "And June thinks she's been seeing her—at Whole Foods, outside our house. Her mom had this scarf that apparently June's been seeing her in." He caught Kirsten watching him with an odd look on her face, but he continued. "If she has some of these symptoms, she could have them all. And look." He pointed to another bullet point on the pamphlet. "Life-threatening thoughts or actions. So I have to find her before something bad happens. I know you might not believe me, but that's why I brought Kirsten and—"

Finally, Moretti lifted a hand. "Mr. Gilmore. Ben. There's no need to convince me you want to find your wife. I believe you. And it sounds like you've diagnosed her accurately, which means there are grounds to open an official missing person case. But I have to be honest with you. We've been looking already and we haven't found her."

"But I don't think she's in Maplewood," Ben said. "Or even New Jersey." He'd known that from the beginning really. After he'd done it, he realized that filing a request to locate here was as stupid as continuing to look for June in their house. She hadn't packed a suitcase to camp out at a coffee shop a few blocks away.

Moretti raised her eyebrows. "No? Well, then…" She wobbled her head. "If that's true, the case really wouldn't be within our jurisdiction…"

"But—"

Moretti held up a hand. "I'm not saying I won't help you.

I will. But it sounds like we'll have to loop in another city's department. And to do that, we'll have to narrow it down. So you said you've been reading your wife's journal and"— she threw a look at Kirsten—"you've been talking to her friends. Do you have any knowledgeable guesses about where she could be?"

Ben dropped his gaze to the floor. The truth was he had no guesses, knowledgeable or otherwise. "No. I don't."

Moretti let out a sigh then stepped to the side, gesturing to the hallway beyond. "Let's go talk. You, too, Mrs. Aimes. We're gonna need all the help we can get."

The three of them settled at the large oval table in the same conference room Ben and Officer Moretti had first spoken in. The memory of that evening, only a few days previous, seemed like years ago to Ben, giving him a strange sense of déjà vu.

"So," Moretti began, "most people, when they choose a place to disappear to, don't just spin a globe. They go somewhere they've been before or somewhere they've always wanted to visit."

As Moretti spoke, Ben's gaze landed on Kirsten, who sat across from him, her hands interlocked tightly on the table. She shifted awkwardly as if she were unsure how she'd gotten there, her lips pressed into a thin line. Ben stared at her, confused. She'd been so willing to help earlier, so collected, but now she seemed anxious and agitated. What could've possibly happened in the past five minutes to make her that uncomfortable?

"So," Moretti continued, "if we can track what's been on June's mind, we may be able to follow that to where she is now." She turned to Ben. "Why don't we start with her journal. What was she writing about?"

"Uh..." All the things from June's journal swam in his mind—that petition, setting a timer to bond with Mikey, her confrontation with Kirsten—but all of those felt like reasons June would leave, not explanations about where she'd go. The one thing that felt like a clue to her whereabouts, convoluted though it may be, was "*Medea*. She wrote a lot about *Medea*."

Moretti frowned. "*Medea?* I'm not sure what that is..."

"It's a Greek tragedy." He sighed then explained, telling her about the Martha Graham Company, about June's role of Medea in the ballet, and about how, in her sickness, she'd grown obsessed with the Greek sorceress.

"All right." Moretti nodded slowly. "And her company performs in New York?"

Ben shook his head. "It performs all over the world. They practice in New York. But I've called the company. They haven't seen her since she left months ago and—I don't know—I don't think June's just in Manhattan somewhere."

"Why's that?" Moretti asked.

He shrugged. "For one, it's expensive. She has cash, but I think it'd be hard not to use her credit card, which she hasn't. And like I said, the Graham Company hasn't seen her. Her old dance studio hasn't either." But more than all that, Manhattan didn't have any connection with *Medea*—at least not one Ben could think of.

Kirsten, who'd been sitting silently, the knuckles of her interlaced fingers white, made a noise from somewhere in the back of her throat. It sounded worried and slightly strangled. Both Ben and Moretti glanced at her.

"Mrs. Aimes?" Moretti said. "Did you have something to say?"

Kirsten looked up, her eyes wide as if she'd been accused of something. "Hmm? No, no, just thinking."

"All right," Moretti said. "Let's go at it from a different angle then. What places does June have connections to?"

Ben sighed. He'd already gone down this road a million times. "Her dad lives in California. I called him and he hasn't seen her. Her best friend lives in DC, which… I could see her going, but Moli says she hasn't seen June and I believe her." He scratched his jaw irritably, feeling like they were getting further and further away from the answer. He thought back to the journal, to *Medea*, to all the times June had written about escaping to Athens. But she'd always written *my* Athens, not simply *Athens*, so he didn't believe she'd meant the actual city in Greece.

"Okay…" Moretti was saying. "So let's expand. Think of people she has a connection with—" But before she could finish, she turned to look at Kirsten, who'd made another strangled sound from her throat. "Yes? Mrs. Aimes, what is it?"

"Oh." Kirsten twisted her wedding band around her finger in fast loops, looking as if she'd been caught stealing. "It's probably nothing…" Moretti raised her eyebrows, but stayed quiet, and Kirsten continued reluctantly. "I was just thinking that—Ben, you mentioned in the lobby that, well, that June's been seeing her mom? Is that right?"

Ben nodded. Was that what had her so rattled?

Kirsten pressed her lips together, her gaze darting frantically around the table in front of her. It was obvious that something was bothering her, but it seemed she wasn't going to say what it was.

Moretti narrowed her eyes at Kirsten then turned to Ben. "Could that have something to do with where she went? Should we be thinking about places associated with her mom?"

"Well, sure," he said, trying to tamp down his frustration. After all, according to June, her mom was her Aegeus, come to take her away. But he had no idea where to go from there. "But her mom's dead. And according to her journal, June thought her mom was there to take her home, which would be the East Village, and like I said, I really don't think she's—" But then he stopped. Suddenly, the visions of her mom, the story of Medea, the relationship between Aegeus and Athens—all the pieces of June's journal fell into place. She had been leading him to the answer all along and now Ben knew exactly where she'd gone.

# THIRTY-THREE

———

*One year earlier*

Seven days after June was offered the role of Medea, she came home from rehearsal, poured herself a glass of wine, drank it, washed the glass, and returned it to the shelf. Then she sat on the couch, motionless, until Ben walked in through their front door.

"Hey, babe!" he called.

"Hi." Her throat was tight.

"What's the matter?"

But June couldn't respond. Her body felt like it was made of metal, immovable and rusty. Her jaw and neck and shoulders had all seized.

"June?" He walked over and sat beside her. "What's wrong?"

She swallowed around the lump in her throat, then lifted her face to look in his eyes. "I'm pregnant."

For a moment, Ben sat very still, searching her face as though looking for some sign that it was a joke. "Wh— Are you sure?"

She nodded.

"Holy shit. How did this even…?" He shook his head. "Never mind. That doesn't matter."

June looked into her lap, her eyes stinging. For seven days, she'd managed to push this back inside her brain, as if ignoring it would make it go away. But it wasn't going anywhere. That evening last Friday, she had taken three pregnancy tests, each one coming back positive, and ever since, it was as if the knowledge of her pregnancy had made her pregnant. She felt exhausted in a way she never had before. She'd started having trouble keeping her eyes open during rehearsal when she wasn't dancing. Her breasts felt painfully heavy.

She'd been so stunned by it all that for seven days, she hadn't been able to find the nerve to verbalize it to Ben. Now that she had, terror coursed through her body. Her arms tingled so painfully it seemed possible they could stiffen and fall off. She was finding it hard to breathe. "What are we gonna do?"

Ben wrapped his arms around her, kissed her temple, and in a voice thick with emotion, said, "We're going to take it one day at a time."

In his arms, her face pressed against his shoulder, June frowned. She'd thought he'd say something along the lines of *What are you thinking?* Then, with a jolt, she realized Ben had already jumped over the huge sea of indecision and landed squarely on the other side, in the land of *We're having a baby.* When he let her go, he was grinning with a look of such goofy bliss it made June dizzy.

"How're you…" he began, but his voice quickly faded and he frowned, leaned away. After a long moment of studying her from that distance, he said, "June? What do you mean *what are we going to do?*"

But June hadn't been expecting this reaction from him—

she felt blindsided and confused—and she found she couldn't say what she'd meant for fear that he'd hate her for it. But it didn't matter; at her silence, it was clear that her meaning had finally landed.

He shifted, turning away from her, and the two of them sat there in silence for a very long time. June's head swam with the disparity between their reactions. Should she have been expecting this? For the past seven years of their relationship, they'd been actively preventing a pregnancy. This was a mistake, so why was he acting as though they'd wanted it all along? She thought back to all the times she and Ben had discussed the possibility of children. In the early stages of their relationship, they'd talked through all the major stuff: religion, politics, finances, procreation. And if these conversations revealed they weren't on the exact same page, at least they showed them they could talk about hot-button issues with open minds and respect.

But they'd been twenty-three and twenty-six at the time, almost a decade ago, and they'd approached the topic of children with a foolhardy assumption that because they were in love, they'd agree about everything. June had said, when the topic came up, "I mean, I definitely don't want kids now. My career is my priority now. But I'm also not saying I wouldn't want them in the future." And Ben had said, "I'd like a family. I always kind of assumed I'd have one, but yeah, I'm totally not ready like, today." Sitting side by side on the couch now, June realized just how different those answers really were.

"So what?" Ben said. "You want to get an abortion?"

"I—I don't know. I guess I just wanna talk."

Ben ran a jittery hand through his hair. "I'm sorry, but I'm really thrown by this. I can't even believe we're having this conversation."

"Ben, how could we not have this conversation? We haven't talked about kids in *years*."

"But an *abortion*? Are you serious? June, we have money and a stable source of income. We have family. And, not that we're old or anything, but we're not exactly young either. I can't think of one reason why we wouldn't have this baby."

June blinked. She understood then just how far apart they were on this, because while he could not think of one reason not to have this baby, her mind flooded with them. And beneath them all, Medea loomed, constant as a heartbeat. Saying yes to this baby would rob June of everything she'd worked for her entire life. Even if she could come back to the company after the pregnancy, Medea—the biggest break in her career—would be gone. Maybe she wanted a baby, maybe she didn't, but what she did know, with absolute clarity, was that she wanted to be Medea in the Martha Graham ballet.

But she couldn't say that to Ben. If she didn't want the baby and she took the role, it would seem as if she'd chosen a ballet over her own child. And it wasn't that simple. Just because she wanted to have a career didn't mean that if she didn't want that same career, she'd suddenly turn into Mrs. Von Trapp and want a houseful of kids. It wasn't either-or.

Because she couldn't say that aloud, she said something else. "A baby changes everything, Ben. What if…" Her voice faded as she chose from the myriad questions in her mind. What if she wanted to stay the center of his love and attention? How did people transition from that to being a parent? What if they couldn't make the transition and parenthood tore them apart? What if they disagreed about something fundamental in raising their child? Or worse, what if they fought over the little things until they lost sight of one another entirely? "What if," she began again, "it changes who we are together?"

Ben gave a little shrug. "I mean, our relationship is always going to change. We don't have the same relationship we had when we first met and we don't have the same relationship as when we got married. That's not a bad thing."

"Well, what if I don't change the right way? Because right now I don't feel like what a mom should feel like. I don't feel...tender or protective. I feel completely devoid of maternal instincts."

To her surprise, Ben seemed to soften slightly at this. "June, you *just* found out you were pregnant."

Her gaze darted to the floor because of course that wasn't completely, precisely true.

"We're gonna have nine months to start feeling like parents," he continued. "And even after we have the baby, there's gonna be a learning curve. It's not like we have to have all the answers and all the right feelings right away. This is an unplanned pregnancy." He chuckled slightly. "It's gonna take a few days to get used to."

June wanted to scream. It seemed as if she and Ben were getting farther and farther away from each other, as if he were standing firmly on the earth and she had floated above him into the sky. "Ben, it's not about whether or not we're going to *get used* to the idea. It's about whether or not we *want* this. I mean, do we really want to bring another human into this world?"

"What do you mean? What are you afraid of?"

June jerked her head back, the question striking her as absurd. After all, what could possibly be more terrifying than bringing a human into the world, for being socially and environmentally responsible for it? What could possibly be more painful than introducing someone you love to a place that

gave birth to Fidel Castro and the Holocaust and the Con-
federate flag? "For starters, I'm scared about climate change."

Ben gave her a wry grin. "I doubt our baby will have to
live through the apocalypse if that's what you're saying."

"But what about our genetic line? If we love our baby more
than anything and it loves its baby more than anything and
on and on for like thousands of years, shouldn't the baby at
the very end of the line also be our priority?"

"I think you're overthinking this."

But how, *how*, could you possibly overthink bringing a life
into the world? Ben had a logical counterargument for each
of her questions, but it seemed to June like he'd missed the
point of her questions altogether. She wasn't trying to convince him of anything. She didn't *want* an abortion—of course
she didn't. And yet, she didn't *not* want one either. She just
wanted to talk through their options and make a decision together, not be steamrolled into one.

"What about our jobs?"

He frowned. "What d'you mean?"

"Who would take care of the baby every day?"

Ben shifted. "Well, for the first few weeks, we'll have
leave…"

"And after that?"

"I don't know. But we can talk about all this."

"We're talking about it now."

"Okay… Well, I don't know. Would you wanna take off
for a while?"

June narrowed her eyes at him. "Take off of what?" The
Graham Company had maternity leave, of course, but they
didn't save places for dancers indefinitely.

"I mean, the company. It's up to you, obviously, but would

you wanna stay in the company with a baby? You're gone all the time and even when you're here, you're always rehearsing."

June stilled. Giving up the role of Medea would be one thing, but quit the company altogether? She had the sudden sensation of being on an operating table, having pieces of her body ripped from her, tearing her flesh. And it stung all the more because it was coming from Ben, her husband, her best friend. Did he really view her career so dismissively? There was another emotion at war with this inside her, but it felt oddly, unexpectedly, like relief, which was vastly more confusing than anger, so she pushed it to the side.

"No, you're right," she said. "How could I possibly work that much if we had a baby I had to take care of?"

Ben shook his head. "I didn't mean—that came out wrong. I was just thinking out loud…" He rubbed his hands over his face. "I'm sorry. Of course I want you to do what you want. I want you to be happy."

She turned away from him and for a long moment they sat side by side, neither meeting the other's eye.

"June," Ben finally said, his voice no more than a croak, his head bent to the floor. "I love you. And we don't have to figure out any of this right now. But I feel like I have to be honest with you. I already love this baby. Because he—or she—is ours. And think about what an amazing combination that would be." He heaved a sigh and when he looked up at her, his eyes were shining. "Is that really something you want to get rid of?"

June walked through the days following their conversation in a blur. Each time Ben brought up the baby, she felt her chest tighten so suddenly it was hard to breathe. One night, after he broached the possibility of moving to New Jersey, where a couple of his colleagues lived, to be within the quote-unquote "good school districts," she'd snuck a glass of wine into the bathroom and drank it, silent tears running down her face. She was having trouble sleeping and her dancing had gotten sloppy. It was as if she were trapped in purgatory. Each time she thought about what this baby would mean to her life as a dancer, she remembered Ben's shining eyes when he told her how much he already loved it. The decision was more complex than simply choosing between herself and her husband, but sometimes that was how it seemed. And if that were true, how could either choice be right? She refused to be the woman who erased her dreams to make room for her husband's, but neither could she imagine forcing Ben to do that for her.

One night, as Ben slept soundly beside her, June stared wide-eyed at the wall, her thoughts turning to her mom. Her mom had walked through the world with such confidence. Nothing fazed her—not showing up in New York from Texas at the age of nineteen with no more than a half-empty suitcase; not getting pregnant at age twenty-four with no one to help raise the baby; not any audition; not even cancer. It had killed her, yes, but it hadn't broken her. June wished she could be like that now, shrug off the worry of what it would mean to have a child and view it as some great adventure.

Suddenly, she felt the need to move. Ben's breathing was like a too-slow metronome; the blankets at her neck felt heavy and strangling. She kicked them off and tiptoed out of their bedroom. She walked quietly to their hallway closet, where she'd stored all those cardboard boxes of her mom's old things. They'd sat unopened for years, but she still remembered their contents as if the item list had been branded on her mind.

She sifted through them gently so as not to make any noise

and finally, she found the box she was looking for, not the one full of clothes, with her mom's favorite turquoise scarf sticking out of the hole, but the heavy one, full of dishes, books, and—what June was looking for now—photo albums. She dug one out, the burgundy one with the black binding, sat cross-legged on the floor, and cracked it open on her lap. The first page was achingly familiar to her, with its mysterious stain on the edge and its crinkled protective sheet on top, flimsy as a bible page. Looking at those first four photos was like hearing a favorite song you hadn't heard in years, but of which you knew every word.

In the photos, her mom was in the hospital, holding newborn June. Her infant self looked tiny, her toes smaller than peas, her skin a mottled purple. Her eyes were screwed shut and her mouth was wide, curling her baby lips into a silent wail frozen in time. Michelle, looking so young herself, was gazing down at her miserable baby with a look of such love and awe that present-day June's throat tightened. She flipped through the pages, watching her own likeness grow from newborn to healthy baby—chubby cheeks, wisps of dark hair—until she found the photo she was looking for.

In it, Michelle was wearing a bulky beige sweater tucked partially into a midlength black skirt, large wooden buttons in a line down the front. On her feet were red ankle boots, and on her head was her signature turquoise scarf. Behind the image of her mom, June recognized the old plaid couch they'd had for years and the coffee table she'd climbed on top of so many times. In the photo, her mom was dancing, a look of bliss on her face. It was clear—her eyes closed, her mouth just barely open in an easy smile—that she was wholly focused on nothing more than moving to the music. In her arms was June, probably six months old, her face smooshed in her mom's palm, sound asleep. The frozen tableau made present-day June laugh helplessly even as tears prickled her eyes. It wasn't as if her mom had been ignoring the sleeping infant in her arms, but rather embracing her as a part of the moment, inviting her into her own private world.

Staring down at her desperately young mom, something shifted inside June.

This whole time she'd thought that saying yes to her own baby, saying yes to motherhood, would change her: she'd forever shift her focus to her child; her love of dance would flicker and pale in comparison; her love of Ben would take second place; her identity in the world would transform into something else. But seeing her young mom in that photo, dancing in red boots and her favorite turquoise scarf, June thought that perhaps she'd been looking at this all wrong. Perhaps she wouldn't have to change her identity to be a mother. She wouldn't have to suddenly start wearing paisley or baking brownies or stop auditioning for strange shows about brokenhearted Greek sorceresses. Perhaps she could be a mother on her own terms. Perhaps opening her heart up to this baby would, rather than use up her finite capacity to love, perhaps it would actually expand it.

That was when June realized that she wouldn't sacrifice her marriage for herself. She would choose Ben and she would choose this baby. Not in lieu of her career, but on top of it. On top of her own dreams and her own life. Although she was still angry at Ben for that conversation, June wouldn't base her decision on anger. She'd base it on hope.

The choice hit her like a wave, like it was coming from some outside source, rather than from within, and in that moment, more than anything, she felt relief. She would have to give up the company for the time being, but she wouldn't have to give up dance. She would tell Silvi and Hiromi that she couldn't be Medea after all, and she knew it would break her heart just a little bit when she did, but in the end, it would be okay because she would do as her own mother had. June would bring this baby into the world and stay the exact same person she'd always been.

# THIRTY-FOUR

———

*Sunday, February something or is it March?*

Dear Mom,

Before the petition and the baby-bonking incident at Whole Foods, there was a birthday invitation. It was from Sydney, inviting me, Mikey, and Ben to celebrate Layla's first birthday and when I got it weeks ago, before all this shit went down, I RSVP'd yes, we'd be happy to go.

The party was today and while I'd totally forgotten about it, apparently, Ben had not. It's Sunday and the only day of the week he hadn't gone into work. This morning, when I walked into the kitchen with Mikey, I found him, drinking coffee, studying the bright invitation.

"So this thing starts at eleven," he said.

I held Mikey out to him and he took him wordlessly, bouncing him as I pulled down a mug for myself. It had felt like a lifetime since I'd been able to do something even as simple as fix a cup of coffee with two hands and it felt deeply luxurious. I took a sip.

"I don't think I really wanna go to the party," I said.

"You don't? Why not?"

The problem is that Ben is such an upstanding citizen. Take exhibits 1 through 3 as evidence: 1) He's the type to give up his seat on the subway to anyone; they don't even have to be old or pregnant; 2) Once, after buying something at a bodega, he realized the cashier gave him too much change and he made us walk two and a half blocks to return it; and 3) He always researches every aspect of something before forming an opinion, whereas I take one look at a headline and know exactly where I stand. And because being a model citizen comes naturally to him, he has trouble understanding when people don't behave as well as he does. This morning, I didn't want to see the inevitable disappointment that would flash in his eyes as I told him everything that's happened between me and Kirsten: the missed vaccine appointment; the destroying of her bananas; the bonking of the babies. "I don't know," I said. "I thought it would be nice to stay at home today. Just the three of us. We haven't gotten any time together recently."

Ben studied my face. "Don't you think getting out of the house would be good, too, though? Plus, the party's only a few hours. We'll be home by one. Then we'll have the rest of the day together."

I felt too tired to push. Plus, it was Sydney's party, not Kirsten's. I had just as much right to show up as she did. Granted, I hadn't spoken with Sydney or Reese since the day of the petition, but they'd both texted. Eventually, I looked up at Ben and smiled a thin smile I hoped he couldn't see through. "Okay, sure. Let's go."

The inside of Sydney's home had been completely transformed. The theme, which I'd obviously missed on the invitation, was, if I had to guess, boho chic. There were peonies everywhere. Tissue-paper flowers the size of dinner plates hung from the ceiling and in garlands draped in doorways. In a far corner was a gauzy pink tent full of pillows. The cake was three tiers with icing flowers cascading down it.

Then I saw it. Across the giant living room, I spotted my three friends, Sydney, Reese, and Kirsten, all in matching outfits. Each was wearing some version of the same thing: a floor-length skirt, booties, enormous floral crowns, and golden glitter that began as eye shadow and swept up on their temples and foreheads in artful designs. I looked down at my own outfit: black jeans, a black turtleneck, and gray high-top Converse. I looked back up again and caught their gaze. Sydney and Reese seemed surprised to see me; Kirsten looked mutinous.

I turned to Ben, who was holding Mikey, but Reese's husband, Will, had already found him and the two of them were laughing about something. "Be right back," I told Ben and he just nodded, happy and oblivious.

I darted into the kitchen and through the side room to the garage. I just needed a moment away from everything. I pulled the door behind me and swallowed hard. But my throat was still tight and before I knew it, that horrible swallowing fit had taken hold of me yet again.

Just then, the door opened and in walked Liam. I could tell immediately that Kirsten must have dressed him with the theme in mind. He was wearing a white linen shirt rolled to his elbows and muted green pants. His wavy brown hair looked deliberately unruly. His eyes scanned the room and when they landed on me, his head jerked back in surprise. "June, I didn't see you there."

"Hi, Liam." He was probably the only person at this entire party who I didn't hate seeing right now. "What're you doing here?"

"I was sent to get more champagne. What're *you* doing here?" he asked with mock accusation.

But I couldn't muster the energy for anything other than the truth. "Just...taking a second."

He nodded, then cocked his head. "Are you okay, June?"

I once heard that humans love the sound of their name more than any sound in the world, and in that moment, I understood why. The way he said mine unlocked something in me. I had cried so much around Mikey, the one person who could do nothing about it and had no responsibility to even try, but I hadn't cried in front of the girls and I hadn't cried in front of Ben, at least not recently. I hadn't given in to my emotions in front of another adult in a long time. And now all it took to unleash them was someone simply saying my name and asking if I was okay.

I shook my head, tears silently streaming down my cheeks. Liam hesitated only a moment before crossing the short distance that separated us and wrapping his arms around me. Oh, God, Mom, how good it felt to be held by someone, to feel someone else's strength holding me up rather than my own. Neither of us said anything. For a long moment, we just stood there.

Then the door opened again and we jumped apart. Obviously, we weren't doing anything wrong, but even in my state, I knew getting caught in the garage, hugging another woman's husband would look bad. When I looked up to see who had come in, my heart dropped because it was— wouldn't you know it—Kirsten, standing frozen in the doorway, mouth open, looking radiant in her colorful outfit that I hadn't known to wear, her blond hair in beachy waves. Her eyes darted between the two of us and then she straightened her back and cleared her throat. She raised her eyebrows at

Liam. "Did you find that champagne, babe?" she asked, her voice steady and sweet.

Liam looked from his wife to me and then back again. He sighed and it sounded sad. Suddenly, I felt guilty for not asking him if he was okay. "I'll grab it now," he said. There was nothing guilty in his voice, but he didn't look at me as he went to the refrigerator, grabbed a few bottles, and walked back to the door. It seemed obvious to the three of us that he was going to leave and Kirsten was going to stay, and it made me feel like a trapped animal. All I wanted in that moment was for the ground to open up and swallow me.

Once Liam disappeared, Kirsten closed the door behind her with the gentlest of clicks. "You need to leave," she said and her voice was so calm it was unnerving.

"Kirsten, I—"

But Kirsten squeezed her eyes shut, her hands balled tightly at her sides, and shouted, "Get the hell out of this house!"

So I did. I tried to make my trembling body smaller as I passed her, as if somehow that would allow me to escape her gaze and her hatred, but of course, it didn't. As I slipped by her in the doorway, she hissed in my ear, "I never want to see you again." It's ironic, though, because if she only knew how much I don't want to see myself, either, how much I don't want to be myself, she probably wouldn't have felt the need to say it at all.

I found Ben and Mikey right where I'd left them and told them we had to go. When we got home, Ben asked why I'd wanted to leave so early, but all the things I hadn't said out loud felt like an insurmountable mass between us. I knew that if I started talking now, I would eventually get to the moment where I had to explain the inexplicable: that something was deeply wrong with me, that no matter how much I love Mikey, I am all wrong as a mother.

I walked upstairs to get out my journal to write to you, Mom, and as I did, I finally saw you again. You darted from the hallway into the bathroom, your long, dark hair flowing behind you, that bright burst of your turquoise scarf not much more than a blur of color, but it was you. I followed you into the bathroom, but you were gone. I stood, very much alone, staring at my own reflection.

Then it hit me. I had thought the petition was my banishment, but that was simply the warning. Like the king does to Medea, Kirsten had given me time to get my affairs in order and then she'd issued the final decree: "I never want to see you again."

Just as Aegeus appears to Medea at the time of her banishment, you'd finally appeared to me. And I knew you'd only return when I had my plan complete. By now I'd figured out where your Athens is, but there was still the matter of the chariot of flames. So I have some details to sort, but finally, I'm ready to follow you. Finally, I'm ready to go.

Love,
June

# THIRTY-FIVE

———

Ben was rushing out of the police station when he heard someone calling him back. He stopped, spun around, and saw that it was Kirsten.

"Kirsten," he said, running a jittery hand through his hair. "What's up?"

"I just wanted to say—about, you know, June seeing her mom…"

"Yeah?"

She cleared her throat, looking painfully awkward. "Look, I don't want to hold you up, but I have something to show you. I drafted an email the other week to Sydney. I didn't send it—I was more, just, venting, but… It might clear some things up."

Ben had no idea what she was talking about and he didn't want to take the time to figure it out. Here he was trying to find his wife and she was talking to him about unsent emails. "Fine," he said, walking backward slowly. "Yeah, go ahead and send it over. Liam has my email."

He was turning to the parking lot when she called him back again.

"Yeah. Kirsten. What?"

"Remember—I wrote it before I knew about the postpartum, about hers and mine. And I didn't send it." She sighed. "And I'm sorry."

Ben returned home and asked his mom to take Mikey for a full week. Then he held his son for a long moment, whispering assurances he desperately hoped were true that he was going to find June and bring her back. He packed a bag and bought a plane ticket, and it wasn't until after he'd finally sunk heavily into his airline seat that Ben remembered Kirsten's email at all. When he did, he pulled out his phone, opened his inbox, and skimmed through the hundreds of unread messages to find the right one.

Sydney!

Hi, love, how are you?

I'm writing to ask you a favor. I'd really appreciate it—nay, I'd love it and owe you for the rest of my life—if you would find it in your heart to uninvite June to Layla's party. This probably sounds mean-spirited, but I think once you hear my side of things, you'll not only understand, but jump at the chance to show her whose side you're on.

What I'm about to share with you is top secret, never to be spoken of outside the two of us, even to Reese, because if I'm being totally honest, what I'm about to share is my ugliest truth. I do not look good in it. But I think June has finally pushed me to the point where the benefits of sharing this outweigh the drawbacks.

June is having an affair with Liam. Yes, you read that right. I don't know when it started, but I started suspecting something was up, actually, during wine night at June's.

Do you remember how I got to her house late that night? Sort of a little tipsy and disheveled, and everyone thought it was because Liam and I had just had sex? Reese said something to that effect and I was actually grateful for her misinterpretation because the truth was much worse.

Liam and I, far from having sex, had just had a blow-up fight. I'd been suspecting him of cheating on me for some time. I didn't have any proof, but he'd been distant, distracted. I thought at first it was because I was so preoccupied with Georgia, but after a while it seemed like it was more than that. He was staying late at work all the time and he was always on his phone. Whenever I'd ask what he was doing, he'd just say work stuff. But that night, I—well, I didn't quite confront him about cheating—but I circled around it, saying I thought something must be going on with how much he's away. He played dumb, of course, and then turned the tables on me, saying that ever since we had Georgia, she's the only thing I care about and talk about. I told him he was acting like a child because of course she's the only thing I care about right now! She's our baby. Jesus H. Christ!

Anyway, I chugged a glass of wine and went over to June's and I think I was just fed up with everything and wanted to have a real conversation, so I proposed Confession. If you didn't yet put it together, this is why I broke down when it was my turn. I said Liam was traveling so much I felt like a single parent. In reality, he isn't traveling at all, he's just gone all the time, and I kept thinking, I am not staying with a man who cheats on me. But if I left Liam, I'd be a single mom with no income and when I thought about that, I lost it.

You might be thinking, *Okay, but where does June come in?* Well, she comes in now! Do you remember how weird she was acting during her turn at Confession? She kept almost saying something and then not saying it? And then she ended up saying she was a bad mom all because she didn't like breast-feeding? But it was clear she was hiding something. And I kept wondering what it was she had to hide. The idea that she was having an affair floated into my head like the wisp of a cloud, but once it was there, I couldn't get it out. And then I thought, What if she's having an affair with Liam? It was just a suspicion, of course; I had no proof.

But then I did.

Do you also remember the next wine night we had at Reese's? The one both June and I were late to? Remember how June had texted that she got caught up at the library and lost track of time? Well, guess what? She lost track of time because she was with Liam! That evening, I'd given Liam a stack of books I'd checked out for Georgia to return to the library. As I headed out to Reese's for wine night, I found a book I'd forgotten to give to him so I decided to stop by the library on my way.

When I got there, I saw Liam and June together. They were just talking, but the way Liam was listening to her, the way he was smiling and nodding along—he hadn't listened to me like that in ages. I sat there in my car, just outside the library parking lot, Georgia with me, and watched. At one point, Liam made June laugh so hard, she grabbed his arm as she bent over with it. I knew how much it would boost Liam's ego to have a woman doubled over because of something he'd said and it made me sick. I finally realized how late it was and left, but June stayed, talking to my husband. And as I drove away, I glanced through the rearview mirror and saw them embrace.

Now here's the part where I start to not look so good. But in my defense, everything I'm about to tell you I did because of her. Not to sound childish, but she did start it.

I wanted to know the details of their affair, so I started following June. Obviously, I didn't want her to know it was me, so I sort of wore a disguise. I bought a cheap dark brown wig online at Party City, a pair of big, old-fashioned sunglasses and a black turtleneck from some vintage store, and got my old camel coat out of hiding. And then, the finishing touch: I wore one of June's scarves on my head to keep my wig in place.

Remember all those boxes that were out when we went to her place for wine night? When I passed by them on my way to the bathroom that night, I saw something sticking out and on a whim, I grabbed it. It was this old, threadbare scarf that I'd never seen June wear. Well, I heard somebody coming and I didn't want to be caught with it in my hands so I stuffed it into my bra. I know it sounds insane, but having one of her possessions felt like I was in control of something, like I had a tiny piece of power over her. Plus, if she hadn't even unpacked it yet, I didn't think she'd notice if it was gone.

The logistics of following her were tricky. For one thing, spying with a baby is not easy, so I started hiring a babysitter during the day. But June and Liam were good. Too good. I couldn't catch them in the act. Then something happened that I didn't expect—June saw me. I was standing outside her house one day and I could see through their front window that she was getting ready to go. Right before she reached the door, she looked out the window and spotted me.

And she freaked. I ducked behind a tree and watched as she slid down the wall and sat on the floor by the front door. It was all the proof I needed. Despite my disguise, she must have recognized me. She must have been going to meet my husband and when she saw me, she was overcome with guilt. What other possible explanation could there be?

I saw her again a few days later at Whole Foods and she confronted me about it. I hadn't been following her that time, so I was in my regular clothes and I had Georgia with me, but when

I approached her, her reaction confirmed my suspicion. She was pissed. She told me to stay away from her and then, get this, she grabbed a bushel of bananas out of my bag and threw them on the ground—such a psycho! And then she slammed Mikey into Georgia—Georgia's fine by the way—but the threat was clear. I had to stop following her or else.

So please, Sydney, I'm entrusting this sensitive information to you for the sole purpose of bringing June down. I can put up with many things. But I can't put up with going to a birthday party with the woman who is sleeping with my husband.

Love and thanks,
Kirsten


Ben swelled with anger. This woman had been, albeit unintentionally, gaslighting June for weeks now. June hadn't hallucinated her mom outside their house or at Whole Foods after all; she'd simply seen Kirsten in some cheap disguise and her own mother's stolen scarf. And it had driven her mad.

And yet, according to her journal, there was still that one inexplicable time June saw her mom *inside* their home, darting into their bathroom. It was impossible that the vision had been Kirsten at the time because she would've still been at the party. There was no explanation for it other than a hallucination, which meant that postpartum psychosis was still a very real possibility.

With a mounting sense of dread, Ben pulled out the folded pages of June's journal from his pocket. He wanted to understand everything before he saw his wife face-to-face. He flattened them out on the little airplane tray table and flipped to the last entry, the only one he hadn't been able to make himself read.

★ ★ ★

*Addendum to previous entry.*

*Dear Mom,*

*Medea is a controversial character. On the one hand, she's sympa-thetic. She's betrayed by her husband, the man who has vowed to love and respect her. As the audience watches the ballet, they are on the side of Medea. They watch as her heart gets broken. They watch as Jason chooses wealth and status over the wife he's grown with, the woman who's stayed true to him for years, the mother of his children. He parades around the stage, holding the princess on his shoulder, and as Medea writhes in anguish on the floor, he never even looks at her.*

*But then a light comes on in Medea's eyes and the audience watches as her grief morphs to rage. She transforms into a thing of power once again, placing a loop of thorns onto the princess's head, watching as the princess's adoration of the crown turns to confusion and then to terror. The crown is poisoning her, melting her skin, and despite all her fighting, she cannot pry it off.*

*This is where the ballet differs from the play because in the play, things get even more tragic. I've been avoiding the next part in my mind, because I've wanted to rewrite Medea's story. But each time I read it, no matter what translation, it ends the same way. Just before she escapes to Athens, Medea kills her own children.*

*Hard as it is to understand, she doesn't do it out of anger or hate, but rather love. Because of their connection to her—the murderer of the princess—her children are doomed to death. Rather than watch them suffer at her enemy's hateful hands, she decides that they will die by her loving, merciful ones. But it's complicated. While she's protecting her children from a brutal death, death is their fate only because of the choices she's made.*

*I'd never fully understood Medea until I had Mikey; ironic, see-*

ing as he was the reason I never got to be her on stage. But now I do. These children come into our lives and we vow to do anything to protect them, but the fact is that the thing we most often need to protect them from is ourselves. In trying to keep them safe, we prevent them from learning independence or in trying to make them tough, we beat the softness out of them. We try to encourage them, but we go overboard and the pressure makes them feel trapped. It is so often love that makes us do the things that mess our kids up. So I understand why Medea did what she did. She was trying to protect her children from the consequences of her own actions and as a mother, protecting them is the only thing you can do.

But I think she got it wrong. We have children so they can outlive us, so they can be better than us, so humanity can improve itself one generation at a time. It didn't work with me, obviously, but it would work for Mikey. I know it. He will be better than me, better than Ben.

I stood there in the bathroom, where I'd followed you, trying to work out my next step. As I looked around, my gaze landed on the tub and it finally hit me—you were giving me the same gift that Aegeus gives Medea, the gift of time in which to say goodbye. A sort of calm came over me then and with it, a deep sadness. I went to get Mikey from downstairs where he was with Ben and told him it was time for his bath. I was grateful that was where you'd led me, Mom—bath time was always where I felt closest to Mikey, so it was fitting that it was where I'd say goodbye.

As I carried him upstairs, I tried to memorize him. I rubbed my cheek against his head and tried to catalog that exact feeling of his softness against mine. His wisps of hair brushed against my skin and I let them catch on my lips. I inhaled his scent. I wrapped my thumb and index finger gently around each ankle and then each wrist. I wished I could bottle it all up and take it with me.

I started to run the bath, dipping my fingers into the spray to make sure it wasn't too hot or too cold. I undressed him and put him in the tub, cupping my hand under the water and drizzling it onto his head then wiping it softly from his brow. I'd never taken such care in the bath before. I drew it out and the water rose. I traced his shoulder blades with my fingertips, those tiny, precious shoulder blades. I touched his cheeks and his ears, running my finger around them; they were like little shells.

"Mikey?" I said and the moment I did, tears filled my eyes. "I have to go now."

My mind jumped to Medea, how she had escaped to Athens with the knowledge that she'd been with her children throughout their entire lives—a small mercy, it seemed to me. She'd known every intimacy of her children while I would be left to wonder about mine. What kind of childhood would Mikey have and who would he grow up to be? What things would he love to do? What people would he hold in his heart?

"You won't remember me," I continued, my throat so tight I had to force the words out. "But it's better that way. And maybe, because I'm not here, you'll think I don't love you, but that's just not true. I love you very, very much."

I was really crying then, tears falling into my mouth. I leaned over to press my lips against his head one last time, but I had to shift to do it and as I did, my knee got caught behind the side of the toilet and I fell into the edge of the tub, catching myself with my hands.

But Mikey wasn't in his little bath support seat, the thing that lets me use my hands when I need to. I always use the support—always, always—but I hadn't this time because I'd just wanted to say goodbye. And so when I used my hands to stop my fall, I'd pulled them away from Mikey. Without me to support him, he slipped backward into the water and for one heart-stopping moment, he was completely submerged. I saw him under there, his tiny body distorted by the rippling water. His little legs kicked against it.

I cried out, thrusting my hands into the bath as fast as I could to *grab him. When he came back up, he coughed up a mouthful of water then started wailing. I held him to my chest, heaving with my own sobs. "I'm sorry," I cried. "I'm sorry, I'm sorry, I'm sorry."*

*But my apologies were worthless and I was terrified to be near him. I didn't want him with me for one more moment. I couldn't trust myself. I rushed with him, soaking wet, down the stairs to where Ben was sitting at the dining room table with his laptop. "Take him," I called over Mikey's cries. Ben looked startled, but reflexively grabbed Mikey from my outstretched hands.*

*"June—he's soaking wet."*

*But I just walked away. I couldn't be in the same room as Mikey anymore. What happened had been an accident, but that didn't matter. I was Medea through and through. I was a danger to my own son.*

*So, Mom, the plan has changed, but I finally understand. I have to protect my child from myself. Medea was right after all; a sacrifice must be made, but Mikey is not—*

The rest of the line had been torn off, but Ben knew what it said. He had memorized the words days ago: *the one who needs to die.*

Ben felt as if someone had reached through his chest and squeezed a cold hand around his heart. The hazy cloud of dread he'd been feeling ever since he woke up to an empty house a few days ago finally crystallized into the sickening impossibility of what June had done.

His hands shook as he envisioned Mikey, their four-month-old son, submerged in water. But it had been an accident, Ben reminded himself, a moment of forgetfulness induced by that fucking disease. June was sick. Her presence of mind was missing, leaving a gaping hole in her head where it had once been. Panic crept up Ben's chest at the thought, wrapping its fingers tightly around his neck. Because while Mikey was now safe at home, June was not.

The flight attendant walked by with a garbage bag and Ben grabbed the four unopened airplane-size bottles of whiskey he'd ordered and tossed them in. His body jumped with nerves that needed numbing, but he wouldn't have any alcohol in his system when he saw June, not a drop.

The tarmac arrived suddenly, as if it had leaped up and hit the plane. Finally, he was here. Finally, he'd be able to see his wife.

He just hoped he wasn't getting to her too late.

# ATHENS

# THIRTY-SIX

——

*Five Days Earlier*

June paid for the rental car with her new, shiny debit card, marveling at her own name printed in the little raised letters. It had been so long since she'd felt like June Maxwell, the words seemed almost meaningless to her now. It wasn't that she felt different from who she'd been before exactly, but rather that who she'd been before was fading away, leaving nothing but the husk of her behind. Just like Medea, June had prepared for her departure with a sort of detached determination. The first thing she'd done, three days earlier, was drive to her bank, open a new account, and request a five-thousand-dollar withdrawal from her and Ben's joint account to deposit into her own new one. Then she created a new email address, reserved a rental car, and bought a one-way plane ticket. Finally, she'd been ready to escape on her chariot of flames.

June scanned the rental car section of the airport for her mom, but the only other people there were a couple with their kids and two businessmen in ties. She chewed the inside of her cheek. Her mom wouldn't lead her here then abandon her, would she? Or, was it possible she'd gotten it wrong, that this wasn't Athens after all? But June shook the doubt from her mind. It wasn't the place that was the problem. The problem was that she'd already reached the end of Medea's story. In the final scene of the Euripides play, the Greek sorceress rides off to Athens to start her new life, but there's no epilogue to show what that actually looks like. It would've been nice to have some sort of road map with which to navigate what came next.

"Ma'am?"

The voice pulled June from her thoughts. She looked up to see the woman in the navy Budget polo staring at her with raised eyebrows.

"Sorry," June said.

"Not at all. We see lots of tired travelers in this line of business. I said your car is in section J." The woman smiled. "Welcome to Texas, Ms. Maxwell."

An hour and a half later, June was standing outside her Airbnb on the outskirts of Marble Falls in the Texas Hill Country. The house was small and old, but it had been cheap, and the property it sat on was thirteen acres of nothing but trees and grass; the driveway alone had to be a quarter of a mile. She'd originally wanted to stay in town, but when she'd stumbled upon the aerial view of this property on its Airbnb profile—the house no more than a tiny dot among a sea of green—she'd envisioned herself disappearing under the canopy of leaves and had booked it then and there.

Now, she typed in the code the property owner had provided for the little lockbox looped around the front door handle and retrieved the key inside. Then she unlocked the door and walked through. The house, which would've been better characterized as a cabin, had walls of enormous wooden beams separated by thick slabs of what looked like concrete. In the living area was a plaid couch flanked by two floral armchairs. Across from it was a fireplace, accompanied by a bundle of logs Saran-wrapped in plastic, a stack of old newspapers underneath and a matchbox on top. Above the mantel hung an enormous set of antlers. June assessed her emotional reaction to the antlers and was surprised to find she had none. She neither felt anger at the hunter nor sorry for the deer. Perhaps her overrun emotional triage system had taken one look and declared it unworthy of her heart space, and for that, she was relieved.

Despite her exhaustion, June allowed herself a slow tour of the cabin. She'd envisioned Marble Falls, TX, so many times over the past few weeks, it felt impossible not to explore it now that she was here. She knew this wasn't her mom's childhood home or anything, but that didn't matter. Her mom's parents had died many years ago and anyway, they'd disapproved of Michelle's move to New York, so after she left, they'd virtually disappeared from their daughter's life. Traveling to Texas wasn't so much about exploring her mom's past as it was about simply inhabiting the same space she'd lived all those years ago.

June walked through the little house, touching her fingertips to each surface. To her surprise, she found everything charming in its utilitarianism. The stems of the wineglasses were thick and sturdy. The crocheted orange blanket strewn over the back of the couch was warm and soft. The stove was probably twenty years old and worked just fine.

After she'd explored inside, June let herself out onto the enormous back porch that overlooked the property. As she stood in the mild sixty-degree Texas winter air, gazing toward the rolling hills of her new temporary home, she realized she couldn't see a single man-made thing and suspected this was the first time that had ever happened to her. Even when you looked out at the ocean, there was always some oil tanker dotting the horizon. The sight now was unimaginable, luxurious, and healing.

After a moment, she walked back inside and into the dim master bedroom where she'd already dropped her suitcase to the floor. The glowing red numbers on the bedside clock read 4:16 pm. June looked from it to the bed, a king-size topped with an impossibly soft-looking quilt. The opportunity for sleep, deep and dark, pulled at her like an undertow. She wanted nothing more than to let it take her, to let herself sink. She hadn't come to Texas to rest, of course, but she felt too drained at the moment to do anything else.

She walked slowly to each window in the room, pulling the curtains closed until she was standing alone in darkness, then she grabbed her toiletries bag and headed into the bathroom. But the moment she walked in, the sight of the bathtub kicked the breath from her lungs. The image that had branded itself on her memory three days earlier filled her brain: Mikey, submerged in water, the rippling surface distorting his edges. She saw his tiny limbs twitch beneath the water, saw the mouthful he'd coughed up when he resurfaced. Her stomach turned. She squeezed her hands into fists, her nails digging into her palms, and pushed the image from her mind.

June realized then, as she caught her breath in shuddering gulps, that although what she'd come to Texas to do loomed ever present in her mind, a small part of her had been holding on to the possibility that when she got here, something would change her fate. She'd thought that because her mom had led her here, she may also have had some sort of plan with which to save her. But as June stared at the old, yellowed tub,

# THIRTY-SEVEN

——

June awoke fifteen hours later, feeling more rested than she had in months. She turned onto her back and stretched, and for one blissful moment, her mind was completely blank. But then, as she blinked up at the unfamiliar popcorn ceiling, all the bad things she'd left behind began to creep at the edges of her consciousness. She flung off the covers, desperate to move, to escape her own thoughts. Without first brushing her teeth or washing her face or eating one of the protein bars she'd stuffed into her carry-on, June threw on some clothes and her tennis shoes and walked out the back door into the morning light. The moment she was outside, the invisible hands around her neck loosened and she gasped in the cool air with thankful gulps.

On the back porch, she scanned the property for a sign of her mom—a flash of her turquoise scarf, a glimpse of her dark hair, any hint of her Aegeus come to guide her. But as she gazed out over the Texas Hill Country, she saw nothing but wilderness and was again struck by the unexpected beauty of it all. It was odd; each piece of the landscape was not beautiful in and of itself—the oak trees were gnarled, the that terrible memory lingering in her mind, she realized how naive that had been. Just as Medea did not suddenly turn into another woman when she landed in Athens, June was still June in Texas. Her mistakes were still her mistakes and she'd never be able to escape the guilt that plagued her every time she thought of them. She needed to make an atonement, but more than that, she needed to ensure she never put Mikey in danger again.

For now, though, that would have to wait. She swallowed everything down, walked back into the bedroom, and slid under the covers. Like a stone through water, June fell into sleep.

long grass was brittle-looking and yellow, the ground was patchy with dirt and rocks—and yet, taken in all together, it was one of the nicest things she'd seen and she had the urge to disappear inside it.

She set off down the grassy slope toward a little plateau and walked along it, running her fingers through the tall grass, and she felt her body begin to relax into the nature around her. She walked past solid oak trees, wispy trees riddled with thorns, squat little cacti that bloomed like alien pods from the dry earth. Eventually, she stumbled upon an animal trail leading down into a ravine and she followed it, twigs cracking beneath her feet. When she stopped and stood still, she could hear nothing. Not the sound of a car or a plane, not even the chirp of an insect or bird. In her isolation and silence, she felt she almost ceased to exist.

But when she stopped moving, her thoughts began to catch up to her, so she continued walking as if she could physically outrun her own racing mind. She walked until she came to a rusted barbed-wire fence—had she already crossed the entire property?—so she changed directions and walked alongside it, out of the ravine. When she emerged from the tree line, she could clearly see the neighboring property. It was a ranch with hay bales and horses, and sitting among them were two alpacas. June had visited Dallas before to perform with the company on tour, but this part of Texas was nothing like that had been. She wondered if Athens had seemed as strange to Medea as this place seemed to her.

"Mornin'!"

June jumped. She turned to look for the source of the voice and saw, a ways off on the neighboring ranch, a house, its back porch facing June. On it, sitting in a rocking chair and holding a mug, was a woman about her age. She had straight blond hair and was wearing a gray sweatshirt pulled tight over big breasts.

June had the urge to look over her own shoulder, to see if there was anyone else around the woman might be talking to. But there was probably no one for miles. "Morning," June called back.

The woman took a sip from her mug. "Good time to be out. This temperature won't keep for another two hours."

June didn't know what to say to that so she smiled and nodded, exaggerating both to make sure the woman, who was twenty feet away, was sure to see.

The woman nodded vaguely in June's direction. "You stayin' at the Dixon property?"

"If you say so. I just found it online."

"On what?"

"On—" June stopped midword. Was it possible this woman had never heard of the internet?

But then the woman started laughing, her chair rocking back and forth. "Sorry!" she shouted, still laughing. "Couldn't help myself. The way you looked at my horses, it seemed like ya'd never seen one before. Didn't think it'd be too hard to mess with ya and turns out I was right!"

June couldn't help it: the woman's laugh was so delighted, for the first time in weeks, despite all the badness roiling inside her, June felt laughter bubble up through it all. "What's a horse?" she called and her neighbor starting laughing all over again.

After a moment, the woman wiped a finger beneath both eyes. "I'm Brandi."

June took a few steps up the slope to get closer. "June."

"You gonna be here for a few days, June?"

"I'm here the whole week."

"And are ya here to relax or do ya have any plans?"

Suddenly, unexpectedly, June's stomach twisted. At Brandi's question, she was reminded of what she was here to do and the thought of it filled her with fear, so complete and visceral, her body flushed hot with it.

"I have one thing," she managed to say around the lump that had formed in her throat. "But it's not for a few days."

Brandi smiled and it looked so kind and bright, June wanted to bathe in it. "Well, holler if ya need anything. We'll be here."

Back at what was apparently the Dixon property, June felt jumpy and agitated. She'd had such purpose in getting here, to her mom's birthplace, her Athens, but now that she was, she felt as lost as ever. Had her mom, her Aegeus, appeared simply to guide her here and nothing more? Yes, she knew what she was ultimately supposed to do, but she didn't want to do it feeling…incomplete. Wasn't she supposed to have some sort of transformation, or at the very least, to learn something before she left? Had she missed something, some sign?

June went over every moment in *Medea*, racking her mind for something she hadn't done, something she hadn't thought of. But after Medea flies to Athens, there is nothing but a blank page. June wished she could reach back through thousands of years, grab Euripides by the shoulders, and shake him. *What comes next?* she wanted to scream in his face. *What does Medea do when she gets there?*

She dragged her fingers through her greasy hair and was reminded of the day last week when she'd washed it so many times, it bled. She'd been trying to purge the Corinthian princess's poisoned crown from her head, but what if she'd done it wrong? What if she wasn't supposed to purge it, but to welcome it, to embrace the poison as a mechanism of transformation? An idea formed in her mind and without hesitating, June went to search the house for scissors, which she found quickly in the first kitchen drawer she opened. It was all the sign she needed.

Back in the bathroom, she grabbed a handful of her hair, slipped her fingers through the handle of the scissors, and cut. In the mirror, she gazed at the freshly blunt edge of her hair, hanging above her collarbone. She'd probably taken off ten inches. As a performer, she understood that transformation sometimes came from the outside in, and she was determined to achieve it. She grabbed another chunk of hair on the other side of her face and cut that too. This side came up a bit higher than the other, but June didn't mind. A crown of thorns wasn't supposed to be beautiful; it was supposed to change her. The idea that she'd ever strived for physical beauty struck her as absurd. It was so obviously meaningless. She'd been pretty before and still had almost accidentally killed her own child.

She started to feel almost manic as she grabbed handfuls of hair and chopped them off. She accidentally nicked her neck a few times with the scissors, but she hardly noticed. The back portion of her hair was the hardest because she had to wrap it around to the front and cut it at an angle, but soon enough, she'd done her whole head. She scooped up the ends of her hair from the sink and threw them in the trash, long, dark strands sticking to her fingertips then falling in silent wisps.

But when she looked in the mirror again, June's stomach sank because nothing had changed. She didn't feel transformed or even altered. Guilt still pressed down on her with such force she thought she might buckle beneath it. Her throat tightened and tears burned in her eyes.

It wasn't Euripides she wanted to talk to now, or even Medea, but her mom.

"Why am I here?" she said aloud, her tears choking her voice, her eyes cast upward, searching the popcorn ceiling for some sort of sign. But there was nothing. All around her was quiet. June pressed her palms into the counter and opened her mouth into a wide, silent scream.

# THIRTY-EIGHT

———

It was early the next morning, as June was taking another walk around the property, when she heard a familiar voice call to her.

"Good mornin', June!"

June, who'd been retracing her steps from yesterday, through the ravine and along the barbed-wire fence, walked up out of the tree line. When she emerged, she spotted Brandi, sitting in the same rocking chair she'd been in yesterday, on her back porch twenty feet away.

June smiled. "Morning."

"We got another nice one, huh?"

It took June a moment to realize Brandi was talking about the day. It was another nice day. "We do." And to June's amazement, she actually meant it. That morning, she'd woken, feeling a little bit better than she had the day before. The previous night, a few hours after she cut her hair into the crown of thorns, she'd stumbled into bed and slept for fourteen hours straight, and for the second time in probably six months, she'd actually slept through the night. Now her brain, which had previously seemed as riddled with holes as

a slice of Swiss cheese, felt as though it had begun to regen-
erate. She didn't want to feel happy exactly—she didn't deserve that—but she thought perhaps it would be okay to feel
less sick. Maybe that was why her mom had led her here, to
let her get some rest before she left for good.

Brandi took a sip from her mug and sat quietly for a moment before calling back, "Now, June, I hope you don't take
this the wrong way, but your hair looks a lot worse than it
did yesterday."

Laughter, loud and unexpected, burst out of June. She
shook with it as she ran her fingers through the jagged ends
of her hair. "Oh, yeah," she called. "Turns out it's pretty hard
to cut your own hair."

"Well, I coulda told you that. What'd you do? Go at it with
a chainsaw?" Grinning, Brandi took another sip from her
mug. "You know," she continued, "my aunt's a hairdresser."

June's lingering laughter died abruptly. The idea of getting into a car, driving into town, and sitting across from her
own reflection in a mirror for an hour was the very last thing
she felt capable of at the moment. "Oh, Brandi, thanks, but I
don't really want to go to a hair salon right now."

At first, Brandi frowned in confusion, but then she bright-
ened again. "Oh, no, I meant I could take a swing at it. I'm
not as good as Aunt Lisa, but I could even out those ends. I
have to go into town for some fertilizer later, but I have some
time now. If you wanted."

June melted a little at the suggestion. She didn't care that
her hair looked bad—in fact, she sort of relished it—but the
idea of having Brandi bustle around her, talking to her in her
slow, contented voice was something she couldn't say no to.
She smiled. "Thanks, Brandi. I'd like that."

It took June almost ten minutes to make it over to her

neighbor's property. Brandi had told her the barbed-wire fence was easy enough to cross, but after she'd watched June begin to try, she'd said, "You know what? Maybe it'd just be easier to walk around." So June had circled back to her front gate then walked along the road to the entrance of Brandi's ranch. By the time she arrived at her neighbor's back porch, Brandi had already set up. Out in the middle of the grass was a metal chair, a black plastic comb and a pair of scissors on the seat. Draped over the back was a stained towel with the words Sea World surrounded by dozens of playful-looking oceanic creatures, including a flipping dolphin and a sea turtle smiling ear hole to ear hole. As June walked up, Brandi passed through the sliding glass door, carrying a big plastic cup full to the brim with water. On it were peeling gold letters that read, Sandra's Found Her Man-dra.

She smiled. "Hey, June."

"Hey, Brandi. It's good to see you up close."

Brandi walked over, bent down to put the cup on the ground, then stood back up, her hands on her hips. "You too. Well, not that hair, but we'll fix it."

June laughed. "Thanks for your help."

"Hey"—Brandi shrugged—"what are perfect-strangers-turned-temporary-neighbors for?" She grabbed the towel from the back of the chair along with the scissors and comb, and motioned June to sit. She'd positioned the chair facing away from the house, so when June did, her view was of the Hill Country, awash in different tones of green. Again, she had the rare sensation of gazing out onto nothing but the natural world and she felt something inside her grow pleasantly still.

"Let's drape this guy on ya," Brandi said, wrapping the towel around June's shoulders neither tenderly nor roughly.

June grabbed her hair and tugged the shorn ends out from under the fabric. "Now, I'm just gonna get your hair wet. I'm not gonna wash it or anything because, well, I'm not *that* nice."

June grinned and Brandi poured, the cool water running over June's head and into rivulets down her neck. She closed her eyes and as she did, her mind flashed to Medea's crown of thorns melting the princess's skin off, but she took a breath and focused instead on what was really happening—the tines of the comb gently digging into her scalp and running through her hair.

"So, June," Brandi began and June's heartbeat picked up suddenly. It was obviously a conversation starter and she felt incapable of talking about almost anything. Each aspect of her life was an emotional land mine: her marriage, her job, her friends, her baby, her past, her future. But then Brandi continued. "What d'you know about the Russian Revolution?"

June opened her mouth, then closed it again. That wasn't what she'd been expecting, but she was immeasurably grateful for it. There was something refreshing about a conversation that revolved around something completely outside herself. "Um…" she said, trying to dredge up any knowledge she had about the Russian Revolution. "I know Rasputin was involved…somehow, I think."

Brandi snipped slowly at the end of June's hair. "Oh, dear Lord, don't get me started on that man. You know, it took me weeks to figure out what Rasputin's motivation was throughout the whole thing." She snipped again. "And what I landed on was that he was just selfish. His country was falling apart around him, and unlike the royal family, he actually knew the country, ya know? He knew the people. He was one of 'em. But instead of giving advice to the czarina that could make real change, he was basically lookin' for sexual favors and braggin' rights." She sighed heavily. "I'm probably the maddest at him. But then I s'pose that's not exactly fair."

June listened as Brandi talked, feeling as though her neighbor were pulling her back from the brink of something. For almost half an hour, she focused on nothing more than Brandi's fingers on her scalp and Brandi's thoughts about the Russian Revolution, and when her neighbor announced that she was done, June realized it was probably the longest she'd gone without thinking even once about the bad thing.

"Thanks, Brandi," June said after Brandi had whisked the towel off her shoulders and brushed the errant wisps of hair from her neck. June ran her fingers through her still-dripping hair and smiled at how short it was. It fell above her shoulders now, so the ends touched nothing at all. She wasn't sure why, but this filled her with immense pleasure.

Brandi smiled. "No problem, June. I'll see you around."

Back at the Dixon property, June formulated a new plan for her time here. If her mom had led her to this little house in the middle of nowhere Texas, then perhaps she'd also led her to Brandi. And if that were true, June would take her cue from the woman next door. Just as Brandi had unknowingly tugged her from the chaos of her mind, maybe June could do the same for herself. Just as she'd focused on nothing but Brandi's words and the sensation of getting her hair cut, next she'd focus on nothing but taking a shower, then on drying off and then on getting dressed. She'd be mindful of each moment until eventually, she'd get to the last one and when she was there, she'd live in that moment, too, until she had no more moments before her, but only the relief of blackness.

# THIRTY-NINE

_____

June's plan of mindfulness worked, more or less. After her impromptu haircut, she showered and felt, with acuteness, the sensation of her fingertips on her scalp as they gently worked the shampoo into her newly short hair. Once she'd dried off and put on some baggy jeans and a sweater, June found it difficult to focus on anything but how hungry she was. She still hadn't eaten anything but one protein bar two days ago. This time, instead of thinking that she didn't deserve to eat or anticipating that whatever she did eat would turn chalky and tasteless in her mouth as everything had since the bad thing, June decided she'd allow herself some food. And as it was still technically morning, she decided it would be breakfast.

Almost immediately, she began to fantasize about the details. She wanted hot coffee with real cream, scrambled eggs just a little underdone with pepper. A stack of pancakes with cheap syrup. She hadn't drunk orange juice in over a decade—it was so high in sugar—but maybe now she'd drink some. Who knew? She had a cabin in the woods and three thousand dollars in her own private bank account and suddenly, the possibilities for breakfast seemed endless. She felt a wave of guilt at her own giddiness, but swallowed it down. Humans deserved to eat and no matter how bad of a human she was, she still qualified.

The problem was that June didn't have a device with which to look up a nearby grocery store. Before she'd left, she'd turned her phone and laptop off and then, at the airport, she'd slipped them into a trash can. It had seemed dramatic, but she hadn't known what else to do. She was leaving her life and she didn't want to be tempted to reconnect. To get to her Airbnb from the Austin airport, she'd printed off instructions like it was the early 2000s, but she couldn't do that now. She thought briefly of asking Brandi for directions, but then she remembered Brandi was in town getting fertilizer. And also, June found that she wanted to do this errand on her own and that she really didn't mind driving without a known destination.

So, phoneless, she got into her rental car and took a left out of the property toward the main road, which was empty. She sat at the stop sign for a long moment, relishing the feeling of being the only human in sight. To her right, on another sprawling ranch, were, to her surprise, two zebras and a small herd of what looked like antelope. With every passing minute in Texas, it grew more bizarre to her. When she'd first arrived, June had seen nothing of her mom in this wide-open place, but perhaps the two were more similar than she'd once thought; her mom had always had the capacity to surprise her. June watched the zebras for a while then pulled onto the road in search of a store.

It was only a minute or two before she spotted a small brown building on the side of the road with a sign that read, Smithwick: Beer, Ice, Soda & Snacks. That ought to about cover it, June thought, so she turned onto the dirt road and into one of three parking spots.

A bell dinged her arrival as she walked through the door into a shop that was not much bigger than her old favorite bodega in Manhattan. Behind the little checkout counter by the door, a middle-aged white woman with brown hair and leathery skin turned to June.

"Hey there," she said both brightly and slowly as if she were delighted by June's presence and had all the time in the world to tell her so. Her teeth were stained and it was clear she'd never had braces. She was wearing a black T-shirt that said Disneyland in that iconic font. Mickey Mouse stood jauntily to the side, his elbow hooked over the top of the last d.

"Hi. Do you have—"

But the woman was already talking again. "How you doin' today?"

"Fine. Thanks. Do you—"

"Have I seen you around before? You don't look familiar to me."

June stood still and it dawned on her that she was in the middle of an actual conversation, not some phony attempt at one in the name of customer service. "I'm staying at an Airbnb nearby," she said.

"You here on vacation?" the woman asked, reaching out a hand to search blindly for something on the counter. From beside the cash register, her fingers landed upon a pack of cigarettes.

"Yep."

"Good time a year for it. This weather won't last." The woman pulled out a cigarette, lit it, and took a long drag. "I could use a vacation. Someplace sandy. The Bahamas or Hawaii or...*somethin'.*" This struck the woman as funny and she started to laugh, which turned into a hacking cough. June felt unexpectedly charmed. The woman rode out her cough, turning away. Behind the desk was a small, outdated TV set. Playing on it in low volume was a show June didn't recognize but which was set in Manhattan. Her emotions kept surprising her because as she gazed at the little square of city she used to call home, she felt nothing but relief that she wasn't there now.

The woman finished with her coughing, grinned up at June, then took a drag, blowing a plume of smoke from the side of her mouth. "Anyway, I interrupted you. What was it you was lookin' for?"

June opened her mouth, but then closed it again. She'd been going to ask if they had any razors—not for today, she reassured herself, but for later, so she was ready—but something about this woman's wide, easy smile made June change her mind. "I think I'll just look around for a bit."

"Lemme know if ya need any help."

June walked up and down the three small aisles slowly. Everything on those old shelves looked good to her now. And so what if she bought it? She had three thousand dollars for four more days. She grabbed a bag of spiraled pasta, a big jar of marinara sauce for $1.29. She grabbed a bottle of red wine and then a second. She put it all on the counter by the woman, then went to look around some more. She felt suddenly blissed out about the idea of food shopping; it was such a luxury to want to eat something and then to be able to buy it. When she was a kid, there had rarely been enough money to buy whatever she wanted and then when she was older, she was always trying to be just a little bit skinnier. She couldn't remember the last time she'd eaten pasta. This small store in the middle of Marble Falls, Texas, was giving her the freedom to buy and then eat whatever the hell she wanted. She grabbed eggs and shredded cheese and milk and coffee and pancake mix and a plastic bottle of syrup and a carton of

Blue Bell vanilla ice cream. There was a chance, she thought, that Medea had simply gone to Athens and eaten.

"Do you have any olive oil?" she asked and even from the opposite side of the store, she didn't have to raise her voice.

The woman looked up at her. She perched an elbow on the counter, took a drag of her cigarette. "You know, we used to, but the bottles were so small and expensive."

June nodded. That made perfect sense to her. Fuck olive oil. She grabbed a stick of butter instead.

The woman put all of June's things slowly into plastic bags, her cigarette bouncing between her dry lips. "Hope you have a good vacation, now." Then she glanced out the window and announced seemingly to no one, "Daryl's here!"

That night, June sat on her new back porch, surrounded by the sounds of the Texas Hill Country. Grasshoppers vibrated and jumped in the long grass like they had springs built into them. Somewhere nearby, cows mooed. She'd finished an enormous plate of buttered pasta with marinara sauce and was sipping her third glass of wine, gazing at a view that was utterly unlike both New Jersey and New York. There was something about this place that slowed the very frequency with which her body operated and for the first time in a long time, June let herself sink into something that felt a whole lot like peace.

# FORTY

———

Over the next few days, June established a routine for her new, temporary life in Marble Falls. She went to sleep and awoke with the sun. In the mornings, she'd make breakfast—pancakes or eggs or both—and eat on the back porch. Afterward, she'd sit there with her coffee, watching birds flit in and out of bushes. Eventually, she'd pull on her tennis shoes and take a walk, ending with a visit to the property line between her Airbnb and Brandi's ranch.

When the other woman was on her porch, the two of them would talk. Brandi told her about her family—her husband, Teddy, and their son, Hank. June had never seen either of them and found Brandi and Teddy's division of labor enviable. She also learned about her neighbor's schooling; Brandi had studied land management and agriculture at A&M, but the classes she'd loved most were, unsurprisingly, history, and many of their conversations dovetailed back to the Russian Revolution. *You can empathize with Czarina Alexandra because of what she was goin' through with her son, but boy, was she bliiiiind blind.* June continued to find it all fascinating. Once, she almost brought up *Medea*, but stopped herself. Compared to her new friend's passion for history, her own preoccupation felt off somehow. Plus, it seemed to June that the more she slept and ate and talked to Brandi, the less of a hold the Greek tragedy had on her mind and this struck her as something of a relief. So even though a part of her would miss the complicated companionship she'd found in Medea, June began to let her go.

After her morning walk, she would shower, eat a snack, and then curl up on the porch with a paperback copy of *For Whom the Bell Tolls*, which she'd found in the built-in bookshelf in the hallway. She couldn't quite concentrate enough to follow the story, but the individual sentences were nice. Sometimes she'd read, but mostly she'd just hold the book in her hands, staring out into the trees. Throughout the week, when she needed something, she'd go to Smithwick where she'd chat with Darla, the woman she'd met her first day in town and the only person who seemed to work there. At night, June would pour herself some wine, boil pasta, and eat and drink on the porch, listening to the grasshoppers sing.

June awoke in the middle of the night to the sound of knocking. For a moment, the nightmare she'd been having hung in her mind, the details of which were blurred but unsettling, and she couldn't remember where she was. She blinked into the darkness of the unfamiliar room. Finally, her eyes adjusted and she remembered. Texas. Marble Falls. She reached out toward the bedside clock, but when she twisted it to face her, it was dark.

The knocking got louder and beyond it, June heard the sounds of a storm, the battering of rain, the crack of thunder. She sat up in bed, heart pounding. Who could possibly be so desperate to come to her house in the middle of the night?

She walked tentatively across the room in the darkness, arms in front of her, searching for the light switch. Finally, her fingers landed upon it and she flipped it, but nothing happened. This was how scary movies started, she thought. A dumb woman is staying alone in a cabin in the woods. The electricity goes out during a storm in the middle of the night, then a murderer knocks brazenly at her door.

June padded to the front door and peered through the frosted glass window, but all she saw was a dark figure against the dark sky. Whoever it was hammered on the door again and she jumped. She knew she shouldn't answer it, but the knocking sounded so frantic. She unlocked the dead bolt and swung open the door.

But it wasn't a murderer after all. In the darkened doorway stood Brandi and she was holding a baby.

"June, I am *so* sorry," she said over the crash of rain. The sky behind her lit up with a crooked bolt of lightning and June saw an upside-down umbrella on her covered stoop.

"Brandi, hi," June said, stepping sideways. "Come in."

Brandi gave her a look of exaggerated relief. "Ugh. Thank you." She walked past June into the living room.

"What's going on? What time is it?"

"It's just after five. Again, I'm sorry." She bounced the baby on her hip and swiped a hand across his head, brushing some errant drops of rain out of his hair. June looked away. "Normally, I'd never do this," Brandi continued. "But the electricity went out and Smithwick isn't open yet and we apparently ran out of batteries, which we need for our flashlight. Teddy thinks he heard a branch fall onto the pipe of our rainwater collector and obviously we need to be collecting this." She took a moment to look around. "Ooh, I've never been in the

Dixon place before. It's nice." She turned back to June. "Sorry again. Did I wake ya?"

June couldn't help but laugh. "It's fine."

Brandi smiled. She seemed both very awake and very calm. It was oddly contagious. "This is Hank, by the way." She twisted her torso to present the baby on her hip and June's heart contracted to see that Hank was about the same age as Mikey.

"I, uh, I didn't know Hank was a baby."

"You didn't know Hank was a baby?"

June reached out a tentative hand to gently grab his upper arm. "I don't know. The way you talked about him made him seem so...old."

Brandi laughed. "Well, he is an old soul," she said, bouncing him slightly. Like his mom, Hank looked utterly unperturbed to have just traveled through the wildest storm June had ever seen and to now be standing in the middle of a dark living room with a complete stranger. "Anyway," Brandi said. "You think this place has any batteries we could use? I would've gone to the Jeffersons', but they're like a mile away and frankly, I was less scared to wake you up than Betty and Sam."

"No, it's no problem. I don't know about the batteries, but we can look."

The two women walked into the darkened kitchen and started opening drawers. Every once in a while, the sky outside the windows would light up with a bolt of lightning and they'd get a good view of the drawer they were looking in, but mostly they dug around blind.

After a few minutes, June heard a sharp intake of breath from across the kitchen. "Ow!" Brandi said.

June looked up from the drawer she'd been searching. "You okay?"

Lightning struck and illuminated the kitchen, giving them both a clear view of Brandi's finger, which was streaming blood. Brandi glanced into the drawer. "There's an open safety pin in here." She sighed, looking down at her finger. "Goodness, how could there be so much blood from that? Here, would you take Hank for a sec while I mop this up?"

June's heart jumped into her throat and her arms began to tingle. With every inch of her being she didn't want to hold Hank. It was as if her very skin was saying *no no no*. She should not be allowed to hold babies. She couldn't be trusted. But she buried all of her protests and reached out her arms. "Of course."

Brandi handed her son to June, and his weight was like an anchor pulling her down. The edge of his pajama shirt rode up over his baby belly and June could feel the inches of soft skin on his wrists and feet brush against her. Mikey's had done the same thing when she used to hold him. She rolled her head around her neck. The sound of her blood rushed in her ears and she swallowed hard. It turned into another swallow and then another. In her arms, Hank started crying and June was back in her bathroom in Maplewood, kneeling before the bathtub, Mikey beneath the water, the tiny waves distorting his body. She was trying to get to him, but her hands were stuck to the side of the tub. Mikey's little legs kicked against the water. Her arms went numb around the baby's body— was it Hank's or Mikey's?—and just as the rushing in her ears reached a fever pitch, the baby was pulled away from her.

"June? June." Brandi's voice seemed to come to her from beyond the surface of water. June's head swam. "You okay?"

Finally, without the weight of the baby in June's arms, the

nausea that had been rising inside her fell away. "Sorry," she said, her voice weak. She blinked hard and her vision cleared.

She saw Brandi, holding Hank easily on her hip, her finger wrapped in a paper towel. "Is it the blood? Sorry. That little prick really gushed, didn't it? Thanks for holding Hank for me."

June felt the color come back into her cheeks. "No problem," she said and seized the cover story her friend had offered. "Yeah, I'm just bad with blood."

Brandi grinned, lifting her wrapped finger. "All gone now! Oh, and I found batteries!"

After Brandi and Hank left, June didn't go back to sleep. She'd been holding all her memories at bay for days, but as she'd held Hank in her arms, she realized that they would never relinquish her, no matter where she went or how much she nursed herself with food and rest and walks through the Hill Country. With everything she'd done, she didn't fit into the world anymore; she didn't deserve it. And now, finally, she had the resolve she needed to leave it. That was what she'd been so diligently swallowing down for days now, the reason she'd come here in the first place. Like a sick animal who left its family to die, June had fled Maplewood to end her life in the place her mom had been born. She hadn't quite been able to articulate that, even to herself, but now she knew it was time.

She stood in the darkened living room, unmoving until the storm subsided and the sun came up, and then she drove to Smithwick where she bought more wine, painkillers, a hammer, and a pack of razors.

Back in her little cabin, her unformed plan swam sickeningly before her eyes. She didn't know precisely how she would do it, but she would try to treat this morning as mindfully as she'd treated all the previous mornings she'd spent there; she'd live inside each moment until she had no more left to live. The prospect made her shake with fear and she poured herself a glass of wine, splashing some accidentally over the rim. She felt a knee-jerk reaction of guilt for drinking so early, but then her rational brain kicked in to remind her that it didn't matter what you drank right before you took your own life.

With trembling hands, she opened two foil packages of Advil PMs and swallowed them down with wine. At Smithwick, she'd slid every little square of painkillers off their hook, without counting them or particularly caring how many she got. She'd simply craved numbness and had grabbed whatever she could find to achieve it. Now, she swallowed another couple of pills and then for good measure, she swallowed two more. When that finished the last of the wine in her glass, she refilled it back to the top.

From the little plastic bag Darla had placed her items in, June pulled out the hammer and the pack of razors and laid them on the counter in front of her. Her mind flitted yet again to bath time with Mikey, but it made her too emotional and she pushed the memory away. She wasn't ready to think about Mikey or Ben, not yet.

She pried open the four-pack of orange-and-white razors and they popped out, skittering along the Formica top of the kitchen island. She felt almost robotic as she went through the motions of grabbing the hammer, placing one of the razors blade side up against the counter's surface then swinging the hammer down against it. But she missed, denting the countertop. *I'm so sorry, Mr. and Mrs. Dixon*, she thought. And she was; she was sorrier than they'd ever know. She swung again and again, then finally, on the third try, she hit the razor head with the hammer, but it didn't shatter as she'd expected. It simply warped, the embedded blade now twisted inside.

"Dammit!" June snapped. Could nothing ever just be easy?

She dropped the hammer with a heavy thud and gripped the edge of the counter, breathing hard. What was she supposed to do now? She grabbed her glass of wine and drank it, her eyes roving around her little cabin.

And then her gaze landed upon that Saran-wrapped stack of wood by the fireplace with the little matchbook on top and she got an idea. She walked over and plucked the matches up, then went into her bathroom and retrieved her tweezers from her toiletries bag. In the kitchen, she struck a match. There was something pleasurable about the little flame; it was more peaceful than the brute force of the hammer. She held the burning match to the head of the razor and watched as the white plastic began to warp, then melt.

"Ow." The flame had reached her fingers, so she tossed the match into the sink where it hissed against the wet bowl. She grabbed the tweezers and pried the hot, malleable plastic from the blade and almost laughed out loud with relief—it was working. When the blade was fully exposed, she plucked it with her tweezers and dropped it onto the Formica counter with a soft tinkle.

She stared at it, breathing heavily, arms tingling. She raised her glass to her mouth with a trembling hand and took another sip of wine. She picked up the blade and for the first time since she arrived in Texas, June allowed her mind to fill with thoughts of her family.

She sank into the memory of them—Mikey's tiny shoulders, the way Ben looked when he slept, her baby's buttersoft skin, the feeling of her husband's arms around her waist.

God, how she loved them, how she'd miss them. The images swam in her mind and she tried to focus on one of them, something happy and nice to hold on to as she left. Finally, one memory shined more brightly than the rest and she held it in her mind.

Mikey had only been a few days old. It had been morning and Ben had put on some music as he made coffee and breakfast. June had been sitting on the couch, Mikey in her arms. He'd been asleep, but his eyes had been moving beneath his eyelids as if in a dream. That was when June had heard the song change from Joni Mitchell to The Mamas & The Papas, her and her mom's song playing softly around them. She'd gazed down at Mikey and his eyes had blinked open with that fuzzy, unfocused look of an infant. And then he'd begun to pump his legs against her forearm.

She'd gasped. "Ben," she had whisper-yelled across the room.

Ben, who'd been scrambling eggs, had turned, spatula in hand. "What's up?"

She'd gestured toward Mikey with her chin. "He's dancing"—she'd nodded at Ben's phone, hooked up to their living room speaker—"to our song."

Ben had cocked his ear, listening. After a moment, he'd looked back at June and smiled. He'd pulled the pan off the burner and walked to where she was on the couch, sitting next to her and draping an arm around her shoulders.

"Oh, God," he'd said, his voice thick with mock horror. "He's gonna be just like you. Do you think we should take him back?"

June had laughed. "You're the worst."

"Nah"—he'd winked—"you are." Then he'd leaned over

to press his lips to her temple and added almost under his breath, "I think I'll keep you too."

Now, standing over a sink full of burnt matches and chips of broken plastic, June filled herself with the memory. She let herself remember the feel of her baby in her arms, her husband's mouth on her skin, her and her mom's song playing around her. Tears flowed down her cheeks as she pressed the blade to her forearm and into her skin.

And then, from out of the silence, she heard a familiar voice. "Oh, chicken," her mom said. "What the hell are you doing?"

# FORTY-ONE

———

Ben drove down the long gravel driveway toward the little cabin. The land on which it sat sprawled before him like an oil painting. The hills of yellow grass rolled in waves, blending with the wash of green treetops. The sky seemed impossibly wide. He'd been told to look here—Country Road 343, the second driveway on the right—to find his wife, but he didn't quite believe that this was where she was. June—who had grown up riding the subway, who traveled to big cities to do big performances, who knew her way around a Manhattan laundromat better than her own kitchen in Maplewood— would surely descend into madness out here in the middle of the Texas Hill Country.

It had taken under three hours to track June down in the small town of Marble Falls. After asking around in every shop, restaurant, and gas station he came to, Ben had met one woman who said her cousin, who worked at Smithwick Market, had mentioned that a lady from New York had been coming into the store. So Ben went to Smithwick and the woman behind the counter there told him the New York lady was staying at the Dixon property just a few minutes down the road.

Now here he was, heart pounding painfully in his chest.

He got out of his rental car and closed the door with a soft click. He followed the stone walkway to the front door and knocked. But there was no answer. He did it again, louder this time, but still, he was only met with silence. There was no doorbell, so Ben peered through the window in the door, but the glass was frosted and he could only make out the vaguest of shapes and colors. No movement caught his eye and when he pressed his ear to the door, he heard nothing. He knocked for a third time, pounding now, and when no one answered, he tried the handle. To his surprise, it twisted easily, and he tentatively swung the door open.

The first thing he registered was the stomach-churning smell of vomit, sharp with bile. He clapped a hand over his mouth and nose and breathed through his palm. Inside the little cabin, he saw a plaid couch, two floral armchairs, a set of antlers above the fireplace that he knew June would've hated. If she were staying here, that is. And then he saw it, along the far wall: June's tennis shoes. He stood motionless, staring at them. She was here after all. He'd found her. All this time he'd been searching, she'd been here, in this strange place in the middle of these rolling hills.

"June," Ben called, but his voice was choked. He walked fast toward the kitchen and the stench of vomit grew stronger; it seemed to be coming from the sink. He peered into the basin and saw that while it had been haphazardly rinsed, the edges and corners were speckled with burned matches, bits of what looked like orange plastic, and vomit streaked with blood. Beside the sink was a litter of objects and it took a moment for Ben to understand what he was looking at. When he did, tears welled in his eyes. It was a scattering of deconstructed plastic shaving razors. He spotted a matchbox and saw that one of the razor heads had been melted and peeled away. The only part missing in all of it was the blade.

Panic radiated throughout Ben's body as he raced down the hall to the only other room he could see, a bedroom. He stopped short in the doorway, the vision of what lay beyond taking the breath right out of his lungs. On the bed against the wall, on top of the blankets, limbs akimbo, was June. She lay still and silent.

This was the person he loved more than anything, the person he'd chosen over everyone and vowed to keep choosing day after day, the person he had yet to forgive but had never stopped loving, the person from whom he needed the most forgiveness. She could not be dead. This was not how his life was meant to go. This was not how their life together was meant to end. All this flashed through his mind in the moment it took for him to get to her side.

He squeezed June's shoulder with one hand, placed the other behind her head, gingerly, urgently. "June! June!" His voice came out strangled and hoarse, as if he were trying to speak around a stone. "Wake up, June. Wake up."

But she remained motionless.

"June!" he shouted. "Wake up!" What had been a plea was now a command. Desperation morphed to authority.

Still nothing.

He began to shake her. "Goddammit, June, wake up." His terror was making him furious. "You have to wake up."

And then, finally, she did. In his arms, eyes still closed, she moaned ever so slightly and the oppressive squeezing around Ben's chest released so instantaneously it was painful. She was alive.

His arms softened around her frame. He peered into her face. "June. Junie. Wake up. I'm here."

Her eyes finally fluttered open, roving unfocused around the room.

"It's me. You're okay."

After a moment, her gaze settled on him and she blinked hard as if she weren't sure she could trust her eyes. But when the understanding settled in of who he was, her face crumpled. Ben ran his hands along her arms, checking for cuts, for blood. There were a few small nicks on her left forearm, but they were shallow and had stopped bleeding. The rest of her forearms were smooth and intact. He pulled down her sweatpants and inspected her legs, then pulled them back up when he was satisfied. He searched her torso, chest, back, and when he found that the outside of her body was okay, he placed both hands on the sides of her face.

"Did you take anything, June?"

She shook her head. "Some ibuprofen," she said groggily. "But I probably threw most of it up."

Ben felt another wave of relief, but he still didn't feel quite reassured. "Why was there blood in your vomit?"

June frowned, blinking, but then her face cleared. "Oh. It was red wine. I got scared and I thought— I thought it would help."

"How much did you drink?"

She blinked very slowly as if it were hard to open her eyes after closing them. "I might've finished the bottle. I'm not sure."

"And the ibuprofen? How many did you take?"

She made a weak, uncertain sound. "Six? I think."

Ben felt the last of his panic ebb away. She was drugged up on ibuprofen and red wine, which explained why she was so out of it, but even as small as she was, those portions wouldn't kill her, not even remotely. And she was right—throwing up had probably purged the worst of it. His body crackled with unused adrenaline and tears filled his eyes. "I'm so sorry," he said, pulling his broken wife to him, holding her in his arms as if he could fix her that way, as if his touch could suck out all of her pain and reverse all of his wrongdoing. "I'm sorry, I'm sorry, I'm sorry."

# FORTY-TWO

———

They sat like that for a long time, on the unfamiliar bed with the worn quilt, June wrapped in Ben's arms, their limbs so intertwined it was difficult to tell where one ended and the other began. They didn't talk. June let her weight sink completely onto Ben, let him rub his palm in circles on her back, and she realized how much she'd missed her husband, not just during her time in Texas, but over the past year. It felt as if she'd been drying out in a desert and he was holding a glass of water to her lips. She wondered vaguely how he'd found her, but she didn't quite have the energy at the moment to ask or even care.

When they finally leaned apart, Ben searched June's face. "I thought you'd— Were you going to—?" But his voice cut out before he could finish.

June looked down, her eyes on a messy stitch in the quilt where one square connected to another. She understood what he was asking and she nodded.

"Can you tell me what happened?"

She took a breath and then met his gaze. "I decided not to go through with it because… I heard my mom." It had happened just after she first pressed the blade into her forearm and somehow, the sound of her dead mom's voice in the middle of nowhere Texas hadn't startled or scared her. Instead, it had seemed like a thread of hope.

"I know that sounds insane," she continued. Although, she had to admit, it didn't seem as insane as all those times in Maplewood when she'd seen her mom out in the world, very much real and very much alive. Unlike those appearances, this time, her mom had seemed to come to her from within. "It wasn't like she was in the room with me exactly. It was more like I heard her in my head," June tried to explain. "Actually…" she said, thinking back to her mom's words: *Oh, chicken, what the hell are you doing?* "She sorta made fun of me."

That had been her mom's only message, but hearing it had jolted her. Suddenly, she could no longer hold the blade, almost as if an invisible hand had clasped around her wrist to physically prevent her from doing so. Whether that had been her mom reaching through the ether or simply her subconscious pushing against what it knew she no longer wanted, June couldn't be sure.

Ben's gaze flicked over her face. She couldn't tell whether or not he understood, but it was hard to put into language what she'd experienced. "And do you—" he began but then started over. "You don't think you'll want to do it again, do you?"

June opened her mouth, but nothing came out. Instead, her eyes filled and she simply shook her head. While she didn't know how to move forward in her life, she no longer wanted it to end. Because in the moment when she thought it was all over, she hadn't felt anger or guilt or even grief; she'd felt love. She'd felt her mom's love pouring through her like sunlight in a cave; she'd felt the love that bound her to Mikey and Ben.

And maybe love wasn't always enough and maybe it wouldn't fix everything, but it did feel like something worth living for.

"Okay," Ben said, his voice thick. "That's good." He took another breath and June steeled herself for the inevitable questions and accusations about why she left—she deserved them all—but none came. Instead, he pushed her hair away from her face and said, "Are you hungry?"

June blinked, relief flooding through her. The question felt like a precious gift. Hunger was too benign a feeling for her to register beneath everything else, but she nodded. "I could eat."

In the kitchen, she slid gingerly onto one of the bar stools facing the island and watched as Ben bustled around with casual authority, as if they'd been living there for years. He washed the sink without a word, found a cleaning spray under it and wiped down the counters, tossing the matches and the razor remnants into the trash. June felt questions churning deep inside her, but she didn't want to vocalize any of them. Not yet. She wanted to sit here and let Ben take care of her and, for the moment at least, it seemed that was what he wanted too.

But there was one thing she couldn't not ask. "Where's Mikey?"

Ben glanced up from the cutting board where he was now slicing a fat tomato. "He's with my parents. My mom stayed with us for a couple days, but she took him to New Haven this morning." His tone was light and matter-of-fact.

June nodded. She watched as he placed four slices of whole wheat bread onto two plates. On each, he piled all the sandwich stuff she'd bought from Smithwick: sliced turkey, roast beef, provolone cheese, pickles, tomato. He squirted two Zs of Dijon mustard and two more of mayonnaise then pressed the top slices of bread down onto the sandwiches and cut each into two halves. The gesture felt heartbreakingly tender.

"Thanks," June said softly as he placed the plate in front of her. Ben nodded.

They sat side by side at the bar, slowly eating their sandwiches and drinking glasses of orange juice in silence. June wished this unspoken truce could last, but she knew it couldn't. And finally, as if her thought zipped straight from her brain into Ben's, he turned to her and cleared his throat.

"So," he began, and June filled with dread. "When does your reservation here end?"

"Monday."

"That's tomorrow." But he said it kindly as if he hadn't expected her to know anything as complex as what day of the week it was. "And the rental car?"

"Same."

Ben took a sip of his orange juice. "So," he said again. "I have a proposal."

June rubbed her lips together nervously. What was he going to ask of her? She couldn't think of a single thing she felt capable of right now, not packing a bag, not driving to Austin, not flying to Newark, certainly not going back to her old life. The thought of holding Mikey again made her hands shake. She didn't trust herself in her old life; she didn't think she ever would.

"I propose we stay here for a week," he began. "I'll call the rental car company and Airbnb to see if we can arrange it. I can't imagine March is a busy tourist time in Marble Falls. If I can sort that out, I propose we stay here for seven more days...and"—he cleared his throat—"I propose that it's a week of honesty. I say we talk about what we need to talk about, and that no matter how hard it is to say or how hard we think it will be to hear, we tell each other the truth. The full truth." He hesitated, then focused on June. "What d'you think about that?"

She sat quietly for a moment. That wasn't what she'd been expecting, not at all. And like the sandwich had, this proposal felt like a gift she didn't deserve. All the things she'd held back from him over the past few months spun in her mind. Would he be able to love her after he heard the full, truthful version of them all?

But then, June thought, maybe this gift wasn't just for her alone. Maybe it was a small act of mercy for himself too. Maybe honesty was their only way forward. Because they couldn't be in this marriage for another year, let alone for the rest of their lives, with so much unspoken between them. Their unsaid truths would push them further and further apart, until they wouldn't be able to see the other at all. Honesty might rip their love in two, but that would be better than the slow death of leaving everything unspoken.

Still, she frowned. "Can you take that much time off from work?"

At that, a complicated series of emotions flitted over Ben's face and, while June didn't catch them all, it would have been impossible not to see that her question had made him ashamed. He cleared his throat. "This is more important than that."

"Okay," she said, already heavy with the weight of what was to come. "One week of honesty."

"Great. Okay."

"I don't want to start now," she said, testing out that honesty, "but I do have one question."

"Okay…"

June looked pointedly at the black splint on Ben's right wrist. "What the hell happened?"

Ben laughed, but it came out tired and humorless. "It's a long story. Let's get the reservations sorted and then we can talk."

# FORTY-THREE

———

Ben and June eased into their week of honesty slowly. On the evening of their first night together, after they'd eaten their sandwiches, June took a shower while Ben called the rental car company and their Airbnb host and arranged to extend both reservations until the following Monday. He'd been right about March in Texas; he didn't get any pushback at either request. Then he'd called his parents' home in New Haven and, feeling slightly ashamed and slightly guilty, asked his mom to take care of Mikey for yet another week. Like he'd known she would, she said yes before he even finished the question.

When he had that taken care of, Ben texted Moli and Kirsten to tell them June was okay. Then he called Officer Moretti to cancel the missing person report and to thank her. She had helped him when he needed it most. "I'm glad you found your wife, Mr. Gilmore," she'd said. "And I'd like to meet her sometime. I'm sure, with all the trouble you cause, that won't be too hard to arrange."

Every so often throughout his calls and June's shower, Ben would poke his head around the dripping curtain and check on her, his fingers pressed over the microphone on his cell.

After the second time he did this, June realized he was making sure she wasn't trying to hurt herself.

The next day, the two of them drove into town to stock up on food. June was sick of pasta and Smithwick didn't have much else. That evening, Ben cooked steaks and baked potatoes while she made a salad and they ate on the back porch, drinking glasses of tap water. They talked very little at first and only about the actual physical things that surrounded them—how warm it was in Texas, how pretty the wide-open sky looked, how good the steak tasted. It was easiest that way and easy felt like a reprieve they both needed. They sat in the bubble of their unspoken truce for hours, watching as the sky dimmed then darkened.

Finally, when the features of Ben's face were hard to make out through the night, June turned to him. "How did you find me?"

"I found your journal. Well, I found the pages."

"Oh." June thought of everything that was in those letters to her mom and shame heated her cheeks. And yet, another part of her was relieved. That meant she didn't have to explain it all: Jitterbuggies, Medea, the vision of her mom in her turquoise scarf.

"Yeah." Ben paused, then turned to look at her. "And, June, about all that…"

She avoided his gaze. She knew what was coming. The sandwiches, the dinner, the truce—they had been the calm before the storm. She wasn't sure how he was going to say it—*What happened at bath time? How could you do something so reckless? You almost killed our baby, you bitch*—but to her surprise he didn't say any of it.

"I think you have postpartum anxiety," he said instead. "You're sick, June."

His words felt like dredging up something old and forgotten, as if what he'd said was both a revelation and also a deep part of her. Because of course she was sick. Of course there was an official diagnosis some doctor could give her. And yet, over the past four months, she'd never made it that far in her mind. *Something's wrong with me*, she'd thought over and over, but it had always ended there. And maybe, she thought now, that was a part of the sickness, the inability to see it in yourself. "Yeah," she said after a moment. "Yeah, that's right."

"I think a lot of the things you wrote about in your journal can be explained by it. One of the symptoms of a very progressed case is hallucinations. I think that's one of the reasons you were seeing your mom."

June stared out into the blackness of the night, trying to absorb this. All those times she'd seen her mom and believed she was there to tell her something, to take her away—they had all been in her head? But her mom had seemed so real, so physical. Then Ben's words replayed themselves in her mind. "Sorry. Did you say *one of the reasons* I was seeing my mom?"

Ben sighed. "There's a lot I need to catch you up on."

He went on to tell her a strange series of events. He told her that Kirsten had thought she was having an affair with Liam and had followed her in a disguise to prove it. He told her that Kirsten had created the petition as revenge and that he'd punched Liam for the same, which resulted in a hospital visit and Kirsten's diagnosis, which led him, finally, to June.

"I don't know the exact numbers of postpartum diseases," Ben said. "But apparently, they're very common."

June sat motionless and reeling as all those memories of her mom retroactively morphed into Kirsten. A part of her was relieved to have such a banal explanation—it made her feel more grounded—but another part of her felt duped and let down.

Because, although the visits from her mom had been unsettling, for a few days, June had felt closer to her than she had since before she died. And yet, Kirsten's actions still didn't explain that last time she'd seen her mom, when she'd disappeared into their bathroom, or when her mom's voice had pulled her from the brink two days ago. Most likely Ben was right, she supposed—those probably had been hallucinations—but maybe, just maybe, they really had been her mom, or at least some ethereal version of her watching over June. June knew Ben wouldn't buy into that idea, so she decided to just keep it to herself, to hold it inside her, as something not to fear, but to cherish.

"Kirsten gave me the name of the doctor who diagnosed her," Ben said, drawing June out of her thoughts. "You can go to her, too, or we'll find you a different doctor. Whatever you want." The way he said it, in that light, matter-of-fact tone, made June feel as if she were a child letting some adult tie her shoes. "And you'll get a prescription to help."

She nodded. The thought of walking into a doctor's office, of signing a clipboard with a sign-in sheet, of talking to a doctor in a white coat, of taking a prescribed pill once a day—while terrifying—also struck her as reassuring. She'd felt alone for so long.

The next morning, Ben and June sat on the back porch, drinking cups of coffee. They'd slept side by side in the king-size bed, carefully avoiding each other's edges. At one point in the night, June had turned in her sleep and her foot had grazed Ben's leg. "Sorry," she'd murmured, pulling it back as if he'd burned her.

Now, she glanced at Ben out of the corner of her eye. She wanted to make herself smaller, feeling that if she could just curl up into a tiny-enough ball, Ben's eyes might skip over her and he'd forget that they needed to talk. She knew he was right and they had to start being honest with each other, but the prospect of a conversation had never before filled her with such dread. She cleared her throat. "Where should we start?"

Ben sat still for a moment, looking out over the trees. "With the big stuff, maybe? Why don't you ask me something first."

June thought about it. "Did you ever forgive me for wanting to consider getting an abortion when I found out I was pregnant?"

He reeled back. "What? I didn't blame you for—"

"Ben."

He stopped then, took a breath. She was right, he realized. He'd been angry at her for not wanting Mikey as much as he had and he'd carried that anger inside him like a little flame.

"You held that over me," June continued. "You punished me for so long for wanting to have that conversation. This is all I wanted, to be honest with each other, but you made me feel like a bad person for it. And you didn't stop. After he was born, it felt like you thought you loved him more than I did. But once we decided we were having him, I was in, you know? I don't love him any less than you do now because you loved him first."

Despite the guilt and regret coursing through him, at that last part, Ben's shoulders loosened with relief. He hadn't realized how badly he'd needed to hear her say that. He hadn't realized how unsure he had been about June's love for their child. Now that made him feel monstrous. "I'm sorry. I shouldn't have made you feel guilty for being honest with me." He ran a hand through his hair. "That was really unfair. Fuck. I'm sorry."

June nodded. "Your turn."

Ben dragged his hands down his face. "This isn't a question." He hesitated. "But what you wrote about that first time we had sex after Mikey? I didn't know you were feeling like that. And I'm—I'm sorry." He bent his head then looked at her. "Also... Look, I obviously don't want to blame you or anything, but you did make it seem like you were enjoying it. And if you're acting like you're into sex, I'm not sure I'm always gonna know when you're not actually into it."

June's throat tightened. "I know. I just kept feeling like if I acted like I was enjoying it, I would, but... I should've just told you what was going on."

He shook his head. "I should've asked. You'd just given birth—I can't imagine how that makes you feel about sex. I'm sorry." He hesitated. "And I have another thing. Another not-question. If you're ready."

June nodded.

"I've been drinking too much."

She blinked. "Are you... Do you mean... Do you think you're an alcoholic?"

"No," Ben said. "I mean, I know that's what an alcoholic would say, but I'm not an alcoholic. It's just that everybody at work drinks all the time, so I just sort of started to as well. And then it sort of became a habit, to self-medicate. I'm gonna stop for a while."

"Okay. Good." June didn't know what else to say. "Are you happy there? At Clark & White?"

"God, no. I hate working an eighty-hour week with a wife and kid at home." His mind flashed to his own absent dad and he radiated with self-loathing for so thoroughly turning into him.

"Then why are you doing it?"

The answer felt like something solid in his mouth, something impossible to articulate. Because while the truth was that he believed he was doing it for her, for their family, there was also something underneath that he couldn't quite put his finger on.

"You know," she continued, "you don't have to be miserable to make enough money for us to live on."

He laughed wearily. "I get paid a lot more at Clark & White than I would at almost any other law firm in the city."

June gave him a confused look. "But why do you feel like you have to make that specific amount? You know *I* don't care about having a big house, right? I grew up in a six-hundred-square-foot apartment. We don't need to make some enormous mortgage payment every month if we don't want to. Yeah, money's great. And we gotta feed the kid, send him to college, but I hope I never gave you the impression that I wanted some sort of life that requires over half a million dollars as an annual salary."

"No, no, you didn't," Ben said. His mind flashed to this past week, to how small he'd felt when he'd walked into Sydney and Jonathan's house, how inadequate. He thought about all those times his mom had all but said June's role was to take care of their baby and his was to make money, and he realized that despite being able to recognize exactly what was wrong with that paradigm, all he'd done with his own family was reinforce it. For the first time, Ben fully understood what June had meant about being Medea, married to a man who left her for the status something else could give him. "I think maybe I've been a bit misguided," he said, which felt like the tip of some giant iceberg. "What about you? Were you happy at Martha Graham?"

June felt the question like a needle in her arm, prodding and uncomfortable. Every part of her wanted to say yes, to reassure him that being in the company was all she'd ever wanted, but the memory of her drive to Marble Falls flashed in her mind. She'd driven by a billboard with the image of a little girl in a pink leotard, her arms in an adorably crude version of fourth position. One was wrapped above her head, the other around her soft tummy. Beside her, the message had read, *Cindy wants to be a ballerina when she grows up. With the Texas Children's Foundation, now she can.* "Don't do it, kid," June had said aloud into the quiet of her car, taking herself by surprise. "It's a lot harder than it looks."

Being in the company was too hard—not in the sense that it was too difficult—but because it simply wasn't malleable. It didn't bend to the rest of the life June wanted for herself. It was too big and wide and unwieldy to squeeze in friends and dinners out and lazy Sundays and a husband and a baby.

"I think I wanted to be happy there, so I let myself believe that I was," June said. "But I think maybe my ambition got in the way of what I actually wanted."

Ben nodded. "Know what you mean."

June wanted to stop there. She wanted that to be the full truth so she wouldn't have to say the other thing. But she'd made a promise to Ben, so she continued. "And I think I hung on because of my mom. She wanted it so badly."

Upon saying it, June realized that was exactly what Ben had done too. He'd stuck with his job at Clark & White for her and Mikey and some sort of outward validation, and she'd stuck with her place at the company for her mom. But you couldn't live your life only for other people. Life was a balancing act and maybe both her and Ben's scales had been tipped too far in one direction for too long.

"Your turn," Ben said.

"If I had made more money than you from dancing, when we had Mikey, would you have given up your job?"

"I don't..." He hesitated. "I don't know. I can't imagine staying home all day. I guess, probably not."

"Then why did you think I wanted to give up mine?"

Ben let out a breath. "I don't know. It was fucked up. I'm sorry I made that assumption. And I'm sorry you missed out on *Medea*. I didn't understand at the time how much that meant to you, but...you would've been really great."

June smiled a small, sad smile. "Thanks." For as much as she'd wanted that, for as disappointed as she'd been when she'd given it up, after these past few days in Texas, Medea no longer represented a missed dream to her but rather a nightmare. The Greek sorceress was too wrapped up in everything bad to be anything else.

As if Ben could read her mind, he asked tentatively, "Do you still think about that a lot? About her?"

"Not as much now," she said. "It's like I can understand everything I thought, all the parallels and stuff, but I don't *feel* it as much. If that makes sense."

His face screwed up and he inhaled a shaky breath. "That's good. It scared me—reading about that in your journal."

She nodded. "I can imagine."

They sat there quietly for a moment, then Ben said, "Your turn."

Questions churned in June's mind, but one kept circling back to the forefront. It was the one question she needed an answer to and the one she never wanted to ask. And yet, she'd promised to try. "Will you forgive me?"

He turned to look at her. "For what?"

"For what happened after the party? When I gave Mikey his bath?"

Before she knew what he was doing, Ben was standing up out of his chair and kneeling in front of her. He reached his hands up to grab the sides of her face, staring into her eyes, searching for something she didn't know how to show him.

"Oh, June," he said, forceful and pleading. "I turned you into a single parent and pretended like I hadn't. You got sick and I didn't see you, like really see you, for months." He heaved a tired sigh. "I guess what I'm saying is, you don't need my forgiveness for that. As for everything else... I'll try to forgive you if you try to forgive me."

# FORTY-FOUR

Once they'd gotten the big stuff out of the way, it was easier to talk about the smaller things. It was easier to get angry and easier to say sorry. They kept up their policy of honesty, which was both difficult and liberating. Like June had done in the previous week, the two of them established a slow routine for their time in the Hill Country. They'd fall asleep not long after the sun went down and wake when it first got light. They'd take their time cooking enormous breakfasts together, eating them on the porch, drinking coffee, sometimes talking, sometimes not. They took walks in the afternoons and although June introduced Ben to Brandi one day when she was out with the horses, their neighbor never came over again after that one stormy morning. She seemed to understand they needed to be alone.

Eventually, their careful way of interacting thawed into something more natural. And then one night as they slept side by side, Ben rolled over and his hand accidentally hit June's arm. "Sorry," he said groggily, but before he could pull it back, she took his hand in hers and wrapped it over her chest. He responded, pulling himself around her—her back flush with his front, his mouth against her neck—and they slept like that until morning.

"Where do we go from here?" June asked on their last night in Texas. They were sitting in their favorite spot on the back porch, looking out into the black sweep of the night sky. They each held a glass of water—Ben still hadn't had any alcohol—and they were rocking slowly side by side in the rocking chairs.

"I don't know," Ben said, but ever since June had first asked about Clark & White, a hazy plan had been forming in his mind. "I think I might call Mihir in a few days. He has a buddy who practices civil law."

June smiled. "That'd be good for you."

"Yeah. Nothing's guaranteed, of course, but I think it could be a good fit. I mean that is why I studied law in the first place, to help people. It'd be nice to actually do that at some point. And if you decide you wanna work, I can look into daycares. What're you thinking? Do you still wanna dance with the company?"

"I don't... I don't think so." The admission made June feel like nothing short of a failure, but all week, each time she'd thought about leaving the intensely competitive world of dance for good, it was as though some internal cog had finally shifted into place. It felt like a relief. She sighed. "I mean, I don't regret it. At all. I'm a much better dancer because of it and I think if I hadn't pursued it, it would've haunted me forever. But I don't think I want to go back." She let out a half laugh, half sigh. "I don't know *what* I want."

As healing as this past week had been, June still felt lost, as if she were standing in a forest without paths but dense brambles. The possibilities of which way to go felt both scary and *are.* Love—the kind she'd been waiting on—would bloom fierce and uncomplicated in her chest.

All of this would happen soon, but for now, Ben and June held each other in the darkness of the Texas night. For now, they danced.

★ ★ ★ ★ ★

# ACKNOWLEDGMENTS

I first want to thank my agent, Sarah Phair, who, with one phone call, changed my life. Sarah, thank you for taking a chance on me, for the ferocity with which you represent my work, for your unflagging faith in my craft, and for taking your role of writing therapist so seriously; I consider our phone calls the best perk of my job. You've made many of my dreams come true and I'm forever grateful.

To my editor, Laura Brown, thank you for approaching this book with such enthusiasm and thoughtfulness. I knew very quickly into our first call that you were the perfect custodian to bring it into the world and you proved me right again and again. I'm so happy you saw Ben and June the way I'd intended and I'm beyond grateful for all you've done to make their story shine. You and the rest of the team at Park Row have made my first experience of publishing in print an absolute joy.

To my trusted beta readers, Chris Kim and Courtney Howell, we may not be in the same room often, but y'all are constant sources of inspiration and fellowship for me. Thank you both for all your words about my novel—the encouraging, the constructive, the kind.

There are many people who assisted in my research for this book, for which I'm deeply grateful. First, thank you to Holly Cardiff Thomas, Cheryl Milan, and the other women who wish to remain anonymous for sharing with me their experiences of postpartum anxiety and/or depression. I can't tell y'all how much I appreciate your candor and vulnerability. While June's experience is very much her own, I hope my book reads as I intended: a love letter to all the women who've suffered from a postpartum disease. If this novel makes even the slightest dent in the stigma surrounding mental illness, I will consider it a success.

To the two incredible women at the Martha Graham Dance Company for helping me understand the professional world of dance, Natasha Diamond-Walker and Charlotte Landreau, thank you both for being so generous with your time and information. Martha Graham may not have been the right fit for June, but it was clear from our conversations that it is a beacon of positivity and artistry. Any mistakes I made were very much in spite of your help.

Thank you also to Addie Alexander for all the insight into New York City through the years and to Macy Reeves Strimple for giving me a solid foundation about being a dancer there.

To Drew and Adrienne Moerlein, thank you for your generosity as my Maplewood hosts. A, thanks for showing me around (sorry about that ticket!) and for introducing me to Arturo's. Drew, thank you for sharing all your knowledge about being an artist in New York, especially that of the Broadway scene. Your insight was invaluable.

As always, huge thanks to Matthew Henion for being the best resident police expert a girl could ask for.

And finally, to my dear friends and family, in particular

Nancy Anderson, Kathleen Littlepage, Peggy Crakes, Sarah Farr, Leah McKern, Rachel Kiester, and Matt Stephans, thank you for the boundless support y'all have given me through the years. I'd be nowhere without your help and I love you all very much.

Biggest of thanks to my parents, Kirt Kiester and Mary Tucker, who have done everything in their power to foster my career. Dad, thank you for your patient legal advice, both for my characters and for me. More importantly, thank you for your unbridled excitement for my books and for telling everyone you know to read them. Mom, thank you for being my first-always reader, for bringing me food when I was editing and too preoccupied to feed myself, and for always, always answering the phone. On a daily basis, you inspire me to think big and face my fears. And thank you both for building Songbird, which inspired the ending of my book and surrounded me with beauty as I wrote it. This one is for the two of you.

As ever, endless thanks to my husband, Kyle Ligon. Kyle, you are a constant source of joy in my life. Thank you for picking me up when I'm down, for always helping me brainstorm, for giving me the time and space to write, and for acting like following my dreams was ever the only option. There's no one I'd rather go through this life with.